AWARDS & PRAISE FOR

OPERATION REDWOOD

John and Patricia Beatty Award, California Library Association

National Green Earth Book Award

Carol D. Reiser Book Award

Green Prize for Sustainable Literature Awards (Youth Fiction Award)

National Outdoor Book Award (Honorable Mention in Children's Category)

"One of the finest children's novels of the year." — *A Fuse #8 Production*

"[R]eminds readers that everyone, no matter how large or small, can take action on issues that are important to them." — *School Library Journal*

"Teachers will be able to use this novel for Earth Day discussions and can foster conversations on environmental activism of all types."
— *School Library Journal*

"A highly enjoyable read." — *Kirkus*

"*Operation Redwood* is a book that makes the reader believe that anyone can make a difference if he or she is willing to take on a challenge and overcome the hardships that will be encountered along the way." — *ALAN Review*

"Young readers will learn how courage and passion can make a huge difference, especially if you have good friends and good intentions. It's also about friendship, fitting in and loyalty to a cause. And for adults who care about diversity, French's inclusion of kids from varied backgrounds adds another compelling layer to an already good read." — *Cincinnati Parent*

"The book has a modern multicultural feel that balances the pastoral nature scenes." — *Horn Book*

...ION
...WOOD

S. Terrell French

AMULET BOOKS
NEW YORK

The Library of Congress has cataloged the hardcover edition as follows:

French, Susannah T.
Operation Redwood / by Susannah T. French.
p. cm.
Summary: In Northern California, Julian Carter–Li and his friends, old and new, fight to save a grove of Redwoods from an investment company that plans to cut them down.
ISBN 978-0-8109-8354-0 (alk. paper)
[1. Environmental protection—Fiction. 2. Redwoods—Fiction. 3. Trees—Fiction. 4. Friendship—Fiction. 5. Grandmothers—Fiction. 6. California—Fiction.] I. Title.
PZ7.F889153Ope 2009
[Fic]—dc22
2008030724

Paperback ISBN: 978-0-8109-9720-2

Text copyright © 2009 S. Terrell French
Book design by Maria T. Middleton

Amulet Books are available at special discounts when purchased in quantity for premiums and promotions as well as fundraising or educational use. Special editions can also be created to specification. For details, contact specialmarkets@abramsbooks.com or the address below.

ABRAMS
THE ART OF BOOKS SINCE 1949

115 West 18th Street
New York, NY 10011
www.abramsbooks.com

For William, Clara, and Nathan

"THE BATTLE WE HAVE FOUGHT, and are still fighting, for the forests is a part of the eternal conflict between right and wrong, and we cannot expect to see the end of it. . . . So we must count on watching and striving for these trees, and should always be glad to find anything so surely good and noble to strive for."

—John Muir, Sierra Club lecture at the Academy of
Sciences in San Francisco, November 23, 1895

"EVERYBODY NEEDS BEAUTY AS well as bread, places to play in and pray in, where Nature may heal and cheer and give strength to body and soul alike."

—John Muir, *The Yosemite* (1912)

CONTENTS

I

WAKING UP

Julian Carter-Li opened his eyes and immediately knew he was somewhere he'd never woken up before. But his dream wouldn't let him go. His eyes closed and he was running again, along an abandoned beach, beside a black ocean, searching for someone he couldn't name. He stumbled, and as he fell, a voice inside his head reminded Julian that he was dreaming, and he wrenched himself free from his dark dream world, sat up, and looked around.

A glass wall faced downtown San Francisco. The bright lights of the Bay Bridge shone against the night sky and a computer screen glowed from a massive desk against the far wall. The only sound was the computer's low hum. He must have been sleeping for hours, Julian thought, and he wondered when his uncle would be coming back.

He had never been in Uncle Sibley's office before today. He

looked around at the desk, the clean, uncluttered surfaces, the black leather sofa, the eagle's eye view. Even in shadow, everything about the office said "I'm rich. I'm powerful. Don't mess with me."

The echo of the wind in his ears and the sense of dread left over from his nightmare had begun to subside. Julian stood up and walked across the room. Except for a few fluorescent lights shining in the hallway, the floor was dark and desolate.

Now that he was fully awake, Julian remembered why he was here. It was, of course, because there had been nowhere else for him to go. The assistant principal had been unable to reach Aunt Daphne. When he'd finally gotten through to Uncle Sibley, after being placed on hold for a full five minutes, his already foul mood had grown worse.

"Of course somebody's got to get him," the assistant principal had barked into the telephone. "The kid can't just sit here all day with a fever of a hundred and three! He's *infectious*! Excuse me? No, we don't call taxis! Our students generally don't travel around by *taxi*. If you want a taxi, you'll have to send one yourself!"

Julian had waited in the office for what felt like hours until at last a bright yellow taxi pulled up in front of the school. Julian had never ridden in a taxi. At first, he had enjoyed the smoothness of the red leather seats. It was almost like having a chauffeur. And after years of taking buses everywhere, it was a treat to have the wide backseat to himself.

But as he'd sat, staring at the python tattoo that snaked its way up the fat pink neck of the taxi driver, it had occurred to Julian that he'd just gotten into a car with a stranger and was completely at his mercy.

That was the trouble with grown-ups, Julian decided. How many times over the years had his teachers lectured the class never to get into a car with a stranger, under any circumstance, even if the stranger claimed to be searching for a missing puppy (it was always a puppy). And yet, a taxi pulls up in front of the school with a complete stranger driving it, and he is expected to hop right in. He could have been cut up into little pieces and put in the trunk. Or kidnapped and held for ransom.

Of course, there would be no point trying to get any ransom money from his mother. For one thing, she was five thousand miles away. But even when she wasn't traveling, she was always scrimping to get by. It wasn't just that she didn't have any money, she didn't even *believe* in money.

Uncle Sibley, on the other hand, was rich. Julian wondered how much his uncle would be willing to pay to release him from the kidnapper–taxi driver. A thousand dollars? A million? He imagined his mother calling frantically from Beijing, begging his uncle to meet the evil taxi driver's demands. His uncle would frown, shaking his head: "Five hundred dollars and not a penny more!"

In the end, though, the taxi driver had merely delivered Julian to the gleaming gold doors of a towering skyscraper. There he had been met by some underling, whisked up a sickening fifty floors to the IPX headquarters, and deposited like a piece of lost baggage in his uncle's elegant office. Sibley had motioned for him to sit down. Then, for the next fifteen minutes, he'd spoken into the phone in a voice of such cold fury that Julian could only be grateful it was not directed at him.

"You need a haircut," was the first thing Sibley had said to Julian. His own blond hair was plastered rigidly to the side. He gave Julian another appraising look and added, "You look terrible. Daphne's on a field trip with Preston. Apparently, it's the nanny's day *off*." Helga, the nanny, had been on duty for two weeks, but Sibley still hadn't learned her name. "Listen, I'm already late. I don't know how long this meeting's going to last. There's soda in the refrigerator. You have homework?"

"I'll be fine," Julian had said, gesturing at his backpack. But by the time he'd finished the sentence, Sibley had pulled on his suit jacket and was already walking toward the door.

The moment his uncle left, Julian had realized how tired he was. His head was aching, his bones felt like they were being poked by sharp little needles, and his face was burning hot. He took a ginger ale from the small refrigerator at the back of the room and sipped it slowly as he stared at the photographs on his uncle's desk. There was Aunt Daphne, with the frozen-looking smile that she usually wore when talking to him. There was his cousin Preston's third-grade school picture. And, finally, a black-and-white portrait of the three of them, all smiling wanly from the porch of their old house in Boston.

Julian had almost dozed off in the chair before dragging

himself over to the leather sofa. There, he'd watched the tiny sailboats scuttling under the Bay Bridge until the bright sun forced his eyes to close, and he drifted off to sleep.

Now Julian sat in the darkness, with an empty, sickish feeling in his stomach. He'd barely touched the school lunch—congealed cheese enchiladas and fruit cocktail in a slimy syrup—and it was now past dinnertime. In the dim light, he walked over to his uncle's desk and drank a few sips of the leftover ginger ale. It was lukewarm and flat, but at least it washed the mucky taste out of his mouth.

Sibley's enormous chair sat empty. Julian walked around the desk, plopped himself down onto the cool leather seat, and swiveled around. It had a smooth, silent, satisfying swivel, and he turned himself all the way around three and a half times before he began to feel dizzy.

Facing the wall of glass, Julian looked out at the city lights and the cars crawling along fifty stories below. In the window, he could see his own dark reflection—the wide, slightly upturned eyes, the black hair curling over his ears. Behind him the computer screen glowed in mirror image. He swiveled past a list of e-mail messages, and he was swiveling back toward the window again when he stopped abruptly.

Most of the subject lines said things like "Confirmation of 5/30 meeting" or "Respond ASAP" or "Lunch on the 5th." But it was the last line that had caught Julian's attention, and that was because the subject line of the last e-mail of the day, set out in capital letters, was "JULIAN."

The sender was "awcarter." But the only Carters he knew were Sibley and Daphne and Preston—nobody whose name began with an "A." For a shimmering moment, Julian considered the possibility that the e-mail was from his father—that there had never been a motorcycle accident and his father ("W" for Will) was in hiding, secretly corresponding with his brother Sibley by e-mail. But Julian dismissed the idea so quickly, it was almost as if he'd never thought it at all. His father was dead. He'd been dead for five years and was never coming back.

Julian bent his head and studied the screen more closely. All the other messages had a little check along the left-hand column. But the last one had a circle. His uncle must not have opened it yet. It must have come in while he was sleeping. Could there be another Julian? It didn't seem likely. What if he tried to open the message and Sibley came in? Or what if he accidentally hit some key that erased the entire hard disk? Things like that happened. His uncle was an important man. Maybe there was some kind of iris scanner or fingerprint recognition that would sound an alarm if he even touched the computer.

Opening someone's e-mail was just as bad as opening a letter with somebody else's name on it, but this e-mail had *his* name on it.

He touched the mouse. No sirens. No alarms. He listened for any footsteps or voices. Silence. Finally, his curiosity grew larger than his fear. He dragged the little arrow over to his name and clicked.

Instantly, a block of text appeared:

> ### May 4
>
> It all sounds very trying. Of course, Daphne has her own way of doing things. But sending him away does seem to defeat the purpose somewhat. Whatever your feelings for Billy, the boy is who he is, and perhaps the difficulties may be overcome with time.

Julian squinted and read the message again. It reminded him of the school tests where the sentences are scrambled and have to be reordered into a coherent paragraph. But even after he'd read the cryptic sentences three times, the e-mail still didn't make sense. Who was being sent away? Who was Billy? What did Aunt Daphne have to do with it? And why was it all under the subject line "JULIAN"?

Julian scrolled down the page and discovered a second e-mail:

> ### May 1
>
> Julian's visit is not going as well as we'd hoped. Daphne's at her wits' end—I won't bore you with the details. At our initial meetings, Julian came across as an intelligent boy. It's become clear, however, that he's not used to any kind of discipline and lacks even the most basic social graces.
>
> Of course, none of this should be a surprise—given

his mother's lifestyle. When Cari went off to China, we thought we could do him some good—and certainly we felt an obligation because of Billy. Perhaps the problem is that Julian does resemble his father in certain ways—the sullenness, etc. Daphne says that Preston has just spoiled us for other children.

In any case, Daphne's found an excellent summer camp for him through Fresno University: intensive math—which seems to be his strength. It's a tremendous opportunity for Julian and will get us through mid-July. Daphne's still exploring the options for the remainder of the summer.

The whole situation is awkward—exactly the type of unpleasantness I anticipated when you asked me to look Cari up.

Sibley

From the opening words, Julian's unease only grew. Presumably, this "awcarter" was some kind of relative. But who? And how could his uncle talk about him this way? How could Sibley call him "undisciplined"? Julian had done his homework every night without being reminded and had even gone over Preston's math sheets. What did Sibley mean he lacked "social graces"? It was true he barely spoke at meals, but only because he was afraid of inadvertently triggering one of Daphne's tantrums.

As he read on, Julian's discomfort at prying into his uncle's private correspondence turned into indignation. What did Sibley know about his mother's "lifestyle"? Nothing. He didn't know the first thing about her.

Julian quickly scrolled back to the first e-mail. The pieces of the puzzle were starting to fall into place. "Billy" must be his father. It was the nickname that had thrown Julian off. He'd never heard his father called anything but Will. And nobody ever talked about him in the sneering tone Sibley used. Everybody loved his father. His mother was still in mourning, her friends said, even after all these years.

Sibley never spoke of his little brother, and now Julian understood why. Apparently, in Sibley's eyes, all of Julian's bad qualities—not just rude and undisciplined, but "sullen" too— came from his father.

Although Julian had been staying with Daphne and Sibley for nearly a month, he had seen very little of his uncle. If Sibley had seemed cold—his questions too pointed, his eyes too calculating— Julian had simply assumed this was part of his character. He hadn't taken it personally. But now Julian realized it *was* personal. Beneath his polite veneer, his uncle hated him. Hated him like he'd hated his father. Hated him so much that he was planning to banish him for the entire summer.

Of course, maybe this was all Daphne's idea. "Daphne has her own way of doing things," the first e-mail said. Well, that was a fact. Like her endless rules governing the proper placement of elbows and feet. Like the elaborate point system she'd thought up, in which Julian found his score sinking further and further below

zero with each passing day. Like dinners of carrots and peas ("I can't be expected to come up with a separate menu for him every day just because his mother raised him to be a *vegetarian*," Daphne had scoffed). He could already sense Daphne counting the weeks until his mother's return. Not that they didn't have plenty of room for him. Even with Preston and him in their own rooms, and Helga, the live-in nanny, they still had two spare bedrooms. It didn't matter how little room he took up or how carefully he tried to follow her rules, Daphne just didn't like having him around.

And they couldn't send him somewhere fun, somewhere with sailboats and Jet Skis and rock climbing. No, they were sending him to *math camp*.

Julian already had plans for the summer, involving a bonfire at the beach with his best friend, Danny, and a basketball league at the Rec Center. Even he and Preston had plans. Of course, Preston was just a little kid, but he wasn't bad. He liked to watch Julian draw, and Julian had taught him how to play rummy and Chinese chess. He hardly ever made stupid mistakes, and he never cheated, which was pretty good, Julian thought, for an eight-year-old. They were going to convince Helga to take them to the Santa Cruz boardwalk. And Julian was going to teach Preston to construct a wallet out of duct tape and make origami ninja stars.

Julian couldn't bring himself to stare at his uncle's words any longer. They made him feel queasy, as though he'd opened a gilded casket and found a rotting corpse inside. With a click of the mouse, he closed the e-mail. A siren started wailing, and Julian swiveled the chair around toward the window and watched a tiny fire truck and a tiny police car flashing their red-and-blue lights through the narrow streets below. Then he swiveled back around to the desk and took a large swallow of ginger ale.

The computer beeped. Julian glanced at the screen, and saw a message so astonishing that he sprayed ginger ale out his nose and all across his uncle's computer screen.

The subject line of the newest e-mail read: "SIBLEY CARTER IS A MORON AND A WORLD-CLASS JERK!!!"

2

ROBIN ELDER

After Julian had grabbed some tissues and wiped away every drop of ginger ale, he stared at the computer suspiciously. Did it have a hidden sensor that could somehow read his mind? Surely, he thought, even his uncle's computer couldn't translate his inner thoughts directly onto the screen. It was just an ordinary e-mail. An ordinary e-mail calling his uncle a moron and a jerk. Julian tried to imagine Sibley sitting down at his imposing desk and finding this message. It would be as if he came in and found his computer sticking its tongue out at him.

What kind of person, he wondered, would be sticking his tongue out at Sibley? Obviously, someone smarter than Julian was. Someone who wasn't fooled by his uncle's smooth manners and slick facade. Not another businessman, Julian figured. In fact, it sounded like a kid. But why would a kid write his uncle an e-mail? He checked the name of the sender: Robin Elder.

Julian reached for the mouse, then hesitated. He'd already opened one of his uncle's e-mails. But that one had his name on it. It had practically invited him to open it. This one certainly had nothing to do with him.

Then again, what did he have to lose? And what did he owe an uncle who made up lies about him and slandered his parents and was plotting to send him to *math camp*? Just peeking at one e-mail wasn't such a crime. Especially when the e-mail couldn't possibly be about any important business matter, when it was from some tongue sticker-outer.

Julian got up, crossed the room to the open office door, and looked up and down the hallway. Nothing but darkened cubicles. He felt like a cat burglar about to steal some precious jewel. Stealthily, he sat back down in his uncle's chair, grabbed the mouse, and clicked:

May 4

Dear Mr. Carter,

Maybe I shouldn't call you names, but that's how I feel. I've lived next to Big Tree Grove my whole life and you just come in and buy the Greeley land and think you can cut down all the trees and you don't even care. Maybe you're not really a moron, but it is OBVIOUSLY pretty stupid to take a redwood tree that has been growing for hundreds and hundreds of years and DESTROY it just to make decks for fancy houses or to make more money, especially when you are already probably a lot richer than almost everybody else on the planet! How would you like it if I went to your backyard and started destroying everything with a chain saw? My parents say there's nothing we can do but at least I can tell you that if you do this there's going to be a lot of people who hate you forever, like me!

Yours truly,

Robin Elder

Julian read the e-mail twice. He was puzzled. He had never heard Sibley mention Big Tree Grove, or anyone named Greeley, or anything about redwood trees. His uncle made money. He invested people's money and somehow turned it into more money. When he traveled, it was to places like New York and Chicago. He certainly didn't go tramping through redwood forests cutting down trees. Maybe this girl (he thought it must be a girl) had sent her message to the wrong person.

On the other hand, the e-mail had Sibley's name on it. And obviously, there was a lot about his uncle he didn't know. The girl said his uncle had bought this Big Tree Grove, and that he was cutting down the redwoods to make money. That made sense. Maybe buying the land and cutting down the trees was just part of some business deal.

Julian had been to the giant redwood trees in Muir Woods on a field trip. He liked the ride across the Golden Gate Bridge, through the Rainbow Tunnel, and down into the shady forest.

Those redwoods would have been cut down a long time ago if people hadn't put them in a park. Now they stood behind little fences, as if they were in a tree museum. If those trees were in his backyard, he wouldn't want anybody to cut them down either.

Who was this angry Robin Elder? Julian already had a picture in his mind of her house, out in the country somewhere, with a few chickens running around and some horses. Whenever she wanted, she could walk out her door and into the shade of the giant redwoods. It wouldn't be like Muir Woods, with busloads of tourists tramping about. They would be her redwoods, a place where nobody could bother her or tell her their problems.

Suddenly a light flickered in the hallway. Julian froze and a wave of fear spread down to the base of his spine. Quickly, he closed the e-mail from Robin Elder. When he looked up, a man and a woman were peering in at him through the glass walls of the office.

The man flicked a switch that flooded the room with light. Julian blinked. The man had dark, slicked-back hair and he stared at Julian, then turned and said something to the woman in Spanish. Now, in the bright light, Julian could see that the woman was carrying a bucket and dragging a vacuum cleaner behind her. With relief, he realized that they were the cleaning crew. They kept talking quietly and looking at Julian with suspicion. Julian had been taking Spanish since the beginning of the year, and now he wished he'd paid more attention.

He wanted to say, "I am sick. I am waiting for my uncle. This is his office." But he couldn't remember how to say "sick" or "waiting" or "office" in Spanish. Instead, he said, *"Soy malo . . . y mi tío vive aqui."* "I am bad and my uncle lives here." Close enough, he thought.

The man looked at him, puzzled. *"Qué?"*

Julian repeated what he now suspected was a very foolish-sounding sentence. The man grinned. He nodded and pointed at the picture of his uncle on the desk.

"Tu tío?"

Julian nodded. He felt like he should say something more. *"Me llamo Julian."*

"*Soy Victor*," said the man. And pointing at the woman, "Irene." Then he tapped his watch and said in English, "Your uncle, when he come?"

Julian shrugged.

Irene put her hand on Julian's forehead. She made a little *tsk*ing sound, then unzipped a pocket of her small white backpack and took out a package of peanut-butter crackers. "For you," she said.

Julian remembered to say "*gracias.*" As he munched on the crackers, Victor and Irene set to work emptying the ginger ale–soaked tissues from the trash can, dusting the spotless surfaces, and vacuuming. When they were done, they gave a little wave and moved on down the hall.

Julian was suddenly tired. In the cold, bright light, with the vacuum cleaner humming across the hall, he didn't feel like a cat burglar anymore. He felt like someone who'd been left behind. He wanted to be home. Not in his uncle's high-ceilinged mansion, but in his own house, where he could read with his feet on the sofa and hear his mom in the kitchen frying potstickers—his favorite food, fortunately, because it was the only meal she knew how to cook. The end of summer seemed impossibly far away. Julian put his head down, feeling the cool wood of the desk against his burning cheeks, and closed his eyes.

Almost instantly, Julian was jolted up by the sound of a phone ringing a few inches from his ear. Probably it was somebody calling for his uncle. But what if somebody was trying to reach him? The phone rang five times, then stopped, and immediately started up again. Julian picked up the receiver.

"Hello?"

"Julian! You answered the phone. Good boy." Had he only dreamed about the e-mails? His uncle sounded friendly enough.

"Listen, the meeting went later than I expected. Meet me outside the lobby in five minutes. You can find your way out?"

"Sure. I think so." Julian was not at all sure he remembered the way to the elevator through the unlit corridors.

"Good. I'll see you in five minutes then," his uncle said, and hung up.

Julian looked up at the computer screen. The two messages— "JULIAN" and "SIBLEY CARTER IS A MORON AND A WORLD-CLASS JERK!!!"—now both had checks next to them. His uncle would come to work in the morning and know

Julian had read them. And he wouldn't be pleased. There would be somber discussions about "privacy" and "violations of trust" and "responsibility" and "maturity." There would be "consequences"—one of his uncle's favorite words. And who knows how many points Julian would lose with Daphne. Julian forced himself to focus. He had less than five minutes. What if his uncle never saw the messages? Then he would never know that Julian had been reading his e-mail.

Of course, Sibley would never receive the message from awcarter. But so what? E-mails got lost sometimes, didn't they? Anyway, it wasn't as if it had said much. The line about Daphne. Nothing important.

Julian looked at the clock. Two minutes had already gone by. He didn't have time to think anymore. He clicked the e-mail titled "JULIAN" and pressed the Delete button. The computer prompted, "Are you sure you want to delete this message?" and Julian clicked Yes.

Now there was only the message from Robin Elder. Julian was sure Sibley would never pay attention to some angry kid, even if he knew what she was talking about. But Julian was curious about this Robin, who wasn't afraid to stick her tongue out at his uncle, who loved to walk out her back door into the shade of the redwood trees. He couldn't just let her go.

He pressed the Forward button and typed in Danny's e-mail address. A brilliant inspiration. Now he was in top form! At the top of the message, he typed as quickly as he could with two fingers:

"Check this out. TOP SECRET! We'll talk later." Then he deleted Robin's message. As he was turning away from the computer, he suddenly realized that his message to Danny would appear in his uncle's out-box. He clicked on Sent Mail, deleted his message, and closed the screen. The original list of e-mails in his uncle's in-box reappeared. The subject line of the very last message now read: "Draft press release—please review."

Now everything was in order, exactly the way it had been when he'd come in. Hurrying, Julian slung his backpack over his shoulder and flicked out the light by the door. Where the hallway came to a dead end, he stopped, confused. Right or left? He saw a light and jogged to the right until he came to a small office where Victor and Irene were dusting.

"*Elevador?*" he asked, holding his hands up uncertainly.

They smiled and pointed farther down the corridor and, with relief, Julian saw the red elevator buttons glowing in the distance.

3

THE NEXT DAY

When Julian opened his eyes the next morning, Preston was sitting on his bed in a blue plaid bathrobe and green slippers, reading the funnies in the *San Francisco Chronicle*. Seeing Julian stir, he carefully folded the newspaper and placed it on Julian's nightstand.

"Where were you last night?" he asked, his round face stern.

"I was at your dad's office. Didn't they tell you?"

"No." Preston scratched his head. "My mom didn't know where you were. She called the school and they said you went home sick and mom said we should call the police and then we had takeout Chinese and then I had to go to bed."

Julian sighed. Somehow this was going to be his fault, he knew.

"Well, I didn't exactly go *home* sick. Your dad sent a taxi to pick me up from school. And then he had a meeting and didn't

pick me up until after nine. You were already asleep when I got home. She didn't really call the police, did she?"

Preston shrugged. "I don't think so. Are you still sick?"

Julian did a mental check. Nothing hurt. He was a little tired, but he certainly wasn't going to stay home from school. Not today. He had to talk to Danny.

"No. I'm OK now." He got up and pulled on a pair of khaki pants with lots of pockets and a Beatles T-shirt one of his mother's friends had given him. Preston handed him his watch. "Let's eat," Julian said. He was starving.

He followed Preston along a hall lined with old family portraits, down a wide staircase, and into the gleaming metallic kitchen. Preston took a half gallon of milk out of the giant refrigerator. Julian opened a cupboard full of cereal boxes, pulled out his favorite, and set it on the counter, along with two bowls and spoons.

They ate silently. Preston read the cereal box. Julian emptied one bowl quickly and then poured himself another. The fabulous array of breakfast cereals was the best thing about living at his uncle's, he thought. At home, his mom only gave him organic whole-wheat bread or, worse, oatmeal with soy milk. There were advantages to living the good life.

Daphne walked in wearing a white tennis outfit. Her blond hair was pulled back in a ponytail.

"Elbows off the table," she said to Julian, then gave him a quick once-over. "Well, you don't look so sick to me."

Julian shrugged and kept chewing. Daphne stood silently, staring at him, until he was forced to look up and meet her eyes. So much for formalities. She was coming in for the kill.

"Julian. We need to talk." She sighed deeply. "When you first came here, I thought we had a deal." She waited until Julian lifted his eyes from his cereal bowl again before continuing. "Every day, it is your responsibility to inform me where you're going after school and what time you'll be back. Last night, I had *no* idea where you were. I almost called the *police*!"

Julian had just put a large spoonful of cereal in his mouth. "Sorry," he said, half swallowing. "I thought Uncle Sibley told you."

"Please don't talk with your mouth full. It's not Sibley's job to keep me posted about your after-school plans. He had a *very* important meeting yesterday. He is the chief executive officer of IPX!"

Julian heard Danny's mocking voice in his head. "Mr. CEO." That's what he always called Sibley.

"Why are you smiling?" Daphne's voice was starting to rise like a jet plane taking off. "Do you think it's funny that your uncle had to interrupt an important phone call to arrange for your taxi ride? Did you expect him to spend the rest of his afternoon trying to get hold of me? You were in his office all afternoon! There *is*, if I remember correctly, a telephone on his desk. You couldn't leave a simple message on my cell phone?"

It was important to keep in mind, Julian thought, that this was a woman who was conspiring to send him to *math camp*.

22

His aunt was watching his face closely, and she narrowed her eyes.

"What *did* you do there all that time?"

"I don't know. I fell asleep, I guess. When I woke up, everyone had gone home. Then Uncle Sibley came to pick me up."

Just as Daphne opened her mouth, her cell phone rang and she clamped it to her ear. "Hello, Sergei," she cooed. "I'm running a little late for my lesson." She paused and gave Julian an exasperated stare. "Yes, he's *fine*. He forgot to *call* is all." Pause. "I know, I could just *strangle* him." Then she turned and walked into the dining room, holding the phone to her ear. She lowered her voice, but Julian could still hear it echoing shrilly. "Yes, six more weeks." Pause. "Oh, it *will* be." Pause. "Oh, I can't *tell* you what a relief."

When Daphne returned, her face was stern again. "Before I go, I would like an apology for yesterday. And please tell me when you'll be home today."

"I'm sorry for not calling, Aunt Daphne," Julian said evenly. "I'm going to Danny's after school. I'll probably have dinner there."

"I'm deducting two points for last night. Be home by eight. No excuses. And do make sure Preston gets to the bus stop on time this morning. Helga's got an appointment."

She walked over to Preston and ran her hand down the back of his head, where his pale hair was cut short. "Good-bye, darling. Have a fabulous day at school."

Preston's school bus was late. Once he was safely on board,

Julian stood at the corner, trying to decide whether to wait for the city bus or run to school. It was ten blocks, but entirely downhill. The day was cool and clear with a breeze blowing up from San Francisco Bay. He could see the majestic orange towers of the Golden Gate Bridge and a giant tanker moving slowly across the slate blue waters of the Bay.

He decided to run. He flew down the steep hill, his feet pounding against the pavement, his backpack slamming up and down, trying to keep his feet moving fast enough to avoid keeling forward. In ten minutes, he was careening through the doors of Filbert Middle School. He arrived in homeroom still breathing hard.

Danny sat slumped over his desk, his head half-buried in his black Giants sweatshirt. Julian grabbed the seat next to him just as Mr. Snipps began the announcements. He scribbled in one of his school notebooks, "Did you get Robin's e-mail?"

Danny shook his head and made a face that said, *I don't know what you're talking about. And who's Robin?*

When the bell rang to end homeroom, Julian leaned close to Danny. "You're not going to believe this. My aunt and uncle want to send me away for the whole summer. To *math camp*!"

"*Math camp*! Are you serious?"

Julian nodded.

"The whole summer? That's brutal." Danny gave him a pat on the back and knitted his dark brows in mock sympathy. "Hey! What about our basketball league?"

"I know! And I found this crazy e-mail to my uncle from some girl named Robin."

"Come on, boys," Mr. Snipps shouted. "Get going! This is not a café here!"

"Come to my house after school," Danny said. "My mom'll feed you."

"What's that in your hair, Danny? Is that gel?" Julian reached out to touch his shiny black head.

"Hey, back off!" Danny jerked his head away. "It's my new look. It'll make me irresistible. The girls will be crazy for it!"

All day, Julian sat watching the clock creep through each forty-five-minute period. By lunch time, he was starting to feel tired and queasy again. Maybe he still wasn't 100 percent better. When the last bell rang, he headed out to the front steps. The breeze off the Bay cleared his head a little.

"So, what's with math camp?" Danny asked, coming up behind him.

"You're not going to believe this!" Julian grabbed his backpack and the boys started walking slowly toward the bus stop. "I found this e-mail from Sibley to somebody—I don't even know who— and he starts saying all these bad things about me: how I don't have any discipline or any manners—"

"What? That's insane. My mom's always saying," Danny changed to a mincing Spanish accent, "'Julian is un perfecto caballerito—a perfect little gentleman. You should be more like him!'"

"Anyway, it's obvious from the letter Sibley really hates me. I mean, now there's proof. And then he goes on about how Daphne's found the perfect camp for me—*math camp.* And she's looking for another camp for the *rest* of the summer that'll probably be just as horrible."

"That's brutal," Danny said, shaking his head.

"Oh, and it's in Fresno."

"Fresno! My cousins live there. It's so hot in the summer, you'll be dying to get back to the fog."

"And Sibley's saying what a 'tremendous opportunity' this is for me—"

"Wait—how did you find all this out?"

The bus pulled up and they went to the back and sat down. Julian explained in detail the taxi ride, his visit to his uncle's office, the e-mail with his name on it, and his last-minute decision to delete the message. By the time he got to the end of the story, they'd reached California Street and gotten off to wait for the next bus.

"I don't know." Danny scratched his head. "I mean, it's bad. It's brutal. But what can you do? Maybe you should tell your mom."

Julian considered. "She's in China—what could she do? The camp's probably paid for already. Plus, I'm not supposed to know about it, remember?"

"Maybe she'd come home."

"No way." For years, his mom had dreamed of going to China. Finally, she'd gotten a grant that actually paid her to spend five months photographing Buddhist statues and temples. She wouldn't come home without a genuine emergency.

"Then you're stuck. Don't forget, *my* parents signed me up for two weeks of journalism camp."

"But that's here, not in *Fresno*," Julian said. "And you *like* that kind of stuff." He sighed. "Not that I want to stay with Sibley anyway."

"Now that his *true feelings* have been *revealed*," Danny said.

The 1 California bus pulled up in front of them. It was so crowded, they had to stand in the aisle, holding on to the metal poles.

"I should just run away," Julian said as the bus lurched into motion. "Camp out in the Presidio or in Golden Gate Park." There were lots of places in the park where a kid could hide. If you stayed away from the Children's Playground or the Japanese Tea Garden, there were huge stretches of trees and bushes with hardly any people.

Danny looked at him in horror. "Are you insane? Do you still have a fever?" He reached up to feel Julian's forehead. "You want to live in Golden Gate Park at *night*? With all the homeless people?"

Julian shrugged.

"What about your granny? The one we had dim sum with. Couldn't you call her?"

"Popo? I haven't seen her since Chinese New Year. Plus, what could she do?"

"Rescue you from Sibley and his evil plots!"

"I think my mom already asked her about the summer. She couldn't do it. She was traveling or something. Plus, she works." His mother thought Popo was a workaholic. She wrote for the *Chronicle* and was always late for a deadline.

"It might be worth a try. Blood's thicker than water," Danny said with an air of authority.

"What does that mean—'blood's thicker than water'? I never get that."

"You're always so clueless about everything! It's because you don't watch enough movies. Blood is your blood connections, your relatives. They stick with you."

Julian thought about this. Popo was his blood relative, but she lived two hours away in Sacramento and he only saw her on the big holidays—Thanksgiving and Christmas and Chinese New Year. Then there was his mother, but she wasn't exactly sticking with him. His dad—well, it wasn't his fault he died.

"Sibley's blood, right?"

"Of course! He's your father's brother. That's blood. That's DNA."

Julian raised his eyebrows.

"Well, there's another expression," Danny said, laughing. "*La familia no la escogemos.* You can't pick your relatives. Anyway, forget Sibley for now. Who's Robin?"

Julian pulled the cord for the next stop. "You'll see when we get to your house. I want you to read her e-mail for yourself and tell me what you think."

When the bus came to a halt, the boys jumped out the rear door, walked up a block, and turned onto Clement Street. Fruit stands and stalls of kitchenware crowded the sidewalk. They jostled their way past two cafés, an Irish bar, a pizza parlor, a Thai restaurant, a Chinese dim sum place, and the Toy Boat Dessert Café. All around, voices talked and shouted—in English, in staccato Cantonese, in the sleepy murmur of Russian.

They bought two steamed buns at their favorite Chinese bakery, flipped through the sale bins at Green Apple Books, then turned onto one of the avenues and stopped at a pale yellow row house. Once inside, they headed straight to Danny's room where Danny switched on the computer and turned on the television. A sound like screaming chipmunks filled the room.

"Hey," Julian shouted over the commercial. "I want you to pay attention to this. It's important."

"No problem. I can multitask." Danny pulled up his e-mail screen. "Ah, the mysterious Robin Elder! We meet at last!" he said, clicking the mouse. Julian flopped down on Danny's bed.

"Well, what do you think?" Julian asked after a moment, grabbing the remote control and turning down the TV volume.

"Wait . . . wait."

Julian drummed his fingers against the desk.

"Stop!" Danny yelled. "You're making me nuts!"

Julian stopped drumming and impatiently unpacked his school books.

Finally, Danny leaned back in his chair. "Well, a number of

things are clear. First, your uncle, who we all know is an evil, scary, money-grubbing liar, is even worse than we thought. He's cutting down *redwood* trees! Second, this girl has obviously never met Mr. CEO, or she'd never have sent him a crazy e-mail like this. Third . . . I can't remember what's third."

"What should we do? Should we write her back?"

"Of course! We've got to write her back! You *deleted* her message to Sibley. You can't do that and then not even tell her! That would be *rude*!"

"But what should we say?"

"I don't know," Danny said. "You start."

"OK. I'll dictate and you type."

Danny's mom was an office manager and she believed that everyone should know how to type. Danny was the only kid Julian knew who typed with all his fingers, like an adult. And his mom brought home all sorts of useful overstock. In addition to his own computer, Danny had a color printer, a fax machine, and a speakerphone.

Julian lay down on Danny's bed. "Um. OK. How about 'Dear Robin.'"

Danny made a face. "I'll just put 'Robin.' From what we've read, she's not much of a dear."

"We don't even know if she's a she! Maybe we should ask. But we can't start off like that! How about, 'I'm Sibley Carter's nephew and I accidentally read your e-mail to him. Can you tell us more about yourself and explain what my uncle has to do with your redwood trees? I won't show your e-mail to my uncle. He didn't get the last one because I deleted it. Honestly, I didn't think it would do any good and you might even have gotten into trouble.'"

Danny typed quickly. "Go on."

Julian paused for a moment. "I guess we should say, 'Please trust me. Even though I live with my uncle, we aren't very close.' Then how should it end?"

Danny just cocked his head. He was still typing.

"How about, 'You can reach me at this e-mail address. It belongs to my friend Danny, who you can also trust. From, Julian Carter-Li.'"

Danny finished typing and lifted his hands with a flourish.

"Do you really think this is a good idea?" Julian asked. "I mean, none of this is really our business."

"Don't you want to know what your uncle's up to?"

"I guess so," Julian said. "You'd better send it before I lose my nerve."

Danny pressed Send.

"Let me see it." Julian sat up on the edge of the bed and reached for the mouse.

Danny pulled it away. "Before you get upset, I should tell you I changed a few words."

"What do you mean?"

"Just to make it sound better."

Julian grabbed the mouse and clicked:

May 5

Robin,

I am the unfortunate nephew of Mr. Sibley Carter, aka the Great and Terrible Mr. CEO. I have intercepted your recent message to him. Please reveal your identity and spell out in more detail your complaint against Mr. CEO and what sinister deeds he intends to perform. I was forced to destroy your prior message because I feared it might endanger yourself or others. Feel free to speak freely. You can have utmost confidence in me. Although we are related by blood, I am no friend of my uncle's. Please have utmost confidence also in my closest friend, Daniel Lopez. I would trust him with my life. You can contact me through him, at this address. Please do not attempt to contact me through my uncle or it could endanger my life and yours.

Your devoted servant,

Julian Carter-Li

P.S. Are you a girl?

"Are you crazy?" Julian said when he'd finished reading the e-mail. "Are you trying to make me look like an idiot?"

"No, trust me," Danny said with enormous sincerity. "It's better this way. She'll take us more seriously."

Julian put his head in his hands. "Danny! You totally screwed this up."

Danny was silent for a moment. "Oh, come on. It's not such a big deal. If you really don't like it, send a retraction. You can type it yourself." He stood up and offered Julian the chair.

Very slowly, Julian pecked out:

May 5

Dear Robin,

That last e-mail was from my friend Danny. Please ignore it. Sibley Carter is my uncle. I found your e-mail by accident but I don't understand what you're talking about. Who are you and where's Big Tree Grove and what's the Greeley land and what does my uncle have to do with them? I promise I won't give any information to my uncle. We are not very close.

Sincerely,

Julian Carter-Li

P.S. I really did delete your message to my uncle. I don't think he would have listened to you anyway.

Danny watched over his shoulder. "You really think that's better?" he asked incredulously. "Oh, well. You know best. Send away."

Julian sent the e–mail and then said, "I'd better do my homework." He pulled out his math book. "I have two pages of math for tonight and three still from yesterday."

Danny sighed heavily and set to work himself, alternately scribbling furiously and singing along with the TV. Julian lay on his stomach, writing neatly and figuring his algebra almost automatically. He was in the middle of solving a particularly difficult equation when he heard a voice at the door.

"Hola, mi hijito." Luciana Lopez stood leaning against the door frame in her work clothes, a halo of black curls around her face. "How are you, Julian?" she asked with a searching look. "Are you feeling better? Danny said you went home sick."

"Oh, I'm fine. I'm better today."

"Can Julian stay for dinner, Mom? Please?"

"Of course, Julian is always welcome. Papa will be home soon. You boys are doing your homework? Such good boys! But Danny," she chided, picking up the remote control and turning off the television, "no more TV, OK? These shows, they are baby shows anyway."

In half an hour, the sound of the running shower told them that Danny's father, Eduardo, was home. A little later, Luciana called the boys to supper. In the bright kitchen, she questioned them about school. Eduardo told about his afternoon, fixing a backed-up toilet in the middle of a fancy engagement party. Julian wolfed down two platefuls of spaghetti and six pieces of garlic bread, then sat back contentedly.

"Well, you must be feeling better," Luciana said. "You certainly have a healthy appetite!"

"He's a growing boy!" Danny said with feigned pride. "And you know, his aunt only feeds our little *vegetariano* pig knuckles and cow tongue."

"I had cow tongue once," Eduardo said. "It wasn't bad. But you know what they say: You shouldn't taste anything that can taste you back!"

Julian couldn't help twisting his tongue about to see if he was tasting it or it was tasting him, which made everyone laugh. When the boys had cleared the table, they rushed back to check Danny's e-mail, but there was no message from Robin Elder.

"You see," Julian said bitterly. "She's never going to write back now. She's going to think we're just a couple of stupid kids."

"Oh, lighten up!" Danny said. "Who's she? Mother Teresa? She's probably just a stupid kid too."

At ten minutes to eight, Julian opened the heavy door to his uncle's house and found Daphne and Sibley sitting in the living room, with brochures and papers spread out on the coffee table. Julian waved and headed toward the staircase.

"Julian!" his uncle called out. "In a civilized society, it's customary to greet people when you walk into their home."

"Hello, Uncle Sibley. Hello, Aunt Daphne," Julian said. "How are you?"

"Just great," Sibley answered in a decidedly un-great tone. "And you? Are you feeling better today?"

"Yes, thank you," Julian replied. He could do "social graces" as well as anyone.

"You finished your homework?"

"Yeah, I mean, yes. At Danny's."

"I appreciate that you're on time tonight," Daphne said. "One point. But I have to deduct two points for this morning. You didn't clear away the cereal bowls *or* make your bed." She gave him a pitying look. "Julian, I wish I didn't have to keep doing this, but we've talked about it before."

Julian sighed. Another point in the hole. Daphne had promised to buy him a laptop when he reached twenty-five points, but so far, he hadn't even gotten above zero.

And now he really *could* use his own laptop. Now that the mysterious Robin Elder was out there in the universe somewhere and might just decide to write them back.

36

4

BACK & FORTH

Dear Julian Carter-Li,

Thank you for your e-mail. Assuming you are who you say you are and you're telling me the truth, I guess I should thank you for deleting that e-mail. I was having second thoughts about sending it. I guess I thought Sibley Carter wouldn't pay any attention to my letter but I was mad and I wanted him to know.

I am 11 years old (12 on July 29th). How old are you? I live on a ranch (more of a farm, really) in Mendocino County. Big Tree Grove is an EXTREMELY rare stand of old-growth redwood on the land next to ours. It used to belong to Ed Greeley. He loved Big Tree and was NEVER going to cut it down. Your uncle, obviously, is the CEO of IPX, which is now the owner of the Greeley land. IPX is planning to CLEAR-CUT the whole stand! Maybe you can get your uncle to change his mind?

Yours truly,

Robin

P.S. Tell your friend Danny of course I'm a GIRL! And this isn't a JOKE!!!!

May 8

Hey Robin Hood,

I never said it was a joke! Don't you have any sense of humor???

Your everlastingly faithful correspondent,

Señor Daniel Lopez

May 8

Dear Robin,

Thanks for writing back. You are probably right that my uncle wouldn't have paid any attention to your letter, but it might have made him mad and gotten you in trouble somehow. I am 12 and in the sixth grade at Filbert Middle School. I'm staying with my uncle because my mom had to go to China (Sibley is my dad's brother). My cousin lives there too. He's only 8 but he's a nice kid. I don't know if I can get my uncle to change his mind about your redwoods. Probably not. Do you like living in the redwoods? I have been to the redwoods at Muir Woods.

They are pretty enormous. Have you been there?

Julian

P.S. Danny wants to know if Ed Greeley is dead.

May 11

Dear Julian,

That is so cool your mom is in China. What's she doing there? And where's your dad?

My family's pretty boring. I have 3 brothers and an annoying little sister. And a father and mother, obviously. Nobody ever goes ANYWHERE. We are home schooled so I don't go on field trips and I'm not in any grade, but I'm reading on a 12th grade level. We grow most of our own food, so we hardly ever leave the ranch. But I don't actually mind. I LOVE living in the redwoods. Plus, we have a farm with chickens and goats and stuff. I HATE even going into town (I know you shouldn't say "hate" but it's true). It's so crowded and dirty and ugly. Plus you have to drive FOREVER to get there. May is my favorite month. The flowers are out and we've got a new baby goat. When I grow up, I'm going to live right here. My dad's going to build me my own house down near the river. I'm already making the blueprints.

I've never been to Muir Woods but I did a report on John Muir for a contest on California Heroes (unfortunately, I didn't win the Grand Prize). Have you studied him?

Robin

P.S. OBVIOUSLY, Ed Greeley has passed away or else Big Tree would not be THREATENED.

May 13

Dear Goat Girl,

OBVIOUSLY we are familiar with John Muir, founder of the Sierra Club and Yosemite National Park. It may interest you to know that I am reading at the level of a certified genius and my friend, Mr. Carter-Li, has recently been nominated for a Nobel Prize in mathematics.

I don't know if I would actually like to live with chickens. My dad used to have chickens and he says they are not the brightest creatures on the planet. San Francisco is a very cool city. It has the Golden Gate Bridge. And Alcatraz, the famous prison. Don't forget that millions of people come every year just to see the cool things here.

Signing off from the epicenter of the civilized world,

Danny

P.S. Don't you know it's rude to ask people personal questions?????

May 15

Dear JULIAN,

You can tell your FRIEND that a lot of people come to Huckleberry Ranch too. My mom and dad lead seminars on organic gardening and solar power and we're part of the

Farm/Urban Network (FUN). Sometimes in the summer we host exchange students through FUN. Of course, we wouldn't want MILLIONS of people here. They'd just trample everything and ruin everything. Then it might look like San Francisco! (Ha-ha!) But we live so far away from town that it's nice to have visitors. My mom loves all our guests (even the BAD ones) and my dad is a natural born teacher. I like the exchange students best because my best friend moved to Phoenix last year so now there's no kids my age nearby.

Has your uncle said anything about Big Tree?

Did I ask something too personal???

Yours truly,

Robin

May 16

Dear Robin,

I haven't heard anything from my uncle about Big Tree but he doesn't really talk much. He's hardly ever home.

My mom is a photographer and she got a grant to go to China to do a photographic series on Buddhist temples. My uncle moved to San Francisco from Boston last fall. So my mom asked him if I could stay with them while she's in China. He said yes but actually I found out he's sending me away to camp for the whole summer. My dad died in a motorcycle crash when I was 7.

I think your house sounds very interesting. Danny and I looked at the website for that exchange program and there was a picture of your goats! It sounds like FUN (you must get a lot of puns about this!).

Julian

May 19

Dear Julian,

I have to write fast because I have double chores today. I got in BIG trouble yesterday because I forgot that I had made this stupid bet with Molly (my SUPER annoying sister) and I lost (which was basically unfair, but that's another story) and I was supposed to milk the goats. They were FINE, of course, but my dad was super angry!

Anyway, I just wanted to say sorry about your dad. That is a real tragedy to lose your father. Maybe in real life your uncle is not such a moron. I may be unfairly judging him and not understanding things from his shoes. My mom says I have a tendency to do this. But I don't see how anything could justify cutting down Big Tree Grove. I do apologize if what I said in my e-mail about your uncle hurt your feelings. Obviously, I didn't know YOU were going to read it!

Robin

May 20

Dear Robin,

It's OK about my dad. I don't really remember him that much because I was so little when he died.

I get in trouble at my uncle's a lot too. My aunt has this point system for everything I do. I'm supposed to get a laptop when I get 25 points but right now I'm at negative 17. I spend most of my time at Danny's.

If you don't go to school, what do you do all day?

Julian

May 21

Dear Goat Girl,

Since you asked, I'm doing extremely well. Thank you for your concern!

Lose your sympathy for Mr. CEO! I'm sure he doesn't care 2 cents for your redwoods. He actually banned me from his mansion because I didn't get my feet off his couch fast enough to satisfy his evil mate. I kid you not, I was wearing socks!!!! Julian is in DENIAL if he thinks he's ever going to get a laptop because he gets dinged a point for the most idiotic things—like saying "yeah" instead of "yes." And let's not forget that Mr. CEO is sending Julian to MATH CAMP!! In FRESNO, the HOTTEST PLACE OUTSIDE HELL!!

Basically, Sibley's $EVIL$. You should bring him down!!!

On the other hand, at least he doesn't make Julian milk goats!

Just tellin' it like it is,

Danny

May 23

Dear Julian (and Danny),

There's about a million things to do here. Well, obviously, there's a lot of stuff I HAVE to do, like my homework and reports, etc. And planting and weeding and gathering eggs and milking the goats, etc. But there's a lot of fun stuff too, like going to the river or the swimming hole. We bake a lot with my mom and I'm still working on my blueprints for my house. I bet it's a lot more fun than math camp!

Of course my favorite place to go is Big Tree. Nobody ever goes there except me and it's the most BEAUTIFUL place on earth. I can bring a book or a snack (I LOVE chocolate chip cookies, do you?). If you saw it, you'd know why I'm so mad at your uncle and IPX!

Speaking of which, even if your uncle is not the nicest man in the world, he can't be entirely heartless. He's taking care of you, right? Couldn't you at least say something to your uncle about Big Tree? If I could speak to him, I'd have plenty to say!

Robin

5

HOME WITH DAPHNE & SIBLEY

The day after the boys received Robin's latest e-mail, Danny had a dentist appointment after school. Alone, Julian climbed the steep hill to his uncle's house, wondering how he could respond to Robin. Clearly, she still didn't understand a thing about Sibley. Maybe he should just tell her that her cause was hopeless, that it was ridiculous to think that he could change Sibley's mind about anything. But then she'd have no reason to write to them at all.

Near the top of the hill, Julian turned down a wide street lined with ornate apartment buildings and enormous mansions. Robin might like these houses, he thought. They weren't dirty or ugly-looking. They were beautiful and elegant. He tried to figure out why the houses here looked so different from the houses where he and Danny lived. They were bigger, of course, but it wasn't just their size. It was something about money, he decided, that made them look so solid and harmonious, something he couldn't put his finger on that made the houses only for rich people, like his uncle.

His mom had never owned a house; they had rented the same shabby flat since he was a baby—the bottom floor in a gray house with a pointed roof and peeling shingles. Upstairs there used to be an old Russian lady, who would babysit Julian when his mom was away, but then Mrs. Petrova moved to Florida. A couple of Japanese graduate students moved in to her place but they were so quiet you'd hardly know they were there.

The inside of his mom's house was also different from his uncle's. For one thing, the dishes didn't match. And the furniture was mostly odds and ends she'd picked up at garage sales. The walls were covered with masks his mother made—painted masks and red clay masks and white papier-mâché masks, and Julian's favorite, a gnomish green face with horns holding a large purple marble in its mouth. Her portraits—black-and-white photos of brides and grooms and unfamiliar children—littered the hallway and covered the dining-room table.

Sibley's house was like his office, every surface gleaming and smooth, everything in its place. It was quiet and dustless and cool.

Julian remembered how excited he'd been when he'd first seen the house. All he'd known then was that his uncle had moved to San Francisco and wanted to meet him. At first, his mom hadn't wanted him to go. She'd said his father never wanted to see his family, and they never wanted to see him. But then she decided it was time to let bygones be bygones.

It was right before Halloween. Glowering jack-o-lanterns lined his uncle's wide steps. As Julian listened to the doorbell chime, black silhouettes of witches and devils had peered down from the golden windows. Inside, he had been awestruck by the enormous rooms, the gleaming silver, the sophisticated elegance of his aunt and uncle.

They'd set up a formal visitation schedule—dinner on the first Friday of the month—except when Sibley and Daphne had other obligations, which turned out to be often. When his mother got the China grant, Sibley was her only real option. She'd stood, rubbing her slim fingers together, her face nervous and beseeching. Sibley appraised the two of them by the light of the chandelier in the cavernous entryway. "Not a problem," he'd said after an awkward moment. "Plenty of room here."

Now Sibley's steps were lined with urns of gaudy spring flowers. Julian unlocked the front door and found, on the side table, a postcard of a monkey staring at a giant golden Buddha. On the back was scribbled: *Working hard! So many things that would interest you—wish you were here! Love, Mom.* Julian folded the postcard in half and stuck it in his back pocket, then jogged up the wide main staircase and down the hallway to Preston's room.

Preston, still in his school uniform, was sitting at his desk, playing a computer game. Julian came up behind him and gently lifted off his headphones.

"New game?" he said softly.

Preston shot down an alien spaceship. "Gram sent it to me."

Technically, Julian thought, she was his grandmother too. But she lived in Boston and had never even sent him a birthday card.

"Don't you have homework, buddy?"

Preston closed the game with a sigh. "I'm supposed to pick a topic for my final project." He swiveled his chair toward Julian. "On ecology. We were supposed to have one last week, but I don't know what to do."

"Ecology's a pretty big field. There must be a million things you could pick."

Preston slumped down farther in his chair. "I've been thinking and thinking, but I'm stumped!"

Julian laughed. "Well, if you're 'stumped,' maybe you should write about a tree."

"A tree?" Preston said doubtfully. "I was thinking maybe spiders."

"Come on, you live in California, land of the greatest trees on Earth."

"You mean redwood trees?"

Julian had suggested a tree because he couldn't resist the pun. He hadn't been thinking about Robin. But if Preston became an expert on redwoods, all the better! His uncle wouldn't be able to sway him so easily then. Preston's soul was unformed, and still innocent, he thought. He couldn't stand to think of him ending up like Uncle Sibley.

"Redwoods might work," said Preston, thoughtfully. "We went on a field trip to Muir Woods last year. Do you think there's books on redwoods? We have to make a bibliography."

"There must be." Julian sat down at Preston's computer. "You have Internet on this thing, right?"

Preston nodded.

"You can start there." He pointed to the set of encyclopedias on Preston's bookshelf. Preston picked up Volume 21, Ra–Ru, and began looking for "Redwood." Julian opened the online catalog for the San Francisco Public Library. "Here's *The Ever-Living Tree: The Life and Times of the Coast Redwood*," he said. "And *Coast Redwood: A Natural and Cultural History*. You'll definitely have enough for a bibliography."

He typed "redwoods" into the search engine and clicked on one link promisingly titled "Fun Facts for Kids." "The magnificent coastal redwood," it began, "once covered millions of acres, from southern Oregon to the Santa Cruz Mountains in California. Today, experts estimate that about 4 percent of the original redwood forest remains."

Julian frowned. He pictured ninety-six giant trunks lying on the forest floor and only four trees left standing. That couldn't be right.

He read on: "Large-scale logging of redwood began after the California gold rush of 1848 and continued steadily throughout the twentieth century. While redwood forests still blanket vast stretches of Northern California, most of these forests are less than 100 years old. Vestiges of the original, or 'old-growth,' redwood forest are protected today in areas such as the Redwood National Park and Humboldt State Park in Northern California."

Julian leaned back in his chair. Was Big Tree Grove, he wondered, one of the last vestiges of the original redwood forest?

Sibley was home early that night, which meant a formal dinner in the dining room at seven o'clock sharp. Sitting at the long, polished table, Julian tried to think of a way to broach the topic of Big Tree. But his imagined questions all sounded completely fishy ("So, Uncle Sibley, any interesting new projects at work lately?") or too obvious ("So, Uncle Sibley, bought any redwoods lately?")

Julian gave up and concentrated on the food. Besides the decidedly unvegetarian salmon, there were baked potatoes (acceptable), beet salad (dubious), and lima beans (clearly inedible). He was just trying the beets, which were sour and unpleasantly crunchy, when Daphne suddenly said, "Julian, there's something we've been meaning to discuss with you." She smiled the smile of a gracious hostess. "You know, summer's just three weeks away, and we've made some plans we know you're going to be very excited about."

He'd been expecting this announcement ever since he'd opened Sibley's e-mail.

"What's that?" He fiddled with his napkin and tried to look innocent.

"We've found this absolutely fabulous camp. It's going to be a tremendous opportunity for you."

Of course, she wouldn't admit she just wanted him out of the way.

"I know you're going to love it," Daphne continued.

"Anything but math camp, right?" Julian's nerves were making him bold. "I heard they actually have such a thing. What a nightmare!"

Daphne blanched. Julian looked at her with a smile of satisfaction that he hoped would pass for one of pleasant anticipation.

Sibley, who was flipping through the business section of the newspaper, looked up at the unexpected silence.

"Well, in fact . . ." Daphne hesitated and Julian smiled more broadly. "It's called High Sights Academy. It's not *math camp* . . . I would say more sciencey. Four weeks! Take a look!" She handed him a brochure. "And then, when that's done—I just finalized this today—you're off to study *Mandarin*! I mean, Sibley and I were saying how *ridiculous* it is that you don't speak Chinese when you're half-Chinese yourself! Right, Sibley?"

Something about the way his aunt said "half-Chinese" always made it sound vaguely like an insult—or not an insult exactly, but something that made him less than Preston, who, at least in her view, wasn't half anything.

"Language of the future," Sibley said. "In six weeks, you'll know conversational Mandarin."

"You could talk to your mother's family," Daphne gushed.

"They speak Cantonese," Julian said. "Well, some of them. But they all speak English anyway."

"It's not just to speak to them!" Daphne said with a trace of irritation. "Like Sibley says, it's a very important language. A billion people! Your mom's probably learning Mandarin right now. You two can practice together."

Julian doubted that his mom was learning much Mandarin. She'd tried some language tapes before she'd left and never got past "How are you?" He could still hear the counting in his head: *ee, er, san, tse . . .*

"I'm sure your mother will be thrilled," Daphne continued. "Of course, she hasn't exactly been in touch. I sent her an e-mail last week, but I haven't heard back." She glanced meaningfully at Sibley.

Hearing Daphne talk about his mom always made Julian a little queasy. He looked down at the brochure Daphne had given him, which featured a clump of goofy kids standing in front of a chalkboard, grinning broadly.

"Well, Julian, do you have anything to say to your aunt?" Sibley said.

"Thanks, Aunt Daphne," Julian responded. "Math camp. Wow."

Daphne narrowed her eyes, then apparently decided to ignore Julian's tone. "You leave the Monday after school lets out. There's a bus that will take you to Fresno. Did I mention it's through Fresno University? Very prestigious."

"Pricey," Sibley added from behind the newspaper. "But worth it."

Julian stared at Daphne with loathing.

"Of course, before you leave I thought we'd have a little party. Saturday night! We couldn't let you leave without celebrating!" she said, then added with a saccharine smile, "Celebrating what a great time we've all had, of course."

Preston said, "Can we have ice-cream cake?"

"Of course, darling. Ice-cream cake it is. And we'll do take-out from Eliza's. They have that fabulous roast duck and sesame chicken that you love, Sibley." Daphne took out her BlackBerry and punched a few buttons. "Less than three weeks to go!" she said with poorly concealed glee.

6

THE PLAN

Julian sat through the next day of school in a kind of daze. As his teachers droned on and on, he became fixated on a single depressing thought: If he went to math camp and Mandarin camp all summer, he wouldn't have a real summer vacation for more than a year! Two years of school without a break. Meanwhile, there were kids like Robin living in the United States of America who didn't even have to go to school at all! That was injustice!

After school, he just lay on Danny's bed while Danny worked away on the latest e-mail to Robin. When he finished, he read it out loud:

May 25

Dear Robin,

Nothing but bad news here. First, we haven't found out

anything about your redwoods. Mr. CEO hasn't said a word. Are you sure you've got the right guy??

Second, even if you DO have the right guy, we're not going to be able to help you much more because it's official: Julian's being shipped off to Math Camp in three weeks. While you're up there having your vacation from not being in school, the Dastardly Duo—reaching new heights of evilness—are forcing poor Julian to spend HIS summer vacation doing algebra and learning Chinese!!!

So it looks like you're losing your undercover agent!

Lopez & Carter-Li

Julian watched a hummingbird dip into the feeder by Danny's window. "You know, she doesn't like it when you write like that. She thinks you're making fun of her."

"Aw, she can take it! She's a big girl."

"It would be nice to give her some good news for a change."

"What? Like, 'Julian had a long talk with his uncle and convinced him that cutting down redwood trees is morally wrong'? Be realistic! We're talking about Mr. CEO here!"

"Yeah, I guess."

They turned reluctantly to their homework. With the end of school approaching, their teachers were trying to cram as much into their heads as possible. Danny worked conscientiously for half an hour, then began to drum a syncopated beat with his pencil against his desk lamp. Finally, he turned to Julian and said, "Heard anything from your mom?"

Julian reached into his back pocket. The postcard was still there and he unbent it and handed it to Danny.

"Very touching!" Danny said. "'Wish you were here.' Very original."

"Aw, be quiet." Julian studied the golden Buddha. "She's doing good. *She's* not in math camp."

Danny flipped the postcard onto Julian's stomach and turned toward the computer. "New message from Robin Hood! See, if she were offended, she wouldn't write back so quickly."

Julian sat up and looked at the screen:

May 25

Dear Julian and Danny,

I feel for Julian about math camp. Truly that would be my WORST NIGHTMARE to be cooped up in a classroom all day, winter AND summer. I think I would go CRAZY!! I can't even stand to wear shoes for a day!

Hey—I just had the MOST BRILLIANT idea!!! What if you came up here instead?? Then you could see Big Tree Grove for yourself and maybe figure out how to convince your uncle not to cut it down.

On second thought, I guess your uncle isn't going to send you HERE, when WE'RE the ones fighting his logging plan!

OK. Scratch that idea. Maybe it wasn't so brilliant after all!

Robin

Julian hadn't even gotten to the end of the e-mail when Danny cried out, "That girl is a genius!"

"Danny!"

"You can go to her house! Instead of math camp! It's perfect!"

"It's not *perfect*! It's crazy!"

"Why?"

"Well, first, I'm all signed up for High Sights Academy. Second, like Robin says, Sibley's not going to send me off to live with his *enemies.*"

"Say it's an exchange program. Through FUN! He won't even know!"

"Come on. It would take Sibley about two seconds to figure out they live next to Big Tree Grove."

"You always look on the dark side," Danny said in exasperation. "And you have no sense of adventure! You're the most boring person on Earth. You're going to live the boringest life ever and then bore yourself to death."

"I don't see you running off to Robin's."

"Umm," Danny said in his airheaded girl voice, "am I, like, the one being sent to math camp here?"

"Danny, there's no way."

But Julian had pored over the pictures of Huckleberry Ranch on the FUN website until he knew them by heart: two goats, an orchard covered in pink blossoms, a mossy waterfall beneath towering redwoods. And, for a moment, he imagined a summer without points, without shoes, without math camp. He could walk down the shady path. Into the forest. Into Robin's redwoods.

Julian slipped into the house as the clock chimed seven and managed to settle into his designated chair just before Sibley stepped out of his office. After the perfunctory greetings, he was ignored. He picked discreetly at his salad, which was filled with nasty surprises like kidney beans and olives. Daphne was engaged in a long story about Preston's school auction, which Sibley interrupted with sarcastic outbursts.

Sometimes, in restaurants, Julian would see large families gathered together, everybody laughing and talking at once, and he would study them, trying to figure out what made them so happy. Robin's family was probably like that. In his mind, Julian could see them clearly: a family of brawny Vikings, three giant sons, two fair daughters, living off the land and laughing at night around the dinner table.

"You know, we usually strive to be *cheerful* at the dinner table. Not *sullen*."

Julian realized Daphne was talking to him. *Sullen*. Wasn't that what Sibley had called him in the e-mail? Sullen. Like his father.

"One point deduction. I'm sorry, Julian, but am I talking to myself? You really need to work on this."

"I didn't even hear you!"

"That's exactly my point."

Now Julian really did feel sullen. And he'd lost the trail of what he'd been thinking. He'd been going along some pleasant path in his mind, but what was it? Now there was only Daphne's smug expression. "That's not fair," he said softly.

"Julian!" his uncle warned.

"Talking back. Another point." Daphne pursed her lips. "I won't be treated this way in my own home."

"I hate this point stuff!"

"Three points, Julian." Daphne could have been calling out a tennis score. "Camp's not starting a moment too soon," she added under her breath.

Thirty seconds ago, he'd been sitting at the table minding his own business and now, somehow, everything was his fault. He'd blundered into another one of Daphne's invisible traps. "I don't care about these stupid points!" he blurted out. "Why don't you leave me alone? Why do you hate me so much?"

Sibley stared at him for a moment with unblinking eyes. Then he cleared his throat and said in a strained voice, "Julian, you're out of line. This may be hard for you to understand, but the fact that you're my brother's son creates certain obligations."

"You owed him one," Julian said.

"No," Sibley said immediately. "No! *He* owed *me*. I never owed him a thing. I gave. He took. That's the way it was."

Julian's cheeks flushed. He felt like he'd been slapped, and he lowered his eyes and bit his lip.

"But he was your brother, right?" Preston said in a worried voice. "So, you didn't mind giving him stuff."

"Of course." Sibley turned his glassy eyes toward Preston. "Of course I didn't mind."

Julian couldn't breathe. Something was squeezing the air out of his chest. He stood up abruptly and took his half-full plate to the kitchen. Then he ran up the staircase and into his room, locked the door, and threw himself on the bed. He blinked hard three times, then turned on his back and stared up at the blank square of the ceiling.

With each breath, the block in his chest grew smaller and smaller until all he could feel was a dull ache. There was a small knock on his door, a pause, then the shuffling of footsteps down the hall. A burst of Daphne's shrill laughter came from downstairs.

Maybe math camp wouldn't be so bad, Julian thought. It couldn't be worse than Sibley's.

He opened his dresser drawer. There was the High Sights Academy brochure Daphne had given him, and next to it, a small pocketknife. It was longer than a typical pocketknife, and slimmer, with a circle of silver initials at the base: J.S.C. Julian picked it up and ran his thumb along its burnished ivory handle. He had a clear memory of taking the knife from his father's pocket and opening and closing the two blades, intrigued by the satisfying way they clicked into place. His father had said the initials stood for Julian Super Clever.

Julian set the knife back in the drawer and picked up the brochure. Inside, he read:

> Is your gifted child being challenged by the math curriculum at his or her school? At High Sights Academy, we teach the concepts, study skills, and memorization techniques your child will need to succeed in the 21st century. Our unique approach to topics—ranging from probability and statistics to recreational puzzle solving to deep logic—will make this summer a learning experience your child will never forget!

Julian stared numbly at the words. His father would never have sent him to math camp. He loved crashing waves, storms, wild places. After a long moment, Julian picked up the telephone and called Danny.

"Danny? It's me. Maybe you were right."

"Of course I was," Danny said sleepily. "What are we talking about here?"

"Do you really think I could get to Robin's? I mean, were you just being crazy, or do you really think it's possible?"

"Be calm, Julian," Danny said, imitating the voice of Ms. Felicity, their favorite fifth-grade teacher. "Anything's possible."

"Forget it. I don't know what I'm thinking," Julian said. "I should just go to math camp. It's not going to kill me."

"No, no. Be brave! We make good plan," Danny said,

caveman-style. Then in his normal voice he added, "I'll sleep on it. My brain works better when I'm unconscious. I'll have a complete plan by eight a.m."

When he met Danny in the schoolyard the next morning, Julian half hoped that he'd forgotten all about their conversation the night before. But Danny immediately hustled him over to the corner of the chain-link fence and said in a conspiratorial whisper, "I've got the plan all figured out. It's bulletproof."

"Are you sure that's the right expression?"

"First, the night before you go to camp, you sleep over at my house."

"OK."

"You tell Daphne we'll take you to the math camp bus stop on Monday. And pick you up four weeks later. Tell her the day you get back is my birthday or something."

"It's already sounding pretty complicated."

"This way, Sibley and Daphne will never even know that you went to Robin's instead of math camp."

"If I don't show up at math camp, don't you think someone will notice?"

"We'll cancel. We'll wait until the last minute and cancel."

"Cancel how?"

"Just call up and say you're not coming. My mom does it all the time—hotels, car reservations, anything. The people who answer the phone don't care."

"Aw, Danny. I don't know. I mean, Sibley would murder me if he found out. And I'd probably lose about ten thousand points. Plus, how am I going to get up there?"

"Be calm." Danny closed his eyes and struck a meditation pose, floating his hands at his sides and touching his thumbs to his middle fingers. Abruptly, he stopped and said, "Work with me here."

"You think I should go up there without even telling my uncle?"

"You *want* to tell Sibley you're going to Robin's? Are you crazy?"

"I was thinking we'd somehow trick him into letting me go."

"Great!" Danny said. "And how are you going to do that, exactly?"

Julian shrugged.

"As Sherlock Holmes says, 'Once you have eliminated the impossible, whatever remains, no matter how improbable, must be the truth' or, in your case, the Plan. I know it can work. I have a vision. Unless you really want to spend your whole summer being tormented by overachievers!"

All through school the next day, Julian thought about the Plan. Maybe Danny was right. Maybe it would work. Sibley and Daphne would think he was at math camp. He could see Huckleberry Ranch for himself. Robin sounded pretty nice (even if she did have a temper). She'd said her mom loved exchange students.

The more he thought about the Plan, the more he thought it might actually succeed, if he and Danny were very careful and didn't make any mistakes.

During class, he worked on his list of things to do. By lunchtime, it read:

1. Check with Robin if plan really OK
2. Figure out exchange student stuff
3. Arrange sleepovers at Danny's
4. Cancel Math Camp
5. Figure out how to get to Robin's house
6. Figure out how to get home from Robin's house
7. Get $$

Then he couldn't think of anything to add, even though he felt certain there must be more than seven things he needed to do. During math, he added:

8. Get Sibley not to cut down redwoods???

After the last bell, he met Danny in front of school and showed him the list.

"Hmmmm. Very good. Very good. I can see you've given this a great deal of thought," Danny said, pulling on an imaginary beard. "Ze plan can now begin!"

7

DETAILS

Dear Robin,

We think your plan might be brilliant after all! If I came up to your place, maybe I might somehow figure out how to get my uncle not to cut down Big Tree Grove. Do you think your parents would let me?? And where exactly do you live?

From,

Julian

May 29

Dear Julian,

OH MY GOSH! I'm so excited!! Sometimes you should trust your intuition. Like when I said you should come up, but then I thought it wouldn't work, but now I bet we can figure it out!

We live about 15 miles outside Willits.

Under normal circumstances, you'd sign up through FUN. So far we only have one exchange student coming this summer—for 2 weeks in July. When would you be coming??

Yours truly,

Robin

May 30

Dear Robin,

I'm supposed to go to math camp for 4 weeks starting June 14.

Julian

P.S. For OBVIOUS reasons, Sibley doesn't know about these plans so keep them TOP SECRET for now!

Danny

May 31

Dear Julian and Danny,

I've been thinking nonstop about the best way to do this. Usually FUN lets us know way in advance about exchange students but these are UNUSUAL circumstances, so I'll think of something. Download the application forms off the website. Fill them out and put "#32 Huckleberry" as your first-choice placement. Write neatly. In the essay part, say you really want to experience life on a farm because you've never seen a goat, etc. And you're supposed to have a letter of recommendation saying you're deserving and not a criminal or anything. ASAP—we don't have a lot of time!

Yours truly,

Robin

P.S. DON'T mention the name CARTER, or my parents will get suspicious. Just put plain Julian Li.

June 1

Dear Miss Elder,

Julian Li is a remarkable boy, despite the many disadvantages of his upbringing. First, his father was killed in a tragic accident when he was seven years old. Second, he lives in the inner city, where he faces crime, dirty streets, and the other dangers of city life. Third, his mother does not have a steady job. However, he is a very good student and has never been in trouble with the law and he is kind to animals. A few weeks in the country would be just the thing he needs to leave behind his troubled life. I highly recommend Julian for this unique opportunity.

Sincerely,

Mr. Daniel L. Pez

Guidance Counselor

Filbert Middle School

June 1

Dear Mr. Pez,

I think that should do!

Robin

June 2

Dear Robin,

We filled out the forms. Now what??

Julian Li

June 3

Dear Julian,

Make a photocopy and send it to me at Robin Elder, P.O. Box 1667, Willits, CA. Normally, you'd get a letter from the placement center at FUN saying you've been accepted. Obviously, you should tell my parents you left this at home. I'll take care of it from the other end! What time will you get here? I can't WAIT!! Do you need directions????

How is your mom liking China? Even though I want to live here forever I do plan to travel when I'm older and experience different cultures. I am studying Spanish now and have learned a lot even though everything I know is from these boring tapes and videos.

Robin

DETAILS

June 4

Hola Petirrojo,

Trata bien a mi amigo o lo pagarás caro!

Danny

June 5

Dear Danny,

"Treat my friend well or you'll pay" !! Muchos gracias for teaching me how to say Robin in Spanish! (And you don't have to threaten me—I will treat your friend muchos bueno!)

Petirrojo

June 6

Dear Robin,

My mom likes China a lot. I just got a postcard from her today—she said the people are very nice but the air is very dirty.

There's a Greyhound bus that arrives in Willits at 1:05 p.m. on Monday, June 14th. Can you pick me up at the station? Also, what should I bring?

Julian

June 8

Dear Julian,

I got the forms! (We TOTALLY lucked out because my

Dad drove by the mailbox earlier and checked but the mail wasn't there yet so he sent me down to get it later!)

Just bring normal clothes (it's cold here at night). I'll get my dad to pick you up at the bus. We do that for visitors all the time. Even if you're really just coming to help me save Big Tree, I think you'll have a lot of fun anyway. I'll show you the redwoods and the river and everything. You can sleep in the loft, which is REALLY cool.

Robin

June 11

Hey Robin Hood,

I'll be here at headquarters, providing logistical support for Julian's mission.

FYI, today was the last day of school!!! Good-bye sixth grade forever! I suppose that is just one of life's little thrills that you home-schoolers have to miss out on.

Danny

June 12

Dear Robin,

I'll be there Monday at 1:05 p.m. Don't forget!

Julian

P.S. Julian will be the incredibly cool-looking kid with the black windbreaker!

—DL

8

JULIAN'S JOURNEY

The evening of the good-bye party, Julian carefully packed his duffel bag, making sure he had clean underwear and slipping his ivory knife into an inside pocket. It might come in handy in the woods. When he went downstairs for dinner, the take-out Chinese had been placed on platters and Sibley and Daphne were sitting at either end of the table. Preston gave Julian a big smile and called out, "Happy Good-Bye!" Once Julian was seated, however, the celebratory mood seemed to dwindle. Daphne picked at her food and rattled on about her tennis games, while Sibley stared, preoccupied, at the walls. At least the food was good. In addition to the duck and chicken, there were steaming plates of noodles and stir-fried green beans and spicy tofu.

In the middle of Daphne's critique of her tennis partner, Sibley turned abruptly to Preston and said, "So, is that school of yours teaching you anything for all the money I'm sending them?"

Preston squirmed. "I'm working on my final project. It's a poster. With a bibliography."

"A bibliography? Excellent. And what subject did you choose?"

"Well, we had to pick something on ecology. So I decided to do redwood trees."

Sibley's blue eyes flickered into focus. "And what have you learned about redwood trees?"

"I'm still kind of working on it. It's not due until next week. I'm the last one to give my presentation."

It was bad enough when Sibley ignored Preston, Julian thought, but to be caught in his laser gaze was even worse.

"That's quite a coincidence. I've been doing a little studying about redwoods myself. For a project at work."

Julian nearly dropped his chopsticks.

"Do you know, for example," Sibley continued, "that an acre of old-growth redwood can hold more than two hundred thousand board feet of wood. And that old-growth redwood is currently selling at more than two dollars a board foot. That means that one acre of redwood is worth what, Preston?"

Preston swallowed and scrunched up his eyes. "Two thousand dollars?"

"Not two thousand dollars." Sibley's smile failed to mask his impatience. "Think before you answer. What are you calculating? It's basically two times two."

Preston hunched his shoulders miserably.

Julian couldn't stand it anymore. "Four hundred thousand dollars an acre."

Sibley turned his gaze to Julian. "Correct. And if you were to acquire fifty acres of timberland with even half of this density, its gross worth would be approximately?..."

"Ten million dollars," Julian said. Now, at last, he had something to tell Robin.

"Correct. Perhaps we should have you tutor Preston in arithmetic. Although, I suppose we should have thought of that two months ago. In any case," Sibley went on, "there's something concrete to put in your report, Preston. Do you think you can remember that?"

Preston nodded, relieved that the cross-examination was over.

"So, Uncle Sibley, what kind of project is this?" Julian asked.

Sibley gave him a look of pleased surprise. "Oh, small potatoes, really. The property ended up in our portfolio after a number of unrelated transactions. Still, it's good to diversify your assets."

"Enough business!" exclaimed Daphne. "It's time for dessert!"

Daphne retreated to the kitchen and returned a moment later, humming "Auld Lang Syne" and carrying a pink ice-cream cake with SO LONG JULIEN in white letters across the top. Did his aunt not know how to spell his name, Julian wondered, or had the cake decorator made a mistake? Julian was still hoping to get more information out of his uncle, but Sibley waved away dessert and went off to his study. Daphne took a single bite before pushing away her plate.

The cake was too sweet for Julian, but he tried to finish most of his piece so he wouldn't seem ungrateful. Ten million dollars. That was a lot of money for a bunch of trees.

Preston alone seemed to truly enjoy his cake, and when he had scraped up every drop of goo with his fork, he looked sorrowfully at the remainder, slowly melting on a cardboard sheet. Seconds were not allowed at Sibley's house and neither was plate licking.

"Well, Julian, I hope you enjoyed our little party," Daphne said, smiling her glacial smile. "Since you're sleeping over at Tommy's tomorrow, this is our last night together for some time."

"Danny's," Julian said. "And his mom's going to pick me up after camp too. Remember? It's his birthday?"

Daphne checked her BlackBerry. "Back on July 10th. Saturday." She smiled again. Discussing his imminent departure had improved her mood. "Now, off to bed, you two," she said. And she rose from the table, took the remainder of the ice-cream cake into the kitchen, and dumped it in the garbage.

Julian followed Preston up the stairs, then watched him as he brushed his teeth and washed his face. "I wish you weren't leaving." Preston pulled his dinosaur pajama top over his pale chest. "Will you stay with me while I fall asleep?"

Preston's room was painted sky blue. His sheets and bedspread were covered with rocket ships and the ceiling was decorated with stars and planets and comets. Preston climbed into bed and Julian turned out the light. A rocket night-light glowed and the stars on the ceiling shone with a faint fluorescence.

"Will you tell me the story of the Little Astronaut? Please? It's your last night."

"OK. But only a short one tonight." Julian sat down at the foot of Preston's bed and thought for a moment, staring at the night-light.

"Once upon a time," he began, "there was a little astronaut. He had a wonderful rocket ship. It was red, white, and blue and it could travel the speed of light. Every night he would travel around the solar system with his pet monkey, who was also a highly trained astronaut. They'd go to Jupiter. Saturn. Pluto. Because they were traveling so fast, a trip that seemed to take them just a few hours would be hundreds of years on Earth. They would come back and there would be all new people, even new cities."

"Did they meet any aliens?" Preston asked.

"Of course. Outer space is filled with aliens. In fact, one day the Little Astronaut got a message from another space explorer named Gizmo saying that Gizmo's home planet was under attack. The Little Astronaut was across the galaxy in a flash. He used his special force field to repel the alien attackers while the monkey launched high-speed banana missiles. From then on, Gizmo and the Little Astronaut were best friends."

Preston lay on his back with his eyes wide.

"When the Little Astronaut and his monkey came back to Earth, they built a tree house with a special receiver to send messages to and from Gizmo. They visited each other every Christmas and lived happily ever after. The end."

They watched the light from the fluorescent stars grow dim. After a few moments, Preston turned over onto his stomach and closed his eyes. Julian sat still for a long time, listening, until the sound of Preston's breath grew heavy and even, like the sea, and the luminescent stars faded into darkness. Then he walked silently out of the room and pulled the door behind him, leaving it open just a crack.

As soon as he got to Danny's the next morning, Julian felt his spirits rise. The boys shut themselves inside Danny's room and immediately got out Julian's to-do list.

"We've already done everything," Danny said. "We wrote Robin. The sleepovers are set. Robin's taking care of the exchange student thing. We've got the Greyhound schedule. All we have left to do is cancel math camp." He shook his head. "We should have picked something more challenging—like robbing a bank or stopping a terrorist plot. This is child's play."

"So far, I've only escaped from my uncle's for an hour. I haven't made it to Robin's. Oh, and I forgot to tell you the worst part. I think those trees are worth ten million dollars. At least all together."

Danny whistled. "Ten million dollars. That's a lot. I don't think

we're going to be able to put our hands on that kind of money." He furrowed his brow like a cartoon character. "Unless we rob a bank! On to plan B!"

"Well, there's no way that *I'm* going to convince my uncle not to cut down the trees, not for that kind of money. I don't know. I think I'm giving Robin the wrong impression by going up there. She thinks I can actually help her."

"False hope's better than no hope," Danny said cheerfully. "Besides, it's better than *math camp.* Speaking of which . . ." He turned to the computer and pulled up the website for High Sights Academy. "*Ze time has come!*" he said in a Dracula voice. Then, "Give me the phone."

"What are you going to say? Maybe I should do it."

"Are you kidding me? You'll end up confessing the whole plan and next thing you know you'll be on a road trip to Fresno." Danny pushed the button for the speaker phone and started punching in the phone number. There was a tinny ring and then a tired female voice said, "High Sights Academy."

"Hello," Danny said in a British accent. "This is Daphne Carter's personal assistant. I'm calling to cancel the registration for Ms. Carter's nephew, Julian Carter-Li."

"May I ask the reason for the cancellation?"

"Oh . . ." Danny grinned at Julian. "They've decided to go on a safari instead. You know, lions . . . elephants . . . wildebeests."

"One moment, please." There was a long pause and then the voice said defensively, "Julian's session begins tomorrow and is paid in full. There is no tuition refund for cancellations within thirty days of the start of the session."

"Entirely understandable," Danny said magnanimously.

"Well, thank you!" There was a sudden friendliness to the tone. "You have no idea how difficult some people can be about refunds. Even though our policy is stated very clearly in our materials."

"People!" Danny said. "They want to have their cake and eat it too!"

Julian made an exasperated face—what was that supposed to mean?—but the woman laughed and said, "Exactly! But I appreciate your understanding. I'll just e-mail you a confirmation and—"

"No!" Danny shouted.

"Excuse me?"

Danny regained his composure and said quickly, "I'm afraid Ms. Carter is no longer *doing* e-mail. Spam!"

"Ooooh—that spam can be awful. No problem. I'll just mail the confirmation to her home address."

"I'm afraid she's already in Mombasa. No idea when she'll return to the States. Really, we don't need any confirmation. Julian's on safari. Tuition's paid in full. What's to confirm?"

"I suppose so," the woman said dubiously.

"Trust me. Ms. Carter would *not* want to be bothered. She's *extremely* focused on the safari right now."

"In that case, we'll just keep the receipt in our files. Thanks for calling and I hope Julian isn't eaten by a lion or anything," the woman said cheerfully.

"Oh, that wouldn't be the worst thing," Danny said in a confidential tone. "In fact, I rather hope he is. He's quite a holy terror. Well, toodle-loo!"

"Toodle-loo to you too!"

The woman was still laughing giddily when Danny put down the phone. "Am I good or what?" he said with a broad smile.

"You have a real talent for lying. And you've ruined my reputation too. Congratulations!"

"We all have our gifts," Danny said humbly.

After lunch the boys walked down Clement Street to the bank. Julian removed $160 from his college savings account, which left him with $877.32. His grandmother, Popo, always gave him a red envelope with a $100 bill on Chinese New Year. And she sent him $50 on his birthday every year, with careful instructions to deposit it in the account she'd opened for him.

Julian had never withdrawn any money before. He enjoyed thinking of his bank account growing continually fatter with interest and deposits. It had taken him a lifetime to break a thousand, and he was sorry to see the total fall back into the hundreds again. But, he figured, this was an emergency.

By 7:45 the next morning, the boys had said good-bye to Eduardo, finished their breakfast, and finally convinced Luciana—for

79

the third time—that Julian could get himself to the High Sights Academy bus pick-up. They waited for a safe interval after Luciana left for work, then stepped out into the fog and walked toward Geary Boulevard. Julian had his duffel bag, snacks for the trip, the application forms for the exchange program, and $160 in his wallet.

"Don't forget to get off at the Greyhound station," Danny said when they reached the city bus stop. "And e-mail me when you get there. We should have a code, in case there's an emergency and I need to get hold of you."

"How about 'Please call. It's an emergency.'"

Danny looked at him with scorn. "The code will be 'The river is rising.' If you get that message, you have to contact me immediately."

"There aren't even any rivers in San Francisco."

Danny considered. "OK. How about 'The tide is rising'?"

The bus pulled up and the wings of the door flapped open.

"How about 'Call Danny'?" Julian hoisted his duffel bag up the steps and flashed his bus pass at the driver.

"It's 'The tide is rising'!" Danny shouted. "Be strong! Have a good trip."

Julian waved, the doors folded behind him, and the bus lurched forward into the rush-hour traffic.

The long ride downtown was hot and stuffy. Crammed among the rush-hour passengers, Julian could barely see out the window. Still, he got off at the right stop and navigated the Greyhound station without a problem. The ticket agent barely glanced at him, giving him a round-trip ticket to Willits without even a suspicious look. After a few minutes of confusion, he found the correct bus and boarded.

As the bus wound its way through the city streets, Julian pulled out a bag of potato chips and a chocolate bar. His breakfast at Danny's house felt like a distant memory. He made the chocolate last until the bus crossed the Golden Gate Bridge. At the next station, a handful of new people climbed aboard, all looking slightly demented or sinister or both. Luckily, the bus was not full and Julian was able to ward off fellow passengers by placing his duffel bag on the seat next to his.

The chips, eaten methodically, one by one, lasted nearly half an hour. The bus passed an endless sprawl of malls and car dealerships and housing developments. Slowly, the houses grew farther apart, and soon he was looking out at oak trees and fields of grass, already turning brown. Although the day outside looked fresh and breezy, the air inside the bus reeked of disinfectant and old cigarettes and diesel fuel, and the mix of smells—and the constant hum of the engine and the lurching motion of the bus as it went up and down hills and around bends—made Julian feel a little sick.

He had nothing to do but look out the window. He wondered what people did in the towns that were passing by so quickly. There were only a few jobs that made sense to him. Farming, for example, and even logging. Farmers sold their food and loggers sold the trees they cut down. That he could understand.

But nobody in San Francisco was a farmer or a logger and neither, Julian guessed, were most of the people in these towns. They were doctors or truck drivers or librarians or maybe they worked in the gas stations and fast food restaurants he passed along the road. Where did the money for all these people come from? Most people, it seemed to him, had jobs that did not produce anything or create anything useful, yet somehow they lived. And some, like his uncle, produced nothing at all, and yet lived extremely well.

He didn't understand money, Julian decided. His mother, for example, sometimes said— jokingly? he wasn't sure—that money was the root of all evil. She preferred to barter: photographs for babysitting or yoga classes or even teeth cleaning. Yet somehow, she ended up with enough money for food and clothes and camera equipment.

Julian grew bored with thinking about money. Instead, he played a game his fifth-grade teacher, Ms. Felicity, had taught the class: He tried to imagine how the land might have looked five hundred years earlier, when the Miwok Indians lived there.

It was harder than it seemed at first. The telephone poles and buildings and fences and cows were the easiest to erase. But it was almost impossible to imagine away the highway. The road, with cars and trucks and buses racing along it at seventy miles per hour, seemed like something permanent, an eternal passageway.

In class, they'd built roads over model landscapes, weighing how much dirt had to be cut out of the hillsides and filled into the low spots. It was not easy to build a wide, flat road over land that curved and rose and fell. If the highway went between two hills, Julian knew that the hills must once have come together, perhaps with a little creek running between them. In his mind, he had to unearth the creek lying hidden beneath the road.

Even the trees and plants might have changed. That was the trickiest part, his teacher had said. San Francisco, for example, was covered with eucalyptus trees. But those trees came from Australia! They wouldn't have been there five hundred years ago.

Five hundred years wasn't so long. But everything had changed so that a Miwok boy zoomed into the present might not even recognize this land. What would surprise him the most? Television? Computer games? Airplanes? Or just the city of San Francisco—miles and miles of concrete and asphalt, crowded with people. He would be amazed and impressed. Or maybe not. Maybe he would shake his head sadly and ask to be taken home.

The bus wound its way north. Julian lay his head against the window and closed his eyes. His legs ached to be stretched. At the rest stop, he used the filthy bathroom and bought a cold root beer.

Julian had never been so far from San Francisco. They passed vineyards and piles of logs as tall as a two-story house. Then the hills on either side of the road grew higher and more desolate. It was not so hard to imagine away the people now. The landscape seemed barely touched by human hands, a wilderness, with only the highway winding on and on.

Finally, he began to see signs for Willits, and then they were in the town, although it was not like any town he'd ever seen, just a strip of low buildings and stores and an occasional house. There was not even a bus station, just a fast-food restaurant where everybody climbed off the bus for the half-hour lunch stop, blinking in the sunshine. Julian grabbed his duffel bag and stepped into the fresh air.

He stood awkwardly for a moment, scanning the unfamiliar parking lot. There was no girl looking expectantly toward the bus.

Not knowing what else to do, Julian sat down on the curb at the edge of the parking lot, and tried to look inconspicuous. On the main road, cars and trucks sped by indifferently, and Julian waited with a growing sense of despair as his fellow passengers smoked their cigarettes and ate their hamburgers and french fries. He waited while they filed back onto the bus. Then he watched the bus pull away in a cloud of diesel fumes, leaving him alone in the abandoned parking lot.

9

UNWELCOMED

t first, Julian had eagerly scanned every car that pulled into the parking lot. But after nearly an hour, he gave up. His situation, he figured, was fairly dire. According to the Greyhound schedule posted on the kiosk, there would be no bus returning to San Francisco until the next morning. And even if he somehow survived the night in Willits—a daunting prospect—and was able to make it back to San Francisco, where would he go? He could hardly return to his uncle's. And math camp was no longer an option.

A white truck pulled to a stop in front of him. Julian glanced wearily up and saw a barefoot girl wearing cut-off blue jeans and a tie-dyed shirt climbing out of the passenger side.

"Are you Julian?" she asked. She was an inch or two taller than him, with brown braids, straight brown eyebrows, and a scattering of freckles.

The image of the blond Viking girl dissolved. Julian stood up, flooded with relief. "Are you Robin?"

Her blue eyes lit up. She bent toward him and said in a husky voice, "Sorry we're late. My dad's still a little upset. I kind of forgot to tell him you were coming until today."

The driver's side door opened and a man stepped out, tall with graying brown hair cut roughly around his ears. Although he was dressed in jeans and his face was tan and weathered, there was something professorial about him—a keen, inquisitive gaze that left Julian doubting that the plan he and Robin had concocted would ever succeed. The man gave Julian a hawklike glance, then reached out and shook Julian's hand as though he were an adult. His palms felt rough and calloused.

"Julian?" he said. "I'm Bob Elder. I understand you and my daughter have been carrying on a little correspondence."

What was Robin's father talking about? He wasn't supposed to know about the e-mails—that wasn't part of the Plan. Robin gave Julian a nervous smile. He swallowed and said, "I guess so."

"You took the bus here by yourself? All the way from San Francisco?"

Julian nodded and attempted to steer back to the script. "I'm here for the exchange program. The Farm/Urban Network?"

"We do have exchange students," Bob said, frowning, "but there's a long process. A lot of paperwork. It has to go through the main office. Robin knows that perfectly well. I don't know what she was thinking telling you to come up here on your own."

He took several sheets of folded paper out of his front shirt pocket, which Julian recognized as the forms he and Danny had filled out.

"Your mom signed these?" His gray eyes seemed to stare through Julian.

"Um, right now, she's actually out of the country. But she loves nature and stuff."

Bob gave Robin a quick look then turned back to Julian. "Who do you live with, then?"

Julian thrust his hands into his pockets. If he didn't pass inspection, he might be stuck in the parking lot for a long time. "Well, I live with my mom, but she's in China right now. She's a photographer. That's why I'm doing the exchange program. Because she's not here." He waited for Robin to come to his rescue.

"Dad! Be nice! I told you, we were pen pals through FUN and I was telling him about Huckleberry Ranch and he was saying how much he'd like to see it. It was my idea for him to come up! The forms are all filled out perfectly and the other stuff is just paperwork and stupid bureaucracy."

"Robin, I have no doubt you're responsible for this mess, but I'm afraid there's more to it than that."

"All I'm saying is he just spent hours on a bus. Can't we at least take him home and give him something to eat before you cross-examine him?"

"You're not running away, are you?" Bob asked, still weighing Julian with his eyes.

Julian was taken aback. "I'm not running away." He'd pass the lie detector on that one, he figured. It wasn't running away when nobody wanted you in the first place. "Robin wrote to me about your house and the redwoods. She said it would be OK if I came up," he added, glancing at Robin with a hint of accusation. He dug in his pocket for his return ticket to San Francisco and handed it to Robin's father, who studied it closely and handed it back.

"Well, get in the truck. I'd feel more comfortable if I could talk to whoever's in charge of you. But I guess we'll have to straighten that out when we get home."

Bob swung Julian's duffel bag into the back of the truck. Robin gave Julian a quick grin, then climbed into the passenger side, motioning for Julian to follow.

For a while, they rode in silence. Robin and her father seemed to have reached some kind of truce, but Julian felt numb. Here he was, coming to help Robin's family save Big Tree Grove, and her father looked at him with coldness and distrust. He had not realized how many expectations he'd had until Bob Elder crushed them. What had he expected? Certainly not this unsmiling interrogation. He had expected to be greeted with open arms, to be welcomed into Robin's family, to be taken in.

Julian gazed resentfully at Robin, who sat sucking on the tip of her braid, her hand resting on her father's neck. He'd done everything right—filling out all those tricky forms and getting away from Sibley's and finding his way up here. All Robin had to do was account for a few missing pieces of paperwork, but clearly she'd caved under her father's scrutiny. Not that he could entirely blame her, Julian thought, turning away from Bob's stern profile.

After a few miles, the truck took a sharp turn onto a dirt road. All of a sudden, they were inside the forest. But it wasn't at all like he'd imagined from the highway. From a distance, the mountains were covered with an unending line of dark trees, cool and even. Here, the forest was a mess. Clusters of branches and dead tree trunks lay scattered on the ground. The weeds alongside the road were covered with dust.

"They just finished a logging operation here," Robin said.

Julian glanced back at a field of sunbaked stumps, littered with broken branches.

The road continued down, curving along steep hillsides, then abruptly flattened out. They passed a creek and Julian saw a cluster of houses, with tricycles and trucks and old metal parts lying about. Occasionally, when they passed a house or a driveway, Robin would tell him the name of the family who lived there. The farther they went, the more she talked. Her father remained silent but at least he kept driving on and on through the dim, dusty forest, every turn taking them farther away from the bus stop.

At last, they came to an open gate and a sign that said, HUCKLEBERRY RANCH. The dusty tunnel through the forest opened into a green valley. Steep hills rose up on either side of a narrow river. As they made a turn, Julian saw a deer and a little fawn grazing. At the sound of the truck, they lifted their heads from the grass and watched them pass.

"Did you see the deer?" he asked. A deer! He had never in his life seen a deer in the wild. And there they had stood—a little deer family.

Robin just smiled. At last, the truck pulled up to a gravel driveway and Bob turned off the engine. In the sudden quiet, Julian could hear the leaves blowing in the breeze and the high, falling song of a bird. In front of them stood a wooden house with yellow flowers in the window boxes and a deck stretching along the side. Several chickens strutted in the yard and a tire swing hung from a gnarled old tree.

On the front steps, the sun shone on the bare shoulders of a little child, who sat tapping a stick against the railing.

"Is that your sister?" Julian asked, climbing out of the truck.

Robin giggled. "Well, he's *naked*. I'd think you could tell. Don't they teach you anything in the city?"

Julian blushed. Bob grabbed the red duffel bag from the back of the truck. The little boy jumped to his feet and yelled "Charge!"—brandishing the stick like a miniature naked samurai.

"Jo-Jo. Be nice," Robin said. "This is my friend Julian. And put your clothes on, you little savage." She picked a pair of tan shorts off the deck and forced one of his legs, and then the other, through the openings. Even as he lifted his feet, Jo-Jo continued to glare at Julian and block his way with the stick.

"You'll have to excuse him," Robin explained. "He watched *King Arthur* at my cousin's house last month and he still hasn't recovered!"

The door opened, and a woman came out of the house. She wiped her hands on her apron, then pushed wisps of brown hair behind her ears. She had Robin's straight brown eyebrows and her eyes were the same deep blue, but soft and gentle where Robin's were quick and hard.

"You must be Julian!" She smiled as if he'd just given her a bouquet of flowers, then picked up Jo-Jo, who immediately put his thumb in his mouth and lay his blond curls against her shoulder. "We're so glad to see you. Come in. I just made lemonade."

With an enormous sense of relief, Julian followed the woman into a sun-filled room with a high ceiling. Sliding glass doors looked out on a shady back deck. A long wooden table was set with a pitcher of lemonade and a plate of chocolate-chip cookies.

"I'm sorry," the woman said. "I didn't even introduce myself. I'm Nancy, Robin's mother. You must be hungry. Can I fix you a sandwich?"

"Um, sure. I mean, yes, please. Well, I can fix it myself," Julian mumbled.

"Oh, please, sit down." Nancy said. "Now, what would you like? I have chicken or cheese."

Julian remembered the chickens running around the yard. "Cheese would be great," he said.

Nancy sat Jo-Jo down on a stool and gave him a bowl of strawberries and a cup of milk. "We've already eaten. Robin didn't tell us that you were coming until lunchtime. She's a procrastinator, like me!" She layered slices of tomato and cheese on a piece of bread. "Now, you sit here and eat and tell us all about yourself."

"Like I told you," Robin jumped in, "we both signed up for that pen-pal program. Through FUN. And we wrote back and forth a little. And I was telling him all about where we live. And I was saying how it's so beautiful and telling him about the redwoods and about the exchange program. And obviously he wanted to come, but there wasn't time to do all the paperwork and anyway his mom was out of town, so I told him he could just send me the forms and it would be OK if he just came on up. I knew nobody was signed up for June." She looked up as her father came in the door. "I know I should have told you earlier, but I sort of forgot because we've been so busy lately. And he took the bus by himself all the way from San Francisco."

Nancy handed him the sandwich. "My goodness! Your mother couldn't drive you?"

"My mom doesn't have a car," Julian said, swallowing. "And also, she's in China."

"China! Are you Chinese?" A lot of times, people couldn't figure out what he was.

"Well, my mom is. But she was born in San Francisco. My grandmother too. My mom just likes to travel."

"Who's been taking care of you, then?"

Julian had just taken a huge bite of the sandwich. He chewed slowly while trying to calculate the best response. "Well, I was . . .

uh . . . staying with my cousin, but then school got out and Robin said I could come up, so I did."

Bob had been watching them with his arms crossed. "I don't like it that they cooked up this scheme on their own. At the very least, we should talk to someone in his family. We don't want the police at our door."

To Julian's surprise, Nancy just laughed. She had a lovely laugh, like running water. "Oh, goodness!" she cried. "I don't think he's a fugitive, Bob!" She adopted a serious expression and turned to Julian. "Are you a fugitive?"

"Mom! Of course he's not a fugitive! He's just a kid!"

"Are you running away? Are the police after you?" Nancy asked.

"You're a bad guy!" Jo-Jo yelled, pointing the spoon at Julian like a spear. "Charge!"

Julian shook his head.

"There must be someone we can call. Your cousin? Or somebody in your family?" Nancy asked.

"Um . . . I know it sounds a little weird, but my cousin's, um, in Africa. On a safari. I guess my whole family likes to travel."

Nobody spoke.

"You could leave my mom a message," Julian said dubiously.

"OK, let's start there." Bob reached into his pocket and pulled out the photocopied forms again. "There's no home phone listed," he said.

Julian hesitated. His mother never checked her voice mail, he reassured himself. She wouldn't get Bob's message until she came back from China, and then it would all be over. Besides, if he didn't come up with the number, Bob would probably send him and his duffel bag back to San Francisco on the next Greyhound bus.

Julian recited his home number and Bob dialed and listened intently. Julian heard the tinny echo of his mother's message coming through the phone: "Cari Li! Leave a message if you wish, but I probably won't get back to you for a loooong time! Peace!"

"Hello, Ms. Li. This is Bob Elder in Willits," Bob said. "Your son Julian is staying with us for a few weeks on our exchange program. I understand you're out of the country, but if you have any questions, give me a call." He left his phone number and hung up.

"Any other relatives?" Bob asked.

Julian shook his head

"Father deceased?" Bob was still studying the forms.

"Five years ago."

Bob gave a small nod in acknowledgment, and then his face relaxed, so that Julian could see that it wasn't really a mean face. "Well," he said to Nancy. "I guess we can't just send him away now that you've got him under your wing." Julian couldn't tell if Bob was pleased or not. He thought not. "I'll take your bag up to the loft," Bob said. "You'll be sleeping up there." Jo-Jo followed his father across the room to a spiral staircase, chanting, "I want to sweep in the woft!"

The kitchen seemed suddenly brighter. The phone message wasn't in the Plan, but at least Bob had said he would be staying.

Julian was starting to feel better. He finished his sandwich and his lemonade, and Robin's mother passed around the plate of cookies.

"So you have five children?" he asked. So far, he'd only seen Jo-Jo and he'd been wondering where the rest of the family was.

"Yes, I do," Nancy beamed. "John and Dave are in college, but they're both doing a service project in Guatemala this summer. Then there's Robin. And next is Molly. She's spending the night with our neighbors. Then Jonah's our baby."

A white ball of fluff streaked under the table. "This," Nancy said, "is Snowball, the newest addition to our family." She picked up the kitten and stroked his fluffy fur. "He showed up a few weeks ago, and now we can't seem to get rid of him." The kitten squirmed and Nancy placed him gently on the floor and started to clear the table. "Robin, why don't you show Julian around?" she said. "I'm sure he's tired of sitting after being on the bus all morning."

Julian followed Robin out the sliding glass doors and onto the back deck. He studied the scene, adjusting the image he'd been carrying around of Robin's home. He always had a feeling of dissonance when he came to a new place. It was never like he'd imagined. Sometimes, the picture he'd created was more real than the place itself, and the real and imaginary places would coexist in his mind like two separate places.

Robin's family was different from how he'd envisioned them, and her house was too. It was not in a sunny field next to a forest but in a little clearing, with the forest all around. The house

wasn't a barn-red rectangle, but unpainted wood, with different levels and a sloping roof. Of course, the chickens were there, and a lot of other things he'd never thought of. The tire swing. A large picnic table and a fire ring out back. And behind them, a winding creek with a little footbridge. He followed Robin around as she chattered on about the barn where they kept the goats, the greenhouse, the large vegetable garden, still covered with plastic, the berry patches. Altogether, Julian decided, Huckleberry Ranch was decidedly superior to the house of his imagination. It was probably the most beautiful place he had ever seen.

"Where are the redwoods?" he asked after they had toured all the land surrounding the house.

"Well, we have lots of redwood on our property. But it's all second growth. This land was all logged back in the 1920s. They cut down every single redwood tree, if you can believe that! When my grandparents bought this place, some of the trees were growing back. They planted thousands and thousands of redwood seedlings. And the orchards."

"How big is this place?"

"Two hundred and fifty acres. Big Tree isn't on our land, of course. It's next door. Over this way." Robin ran toward the creek and crossed the footbridge.

Julian didn't really know how big 250 acres was. But one of his mom's friends had a house in Marin with an enormous backyard, many times bigger than the tiny space behind his own house. "I'm living the American dream," the friend would boast. "Quarter-acre lot. House in the 'burbs." If that was a quarter of an acre, 250 acres must be like a giant park. Or the zoo.

"Here's one of the apple orchards." Robin pointed to a dozen or so trees standing in a grassy meadow. "Sometimes there's deer here. One of the does is tame. You can feed her out of your hand. She loves green apples."

Robin was moving quickly through a grassy clearing covered with dandelions. "This is where *my* house is going to be! Near the river, so I can generate all my electricity with a water wheel."

"Is your dad really going to build you a house?" Julian asked.

Robin looked at him in surprise. "Of *course* he is. Didn't I already tell you that?" She turned and disappeared down a slope.

"Here's the river," she called back. "The flow's pretty high now, so don't fall in!"

Robin ran across a narrow tree trunk, split lengthwise, which formed a bridge across the water. There were no handrails. Julian stepped cautiously along the trunk, his arms extended like a tightrope walker. He tried not to think about the gray boulders and the dark water rushing below him. When he reached the opposite bank, he realized with embarrassment that Robin was watching him. She took off without saying a word.

The path was covered with dead leaves. It followed the river for a bit, then began to wind up through the forest, back and forth along steep switchbacks. This was certainly not the shady little trail he'd imagined!

"Hey!" he shouted to slow Robin down. "We have trees like

this in San Francisco!" He pointed to a shrubby tree with large pink flowers. He didn't want her to see him out of breath, and he was relieved when she stopped and started pointing.

"That's a rhododendron. My mom's favorite. And there's some Douglas fir and some oak," she said, waving vaguely. "Big Tree's only about a half mile farther."

And with that, Robin was off again, her brown braids flying as the trail snaked up and up. Julian had lost sight of her when he turned a bend and found her lying on the ground, sticking her head under a faucet that came out of the side of the hill.

"Can you drink that? It's not polluted?" Julian said.

"It's spring water. If we bottled this stuff, we'd probably make a fortune. Try it."

Julian hesitated.

She made an impatient little noise. "You see that black hose? That goes to our house. This water's the same stuff we drink all the time."

A faucet coming right out of the ground struck Julian as the strangest thing he'd seen on the ranch. Some of the water running into San Francisco Bay was so dirty you weren't even supposed to touch it. Nobody would even think of drinking it. Julian bent down and put his head under the faucet. The water flowed out, cool and fresh. It sprang out of some deep, clean place inside the earth and into his mouth.

After the spring, the trail started going downhill but still Julian struggled to keep up. Finally, Robin headed down a small slope and crossed the river again. This time, Julian saw with relief, there was a regular bridge made of wooden planks. Robin waited for him on the far bank.

Despite his best efforts, Julian couldn't breathe without panting.

Robin spoke almost in a whisper. "Here, across the river, it's not our land. So, technically, we're trespassing. This used to be Ed Greeley's land. He was nice. He always let me and my brothers play in Big Tree Grove. He did some logging, but it was sustainable." She gave Julian a questioning look. "You know, he didn't cut down more than could grow each year. Anyway, Dad said Mr. Greeley never would have logged Big Tree. After he died, his kids started fighting and they ended up selling the land. And then it was bought and sold by different people, but none of them moved in. Finally your uncle bought it, or IPX did, and they pretty much want to clear-cut the whole place. And we're all just sick about it."

She looked at him appraisingly. "Come on. It's not far now."

The trail followed the river, then turned sharply away. Robin scrambled up a small slope and waited until Julian stopped, breathless, beside her.

"This is Big Tree," she said.

It was a place leftover from another time, from the age of dinosaurs. Giant redwoods soared up to the sky, their tops towering impossibly high above them. On the forest floor, clusters of green ferns were lit up by slanted shafts of sunlight. Huge logs lay sunk into the ground and green plants and redwood saplings sprouted from their mossy tops.

Julian stared. He had not imagined a place so wild, so unhuman in scale, so profoundly silent.

He followed Robin inside a circle of trees surrounding a clearing of brown earth. Robin lay down on the ground, flung her arms to the side, and looked up at the sky.

"This is a fairy ring. Right here used to be a giant redwood. Then hundreds of years ago, it must have died, and these trees sprang up around it. They're like its children."

Julian sat down cross-legged inside the fairy ring. "So what happened with your dad?" He wasn't quite ready to let Robin off the hook for his ordeal at the bus stop. "You said you were going to take care of the paperwork from FUN. And then you change the whole plan without even telling me. You made me look like a liar!"

She sat up and put her arms around her knees. "I know. I'm sorry. But at the last minute, I just couldn't do it. FUN's very organized. My dad would have called the central office if the forms came in at the last minute. I thought it would be better to stay a little closer to the truth."

"Your dad almost sent me back on the bus!"

"It was dicey," she agreed. "But I knew once you got to the house, it would be OK. So long as my parents don't realize you're Sibley Carter's nephew, it'll be fine."

"I guess you didn't tell them you sent my uncle that e-mail."

"Oh, they would have been furious. You know, it's kind of

amazing it got there at all. I was just guessing his e-mail address. My brother's taking a journalism course, and he was telling us how a lot of people, even big CEOs, read their own e-mail and their addresses are just their names and their company web addresses. That gave me the idea. I never really thought he would get it. Or you, obviously. But all's well that ends well, as my mom says."

She flopped back down. Julian watched her curiously. He had never known a girl who talked so much. In fact, he really didn't know many girls at all. He had no sisters, and neither did Danny. His only cousin was a boy. Even his soccer team was all boys. Of course, there were girls at school, huddling together in the halls, giggling and whispering, but they mostly ignored him.

Julian leaned against the rough redwood bark and breathed in the mossy air. The trees in Muir Woods, he thought, were redwoods too. But somehow this place felt entirely different. This forest was not fenced and swept and filled with signs and paths for tourists. It was wild and remote. He and Robin might be the only people around for miles.

"So, what are you going to do about Big Tree now?" he asked.

Robin sighed. "Nothing, I guess. I mean, my parents filed an appeal. And so did a few environmental groups. They had letters from scientists and everything. But my dad says it's probably a lost cause."

"So you're just going to let them come and destroy all of this?" He waved his hand around.

"Me? Them?" she said in astonishment. "It's your *uncle* who's in charge. He could stop the logging in a minute. Why don't you go back to San Francisco and get him to stop?"

He hadn't expected such an outburst. He was beginning to think that Robin's whole family was a little unpredictable. "You always say he's my uncle, like that makes any difference," he said. "But he basically hates me. I mean, he was trying to get rid of me for the entire summer."

Robin frowned. "Then why were you staying with him in the first place?"

"My mom always wanted to go to China," he began slowly. "Finally, she got this grant to go there and study the Buddhist temples and photograph them. And she couldn't really take me and it was too long to stay with Danny. Or anybody else. So my mom asked Sibley if I could stay with them. Of course, my uncle has a big house. Plenty of room. My mom even offered to pay for my food, which was a little crazy because she basically has no money and my uncle's super rich."

"But he *is* your uncle. He can't *really* hate you."

"No. He does. I—" Julian was silent for a few moments. "The night I found your message, I was in Sibley's office. He was at a meeting. And right before your message came in, I found an e-mail from my uncle saying he was sending me to this math camp. And all this other bad stuff. What a terrible kid I was and how I reminded him of my dad."

"Maybe he hates you because he and your dad were bitter

enemies," Robin said in a melodramatic voice. "But now he has to pretend they weren't because you can't speak ill of the dead."

"Maybe."

"Did they have a fight or something?"

"I don't know." In his memory, his father was always laughing. He remembered holding tight to his dad's leather jacket as the wind squeezed his eyes shut, the motorcycle's roar almost drowning out his father's whooping laugh. And his father with his arm around his mother, their laughing faces lit by an enormous bonfire, the wind blowing cold from the ocean. "My mom says my dad never wanted to talk about his family."

Far away, they heard a bell ringing faintly.

"That's the dinner bell," Robin said, jumping up. "Trust me, you don't want to be late tonight!" And she was out of the fairy ring, up the slope, and almost out of sight before Julian even made it to his feet.

10

HUCKLEBERRY RANCH

Julian woke up the next morning to the sounds of a rooster crowing and breakfast cooking. He lay still for a moment, watching the motes of dust float through the sunshine coming in from the skylight.

He was in Robin's loft. This time yesterday he'd been in San Francisco and now he was lying on a futon in a loft at Huckleberry Ranch. If he hadn't gone to Sibley's office that day, he would be at math camp right now and Huckleberry Ranch would still be here, with Bob and Robin and Nancy and Jo-Jo, but he would never have met them. His mom was in China, and she was meeting other people, people he would never know, with lives just as real as his own. It was impossible to keep in your mind. Six billion people, and each of them thinking his own life was the most real life.

He sat up and stretched, then jumped back in surprise.

Three faces were staring at him. There was Snowball,

crouched on the nightstand, looking like he was about to pounce. At the top of the staircase sat Jo-Jo, looking solemn despite his jam-smeared face. And holding his hand was a girl with straight, pale orange hair and pale blue eyes and a pale, freckled face. Even her eyelashes were pale orange.

"Julian!" Jo-Jo cried, only he pronounced it "Juwian." He turned to the girl. "He's waking! He's not sweeping anymore."

Julian rubbed his eyes. "Are you Molly?" he asked.

She nodded and whispered something.

"What did you just say?"

"Chore time," she whispered a little louder.

Outside, the air was cold and fresh. Robin was waiting for him on the steps. He followed her through the wet grass.

"It's my job to milk the goats this month," she said, lifting the latch on a small wooden barn. Immediately, two brown and black goats started pushing against her pockets. "Stop, you greedy creatures!" She pushed their heads away firmly. One bent its horns toward Julian, and he took a step back.

"Oh, Dolly won't hurt you," Robin said. "She just has extremely poor manners."

At the back of the barn, a small white goat stared mildly up at them. Her eyes were like marbles made of amber.

"Hello, Aphrodite, my little darling." Robin bent down the kissed the goat on the nose. "Aphrodite's my very own. I raised her from a kid. Isn't she pretty? That's why I named her what I did."

Julian didn't say anything.

"You know, Aphrodite, the Greek goddess. Of beauty." She gave Julian a smug look, then handed him a carrot from her pocket. The other two goats came rushing toward him.

"Dolly and Gracie!" Robin said sternly. "Stop that immediately, or I'm going to lock you up."

The goats stopped. Julian held the carrot before Aphrodite's nose. She considered it with her trusting yellow eyes, then took it gently from his hands.

"My mom says she has the disposition of an angel. Very ungoatlike," Robin said, holding out another carrot. Aphrodite followed her to a small stall and Robin fed her the carrot, then motioned Julian in and shut the door against the other goats. She placed a bucket of grain in front of Aphrodite, then wiped her udder with a damp cloth. Finally, she sat on a wooden stool and began to milk the little goat, who munched her grain contentedly. The jets of milk made a hard hissing sound in the bucket.

"Here, now you try," Robin said. "There are two teats. Take one teat and squeeze, from the top to the bottom."

The word "teat," which Robin said so casually, made Julian blush. He reached out for the closest one, squeezed, and nothing happened.

"Wait, stop!" Robin said. "Squeeze just at the top. Harder."

Julian squeezed.

"Now, work the milk down with your fingers. Down toward your pinky."

He tightened his grip and a few drops of milk dribbled into the bucket.

"Excellent. Very good for a beginner. Now, let go and do it again."

This time a small spray of milk came out.

"Oh, you're a natural. Now a hand on each teat. Back and forth. I've got to go milk Dolly and Gracie. They're more cantankerous."

Julian could smell Aphrodite's warm animal smell. She seemed to be studying him with one striped golden eye. After a few clumsy dribbles, the milk began to squirt out in a steady rhythm. Steam rose from the bucket. Then, somehow, he lost his rhythm and the flow of milk stopped. He sat back on the stool and waited for Robin to return.

"How'd you do?" she said, stooping close beside Julian and reaching out to rub Aphrodite's udder. She grabbed the two teats, pulled vigorously, and more milk foamed into the bucket.

"Open your mouth," she ordered.

By the time Julian realized what she was about to do, it was too late. The milk squirted into his mouth and dripped down his chin. The warm, goaty taste almost made Julian gag.

"That's disgusting." He spit the milk into the straw and wiped his chin with the back of his hand. "Do we really have to drink this stuff, Goat Girl?"

"It's good, City Boy," Robin said. "You'll get used to it. None of the city kids like it at first. Soon you'll be eating goat cheese, goat yogurt, goat ice cream . . ."

Goat ice cream? What would Danny say to that? Julian had a moment of nostalgia for the mint-chocolate-chip ice cream at the Toy Boat Dessert Café.

When they came out into the yard, Molly was sitting with a tiny goat in her lap, feeding it with a glass bottle. It drank eagerly, paused for breath, then turned its little tan face toward the bottle again.

"That's Molly's baby," Robin said. "She named her Bunny. Have you ever heard a stupider name for a goat?"

"Do you want to feed her?" Molly asked.

Julian sat down on a stump in the yard, and Molly placed Bunny in his lap. The little goat crossed her delicate legs and tugged at the rubber nipple. When she'd finished guzzling down the milk, she lay her head on Julian's knee, and he traced the soft fur on top of her head. Beneath his fingers, he could feel the outline of her tiny skull.

By the time they had finished with the goats and gathered the warm and slightly dirty eggs from the chicken coop, Julian was starving. He wolfed down five of Nancy's blueberry pancakes before he remembered about the goat milk. But the pancakes were free of that unpleasant, sour taste. She must have regular milk stashed away in her gigantic refrigerator, he figured.

After breakfast, Nancy announced it was lesson time.

"You don't have summer vacation?" Julian asked.

"No. We work like slaves all year long!" Robin grumbled.

"We do take breaks," Nancy said, wiping the table with a

sponge. "But we don't follow a regular school schedule. Exchange students don't have to do lessons, though. You're free to wander around."

Julian spent the morning exploring. He found a cluster of apple trees and, beneath them, a deer with a spotted fawn, perhaps the same pair he'd seen from the road. The deer looked at him unafraid. Silently, he sent her a telepathic message saying, "I won't hurt you" and she seemed to nod her head. Very slowly, he picked a small green apple off a low branch and held it out to her. The fawn took a few steps back, but the doe stretched her neck toward him. Her chin tickled his palm as she delicately lifted the apple and crunched it between her teeth. Julian wanted to touch her rough fur but was afraid of frightening her. Even though he was careful not to move a muscle, she suddenly startled, bounding off into the forest with the fawn close behind.

Julian continued down the trail and found Bob by the vegetable garden. He was crouched down on his long legs, his face shaded by a wide-brimmed hat.

"Do you need any help?" Julian asked.

"We seem to have more weeds than vegetables so far. Did you ever weed a garden?"

Julian shook his head.

Bob looked Julian up and down. "Well, there's a first time for everything. This is lettuce." He pointed to one row of the garden. "And that's chard. Everything else is weeds. Weeds are bad. Crops are good."

The lettuces had pale green, wrinkled leaves, with a purple trim around the edges. They were no bigger than Julian's fist. The tall, grassy plants growing around the edges, Julian thought, must be the weeds. He knelt in the dirt and broke a few off.

"Don't break them. Pull them up by the roots," Bob said. "Keeps them from coming back so fast."

Julian tried again. He grabbed another tall weed, but it too broke off at the base. On the next try, he wiggled the plant slightly, and lifted the spidery clump of roots easily out of the damp soil.

"That's better." Bob crouched beside him and they worked together under the warm sun. After a while, Julian could look down the row and see each bright head of lettuce sitting in a clearing of brown soil. Ahead, the tiny lettuces were still choked in weeds. He finished the entire row and stood up to admire his work.

"Not bad," Bob said.

Julian started on his second row. He worked a little faster now, but still couldn't keep pace with Bob, who moved tirelessly down one row after another. The sun began to burn on Julian's neck and he was relieved when he heard the happy sound of the bell, calling them to lunch.

"Let's get these weeds into the compost," Bob said. They carried the tangle of uprooted weeds over to a large black plastic canister. "That'll be good dirt in a few months. In good farming, nothing's wasted. A family can work the same land forever, if they do it right." They began walking toward the house.

"You're lucky to live here," Julian said. "It's so green. Not like the city."

Bob looked toward the ridgeline on the other side of the river. "I'm a lucky man. Sometimes it's like the rest of the world doesn't even exist. My parents bought this land before I was born. A hundred dollars an acre. I helped my father build our house when I wasn't much older than you."

"Robin said you're going to build her her own house." Julian was nearly running to keep up with Bob's giant strides. "Down by the river."

For the first time, Bob laughed. "We've got the blueprints and everything. State-of-the-art solar panels, water wheel. Every piece of timber in Robin's house will come from this land. Same for Molly and the boys, if that's what they want. My parents passed this land on to me, and when I'm gone I'll pass it on to my kids — maybe a little better than I found it. That's all the legacy I want."

His father hadn't had time to leave much of a legacy, Julian thought. All he had of his father's was the ivory pocketknife and a white conch shell from Hawaii. The inside was glistening pink and smoother than glass. People always said if you held it to your ear, you could hear the ocean, but when Julian listened, all he heard was the sound of emptiness.

At lunch, Julian had his fork nearly to his mouth when he realized the rest of the family was sitting silently with their heads bowed down. Even Jo-Jo had his hands folded in his lap and his little eyes scrunched shut. Julian stopped, his fork clattering down on his plate. He waited nervously to see what they would do next, until, at some unseen signal, they all looked up and began passing around the food.

All through lunch, Julian was quiet. Maybe, he thought, the Elders could adopt him. But why would they want him? They already had three sons, although there was a gap just where he would fit in. Of course, he realized, he already had a mother. Maybe he could just be a hired hand, like they had in the old Westerns, one of those tough, quiet guys who was like a member of the family and ended up killing the rattlesnake in the nick of time or saving the child from a runaway horse.

"We do math after lunch," Nancy explained, when everyone had finished eating. "We really should do it first thing in the morning, but like I said, Robin and I are procrastinators!" She raised her voice to be heard over Jo-Jo, who was holding a small plastic truck and making loud zooming noises. "I'm sorry to leave you on your own again, but Robin will be free soon."

Julian stared at the bookshelves lining the living room, filled with serious-looking volumes: *The Encyclopedia of Organic Gardening*, *The Solar Home*, *Applied Silviculture and Forest Ecology*, *Small-Scale Aquaculture*.

The girls had settled down at the kitchen table with worksheets and pencils, but Jo-Jo kept holding the truck up to his mother and shouting, "Mommy, Mommy, I'm broken!" and when no one responded, he called out, "I'm crying 'cause no one will fix me."

"If you want, I can take him out so you guys can concentrate," Julian said after a minute.

"Oh, that would be great!" Nancy smiled with relief. "You know, he used to just play quietly while we did our work, but now he's getting bored. Actually, he should be taking his nap, but he woke up later than usual this morning."

Julian knelt down in front of Jo-Jo. "Hey, Jo-Jo, want to go down by the creek?"

"You can bring your truck and dig a hole in the dirt," Robin coaxed. She brought him a pair of tiny bathing trunks covered with green frogs. "I'll put on your swimsuit!"

Julian followed Jo-Jo down to the pebbly bank. He sat on a log while Jo-Jo happily pushed his bulldozer around and made beeping noises. Jo-Jo made a few holes with his bulldozer and then stood up and put his toes in the water.

"Can I go in?" he asked with a grave face.

"Um. Sure," Julian said. The afternoon sun was warm. "Don't go in too far."

Jo-Jo walked along the side of the bank, laughing and splashing. He found a stick and banged it on the water. Then he cried "Charge!" and started running all about. "I'm charging the monsters!" he yelled. He rushed wildly into the creek and crashed facedown into the water.

Julian sprang up and grabbed him by his slippery shoulders. Jo-Jo was crying loudly, and water streamed down from his hair into his contorted little face.

113

"Don't cry, Jo-Jo. It's OK. Don't cry," Julian said.

"I'm bweeding!" Jo-Jo sobbed.

"Let me see. Show me. Come on, show me. I'll fix it."

"There!" Jo-Jo pointed to his knee. Underneath the mud, Julian could see that the skin was broken and there was a small speck of blood. Julian looked back at the house, but nobody was coming. Maybe they hadn't heard the cries.

"I want my mama!" Jo-Jo wailed.

"Mama's inside." Julian was determined to show Nancy that he could at least handle a three-year-old. "We're going to wash off the blood. And then we're going to make a dam with your truck and dam up the creek with mud."

The words "truck" and "dam" and "mud" worked like magic. Jo-Jo stopped crying. Julian took him to the creek and splashed water on his knee until the mud and the blood were gone.

"OK," Julian said. "Let's get started."

Jo-Jo seemed to understand that Julian was committed to entertaining him. He demanded that Julian use the tiny truck to move all the mud and dirt and that he build the walls of the dam higher and higher. When the water began to spill over the dam, Jo-Jo would shriek "Julian, the water's coming! Hurry!" and Julian would rush to reinforce the crumbling wall.

After what felt like hours, he heard Nancy's laugh behind him. "Well, you're a sight!" she said. Julian looked at Jo-Jo. His blond curls were already dry and the scrape on his right knee was barely visible. Julian, on the other hand, was a mess. His shirt was soaked, his pants were filthy, and he was muddy up to his elbows.

"I think you've found a friend, Julian," Nancy said. "Now he'll never leave you alone."

She rewarded his efforts with chocolate-chip cookies, then led him to the outdoor shower.

"It's solar heated," she said. "There should be plenty of hot water. We usually shower outside, except in the coldest months."

Julian had never taken a shower outside, with the sky and the trees all around. At least there were wooden walls on all sides. The only part of him that would be visible from the outside would be his feet. When he finished, he wrapped a towel around his waist and, still dripping, hurried up to the loft where he discovered Robin lying on his futon reading.

"Hey!" Julian said.

"Aah! A naked intruder!" Robin cried.

"Get out of here!"

Robin scooted, laughing, down the spiral stairs and Julian quickly pulled on his clothes. A minute later, her face reappeared at the top of the stairs, eyes shut tight.

"It's OK," Julian said. "You can come up now."

Robin threw herself back on the futon. "Thank goodness you're decent!"

"How was school?" Julian asked, to change the subject.

"OK, except for having to listen to Jo-Jo scream like somebody was torturing him!"

"I was not! He fell in the creek! If you guys heard him, why didn't you come get him?"

"Mom thought you could handle it. It wasn't what she calls his *bloody-murder* scream."

So much for impressing Nancy. Julian looked over at the computer, sitting on a desk in the far corner of the loft. Lowering his voice he said, "Maybe I should check in with Danny. I told him I'd let him know I got here OK."

"This is the only computer," Robin said quietly, turning it on. "Mom and Dad hardly ever use it. They let me get my own e-mail account so I could write to Ariel. She's my best friend. She used to live down the road, but then she moved to Phoenix." They waited for the computer to warm up, then Robin clicked into her e-mail. "Looks like there's a new message from Lopez."

June 15

Hey Jimmy Carter-Li and Robin Hood:

Just checking in and letting u know that I'm holding down the fort, available for logistical support on an as-needed basis. What's happening in Redwood City? Any dirt on Mr. CEO? How was the grey hound? All's quiet on the home front. Please delete this e-mail and do not attempt to print it or a hidden virus will erase your hard drive.

Danny

"Danny seems like kind of a crazy guy," Robin said.

Julian shrugged. "No, he's OK. He just likes to be funny. Can I write him back?"

Robin stood up and Julian took her seat. He wrote:

June 15

Dear Danny,

Arrived here safe. Everything according to the Plan (well, pretty much). Robin's family is great and the ranch is really great too. Operation Redwood still undecided. Sleep on it!

—J

"What are you talking about?" Robin asked, reading over his shoulder. "What's the 'Plan' and what's 'Operation Redwood'?"

"Well, the Plan was getting me here instead of math camp—getting away from Sibley, figuring out where you live, finding the right bus schedule, the whole exchange-student thing. Operation Redwood isn't really a plan yet. We were just trying to figure out if there was some way to help you, to keep my uncle from cutting down Big Tree Grove."

Julian paused. "I don't get it. In school we're always studying the rain forests in Brazil and Africa. And people are always trying to get you to sign petitions to save the rain forest and buy special rain-forest nuts. And we never learned anything about people cutting down redwoods in California. I mean, can my uncle really just cut down all those trees? Isn't it illegal?"

117

Robin looked at him in disbelief. "Obviously, it's not illegal. Where do you think all the trees went that used to grow on Huckleberry Ranch?"

"But that was a long time ago!"

She shook her head. "I showed you those stumps by the road. All you need to log is a timber harvest plan—a THP— and your uncle's already got that. There are some rules you have to follow. Like you have to replant and maybe there'll be certain trees they won't let you cut down. But it's private property. You can pretty much do what you want."

That night, Julian read Jo-Jo his bedtime story. In return, he received a slightly spitty good-night kiss.

As he lay in his futon in the loft, Julian felt that he had somehow traveled farther that day than he had on the long bus ride the day before. He'd milked a goat, explored Huckleberry Ranch on his own, walked along a river, and even fed a deer.

It wasn't even nine o'clock and he lay awake for a long time, looking up at the stars through the skylight. In San Francisco, the sky was usually hidden by thick fog or clouds. On clear nights, there might be a handful of indifferent stars scattered in the sky, some of which would turn into airplanes homing in on the San Francisco airport. But here, the brilliant stars shone out of the black night like the glittering eyes of some watchful spirit. Julian had never seen stars like this. He hadn't known this was how stars were supposed to be.

11

BRAINSTORMING

A fter a few days, Julian had found a place in the routine of the Elder family. Before breakfast, he would help Robin feed and milk the goats and collect the eggs. Every time he milked Aphrodite, the level of milk in the bucket rose a little higher.

While the girls had their lessons, he and Jo-Jo would feed the chickens. There was an incubator inside the barn, and one day they watched two ungainly chicks struggle out of their shells. By the next day, the slick, limp creatures had been transformed into buttery balls of fluff peeping about the yard. Julian cupped Jo-Jo's hands around one chick. It was almost weightless, a ticking little heartbeat surrounded by yellow feathers. Only the frowning angle of its tiny beak gave a hint of its future as a sharp-eyed chicken.

Nancy came by and admired the little chick extravagantly. Then she asked the boys to come into the garden shed to help

start the new tomatoes while the girls finished their math sheets. Jo-Jo's job was to fill the cardboard egg cartons with soil, but at least half the dirt ended up on the floor. Julian kept waiting for Nancy to correct Jo-Jo, but she didn't seem to mind. She handed Julian a bag of tomato seeds that she had harvested the previous fall and told him to plant twelve tiny seeds in each egg carton.

Nancy worked silently alongside the boys for a while, then said, "So, Julian, how is everything going for you? Are you happy here? Usually I can tell, but with you I'm not really sure." Her usually cheerful face was clouded with worry.

Julian looked at her in surprise. "It's great," he stammered. "You guys are great. Everything's great."

"But you must miss your mom. With her so far away."

He had a sudden memory of his mother leaning against the sink, looking toward the window, her fragile fingers twisting the ends of her long, black hair. "I don't even know who I am anymore," she'd said, and she'd looked at him as if he might know the answer.

"I guess." He cleared his throat. "She wanted to take me with her, but it was really expensive. The tickets and everything. I'm kind of used to it anyway. She always traveled a lot. Working. Or going on retreats."

"Who took care of you, then?"

"I stayed with my friend Danny a lot. Or the woman upstairs—Mrs. Petrova—she used to watch me when I was little."

"My mother died when I was fourteen," Nancy said abruptly. "I cried for a month." She turned away from him and started sweeping the floor beneath Jo-Jo's chair.

"The first time I came to Huckleberry Ranch, I fell in love with it," she said, in her usual light tone. "I was a city girl. I came with my friend—Bob's cousin. I never wanted to leave."

"Well, I guess you didn't," Julian said.

She laughed. "You're right. I told Bob we should get married. At first, he said no. He thought I loved the ranch more than him! But I kept asking, and finally he said yes." She pushed back the strands of brown hair that had escaped her ponytail. "I guess that taught me a lesson: Don't be afraid to ask for what you want."

By the end of the morning, they'd planted two hundred seeds. Nancy said it would be enough to keep them in tomato sandwiches through next fall.

After lunch, Julian was lying on his futon reading *Build Your Own Smart Home*, when Robin flopped down beside him.

"Let's go to Big Tree," she said urgently. "I'm finally finished with geometry! We need to get working on Operation Redwood!"

Downstairs, they found Molly sitting on the sofa, immersed in *Alice's Adventures in Wonderland*. As they walked past, she looked up and said, "Wait for me!"

Robin slammed the screen door shut. "Race you!" she called to Julian, and she flew down the deck steps and across the creek. When Julian got to the bridge, he couldn't help glancing back.

Molly was standing in the doorway calling to him. He waved, as if he thought she was just saying good-bye, then sprinted off.

Maybe today he could catch up to Robin. He hadn't known the trail the first day, he told himself as his feet pounded against the dirt, and he'd been tired from the bus ride. He walked quickly across the tree-trunk bridge, then started up the long switchbacks, pushing until his lungs ached. He didn't even stop to get water at the spigot.

At the second river crossing, he still hadn't caught up to Robin. Sweat dripped down his forehead. He began to wonder if maybe she'd taken a different trail. He crossed the river and jogged toward Big Tree, thinking he might have beaten her after all. But when he'd scrambled down the slope and into the circle of redwoods, there she was, sitting with her arms around her knees, wiggling her toes, and not even out of breath.

"You had a head start," he said.

Robin looked at him with pity. "Next time, I'll give you a head start. You can have a ten-second handicap."

"I don't need a handicap." Julian sat down next to Robin, still breathing hard. He picked up a thick stick and began sharpening the end with his pocketknife. "Oh, that's a pretty little knife," Robin said. "Can I see?"

He handed her the knife and she opened and closed the two blades. "Who's J.S.C.?"

"It was my dad's," Julian said. "I think he got it from his father."

"It's old, then. I bet it's real ivory. From elephant tusks," she said, handing it back.

Julian opened the larger blade and whittled the stick into a point. "That wasn't very nice, leaving Molly behind," he said at last.

"Molly! I thought we were going to start planning for Operation Redwood. We can't have Molly here. She'll tell Mom and Dad everything. Even Jo-Jo can keep secrets better than she can!"

"Well, OK," he conceded. "So, what are you thinking?"

Robin heaped his wood shaving into little piles. "Even if you can't convince your uncle not to cut down the trees," she said after a moment, "maybe you could get him to come up here. If he saw Big Tree for himself, he might change his mind."

"No way." He stopped whittling. "My cousin Preston was supposed to write a report on redwoods and—I meant to tell you this earlier—Sibley starts talking about how many board feet an acre, how many dollars per board foot. He says this place is worth ten million dollars!"

"Ten million dollars!" Robin frowned. "I don't think that's right."

"Well, that's what Sibley was saying. Or I think he was. Anyway, he's always working. He would never come way up here."

"We could write a letter to somebody," Robin suggested. "The president. Or maybe the governor."

"You think they're going to care about some little pocket of trees way out here? They wouldn't even read it."

"OK, then. You think of something. We'll take turns."

Julian began sharpening the other end of the stick.

"It doesn't have to be a good idea," Robin said impatiently. "Just throw out any idea. It's called brainstorming."

"How about a protest?"

"Who's going to be protesting. You and me? And Molly? And Jo-Jo?"

"Your turn, then."

"We'll chain ourselves to the trees," Robin suggested. "So they can't cut them down."

Julian grimaced. "How long can you stay chained to a tree anyway?" He clicked his blade closed and put the knife back in his pocket. Robin sighed and flopped down on her back. The trees soared up around them, letting in a jagged ring of blue sky. They could hear the hollow sound of a woodpecker drilling high above them.

"I just thought of an idea," Robin said, sitting up again. "But it's a secret."

"What kind of secret?"

She looked at him with her fierce blue eyes. "A big secret. If I tell you, you have to promise, cross your heart and hope to die, that you won't tell."

"I promise."

"Cross your heart and hope to die."

"OK. Cross my heart and hope to die."

"Right in the middle of Big Tree Grove, there's a secret tree house."

"Where?" asked Julian, looking up at the canopy around him.

"Not far. But I've never been inside. My brothers *refuse* to bring me up until I'm twelve. That's July twenty-ninth. There's some big initiation ceremony." She was quiet, sucking on the end of her braid for a moment.

"Well, so what? So what if there is a tree house?"

"We could go up in it. Like Julia Butterfly Hill."

"Who's that?"

She sighed with exasperation. "You don't know anything! She's this woman. And she was trying to protect this big old tree near Humboldt, way up north of here. And she went on this platform way up high in the tree where nobody could reach her and she lived there for more than two years so nobody would cut it down."

"Did it work?" Julian asked skeptically.

"I think it did. The logging company didn't cut down the tree. And a lot of other trees ended up being protected. It was called . . ." She paused. "Headwaters. I think. Anyway, the point is, we could do the same thing. We could go up in the tree house and stay there and then nobody could get us down until they agreed to save Big Tree Grove."

Julian turned this idea over in his mind. Staking out a tree house was much better than chaining himself to a tree. "How do you get up in it?"

"Well, that's the only thing. It's pretty high up. I think my brothers must use ropes or something."

"So we don't even know how to get into this tree house?"

"My birthday's next month. Maybe you could come back."

"Even if I could, then what? The two of us just stay there until Sibley changes his mind?"

Robin gasped suddenly. "Oh, I know!" she said. "Oh, this is the best plan ever! My friend Ariel is coming to visit from Phoenix for two weeks in August. It's all set. And you could come back up and we'd all do it together."

"I don't know." His mom was coming back sometime in August, but he didn't know the exact date. And he wasn't sure about spending all that time with two girls. Three, actually, counting Molly.

"It's too bad Danny couldn't come. He's got really good ideas. And he's good with tools and stuff like that." This was true. He had watched Danny take apart the pipe under his kitchen sink once.

Robin opened her eyes wider. "Maybe he *could* come. It would be much more fun with four of us!"

They were talking so intently that they almost didn't hear the muted clanging of the dinner bell.

"Oh, we've got to go home," Robin said. "Now I can't show you the tree house!" She looked up hopefully, as if it might suddenly materialize out of thin air. "Next time." She looked at him and smiled. "Ten-second handicap?"

Julian started to protest—they'd run all the way to Big Tree already—but the look on her face made him change his mind. As he ran up the slope, he could hear Robin counting backward from ten, with exaggerated slowness. He was almost to the river by the time she got to "one." He listened for her gaining on him, but there was no sound but his own footsteps. He had more endurance, he thought. He was more of the long-distance type.

He pounded on and on, reaching the top of the long hill and tearing down again, his legs flying. He got his second wind and was sure he was running even faster than when he'd started. He was almost at the house and she still wasn't anywhere close.

Finally, as he turned around the last bend toward the house, he saw the red of her T-shirt. She was sitting in a wooden chair on the deck, smiling triumphantly.

"I took another route," she explained when he'd trotted across the creek and climbed slowly up the stairs. "It's a little longer, but it has a nice view of the river." He did notice with some satisfaction that her forehead was glistening with sweat.

12

INTO THE
REDWOODS

"I got a notice in the mail today," Bob said that night at dinner, after they had finished their silent grace. "We lost the appeal for the THP for Big Tree Grove."

"A THP is a timber harvest plan," Nancy explained to Julian. "Robin probably told you they're planning to log on the neighboring property."

Julian nodded.

"It was bought by an investment firm in San Francisco. And they got a THP approved by the Department of Forestry. We were trying to fight it. At least get them to save the old-growth in Big Tree Grove. We filed an appeal. Bob went to the hearing and spoke and some scientists talked about how logging would affect the coho salmon and other wildlife. But I guess it didn't do any good."

"Another takeover by corporate America," Bob said

angrily. "Sometimes I think they just rubber-stamp those plans. Outside of the parks, the big trees are practically gone around here."

Everybody sat gloomily for a few moments. "Julian thought it was illegal to cut down redwoods," Robin said. "I wish it were."

"I guess they don't teach much forestry down in San Francisco," Bob said.

Julian shook his head. "We're always learning about the rain forests in Brazil. I didn't know people were still cutting down redwoods. I thought it was against the law, or they were all preserved in the national forests."

Bob gave him a puzzled look. "The national forests?"

"You know, I thought they were protected. I mean, if Big Tree Grove were in a national forest, they couldn't cut it down, right?"

Bob and Nancy exchanged glances.

"Julian!" Robin was giving him that superior look again. "The national forests aren't like parks. They log there all the time. Right, Dad?"

"Well, that's true," Bob said slowly.

"That was the whole reason the national forests were set up in the first place, to make sure America would have enough timber." Robin gave him a look of exasperation. "Haven't you ever heard of Gifford Pinchot?"

Why did she always know things that he didn't, Julian wondered.

129

"The founder of the Forest Service? 'The greatest good for the greatest number of people in the long run'? He and Teddy Roosevelt put millions and millions of acres into the national forests to protect them from profiteers. Doesn't ring a bell?"

"Robin, that's enough," said Nancy.

Julian decided it was time to get the conversation back on track and away from his educational deficiencies. "So if you lost the appeal, does that mean there's nothing else you can do to stop the logging?"

"Well," Nancy said. "My mother always said, 'A way will open.' But I'm not sure how it can here."

"Mom, don't you think we should do everything we possibly can to stop them?" Robin asked. "I mean, some of those trees could be a thousand years old."

"Of course. But Daddy and I worked pretty hard on our letter to the Board and they still approved the THP. I'm afraid there's nothing more we can do."

"But Daddy, don't you think we should try everything?"

"Like your mom says, we've done what we can. It'll break my heart to see that grove cut down and sold off to the highest bidder just to line some investor's pocket—some guy in Texas or New York who's never even seen this place."

There was another long silence, and then Nancy said, "What did you two do this afternoon?"

"They left me behind," said Molly. "They ran away from me."

"No, we didn't," Robin said innocently. "When?"

"When you ran off across the creek." Molly's eyes started to fill with tears.

"Julian and I were having a race. We didn't know you wanted to come!"

"You did too. You liar!"

"Liar! Liar! Liar!" Jo-Jo called out.

"Hush now, Jo-Jo," Nancy said, then turned and looked at Robin severely. "You know what I've told you about leaving Molly out. Imagine how you'd feel if you were the one excluded."

"We didn't exclude her, Mom!"

Nancy gave her a look.

"OK, next time she can come," Robin said reluctantly. "Mom, can I ask you a question?"

"Ye-es," said Nancy, already suspicious.

"You know Ariel's coming in August, right?"

"Right."

"Wouldn't it be fun if Julian could come too? And maybe even his friend Danny? It would be like camp. And we'd be doing a public service. We could educate them."

Nancy glanced quickly at her husband. "I don't know, Robin. Daddy and I would have to talk it over."

"Please, Mom?"

"It's true when the boys were your age we used to have their friends over all the time. Remember, Bob, the summer the Larsen boys came?"

"That was different. The Larsen boys were like family."

There was an embarrassed pause.

"I'm just saying we don't even know Julian's friend," Bob said. "And we still haven't spoken to Julian's mother."

"Well, that's true," Nancy conceded. "The circumstances are different." She turned to Julian. "You've been awfully quiet. Do you really want to come back, or is this just another one of Robin's crazy schemes?"

"No. It would be great." Though he couldn't imagine how he would get away from Sibley twice.

"You know, August is harvest time. We'd keep you boys working pretty hard," Nancy said.

"That's OK. Danny's my best friend. He wouldn't mind working. He's got a lot of energy."

Bob gave Nancy a look, as if the word "energy" had some special significance for him.

"Well, August is a long way off," Nancy said. "And Julian may change his mind after he's had to put up with us for a couple of weeks." She smiled gently at him. "But it really has been wonderful having him here. He's been so great with Jo-Jo."

Jo-Jo was stirring his soup and talking under his breath in what sounded like Russian. Julian leaned closer and could barely make out Jo-Jo whispering over and over, "Julian's my best friend."

Bob began a new project the next day: extending the old deer fence in the far garden. Julian was relieved from watching Jo-Jo

to help him. Every morning for a week, they'd set off early for Bob's airy workshop, open on all sides and covered with a tin roof. A small sawmill stood at one edge, powered, somehow, by the engine of an old Ford pickup truck that was set on blocks.

In the workshop, Bob seemed less preoccupied and the professorlike quality, which Julian had felt at their first meeting, was even more pronounced. He explained each step of the process with good-humored precision, from choosing the right trees for the lumber to deciding the correct height of the fence. After a few days, Julian had learned how to debark a small tree and how to place the trunk on the log beam and guide it toward the enormous circular saw. He could tell the difference between fir and redwood, cut a two-by-four, and saw the lumber to the right specifications.

Julian liked the work shed, with the tools all hung neatly in their places and the sweet smell of wood shavings in the air. A large bin of wood scraps stood near the sawmill, and Julian started to think that maybe he could use them to build something of his own. He thought for days about what to make, rejecting a toolbox (he didn't have any tools) and a birdhouse (too big to hide from Daphne). Finally, he decided on a simple wooden box with a lid, just a little bigger than his hand.

The next morning, Julian lingered next to Bob in the workshop, watching him sharpen an ax blade. Finally, he worked up the courage to say, "Could I ask you a question?"

Bob gave a curt nod.

"I was wondering if you'd mind if I tried to build something of my own. Something small—it wouldn't take a lot of wood. And I'd do it after we were done working."

"What do you have in mind?"

Julian handed him a rough sketch he'd drawn of the little box.

"Did you ever take drafting?" Bob asked.

Julian shook his head.

"Shop? Do they still teach shop in junior high?"

"No. At least not in my school."

"Too bad," Bob said. "You have a knack. You learn fast and you work hard. I've had college students out here for a month who couldn't do what you do. I couldn't trust them with a handsaw."

Julian felt his face grow warm and realized he was grinning foolishly. He turned away and looked over toward the sawmill.

Bob glanced at the paper again. "A box is a good place to start. Take anything you need. Here, come with me."

They went to the woodpile and Bob helped Julian select a few pieces of wood—oak for the sides and bottom, and cherry for the top. The next afternoon, they guided the wood carefully through the sawmill and Julian, by himself, cut it to size. He would join the pieces together in a perfect little box, then sand it smooth to the touch.

By the end of his second week, something clenched and anxious inside of Julian had begun to melt away. In its place, he felt an easy

contentment. He would wake in the morning to the sun shining in through the skylight, or to Jo-Jo's round face just a few inches from his own, and wonder what the new day promised. His stark bedroom at Sibley's seemed like another world.

Late Friday morning, Nancy announced that the girls had been so productive in school that they could take the rest of the day off. Robin gave Julian a significant look, and they managed to sneak out while Molly was in the bathroom.

It was hot, even in the forest. At the river, Robin pulled a white bandana from her pocket, dipped it in the water, and wrapped it around her forehead. It gave her a fierce, savage look.

When they had crossed into the Greeley property, Robin turned off the path. Julian tried to search the canopy for the tree house, but the forest floor was full of obstacles—broken branches, roots, and crumbling logs. The ground rose and fell unexpectedly. Julian's foot sank into a hole and he fell to the ground, cutting his left knee on a sharp rock.

The sight of the blood trickling down into his sock made him woozy. Robin grimaced, took off her bandana, and wrapped it expertly it around his knee.

"Are you OK?" she asked. "Do you want to stop for now?"

"No. Let's keep going." His knee pulsed with pain but he didn't want Robin to think he was a wimp.

They trudged on until their way was blocked by a giant log stretching a hundred feet on either side of them and almost as high as their heads. Julian ran his fingertips along the thick cords of reddish bark. Robin clambered up some branches to the top of the log, which formed a wide bridge across the cluttered forest floor.

"Come up here," she said. "It's easier." Julian got a toehold on a broken branch. As he pulled himself up, he banged his cut knee, flooding his body with pain. The white bandana was now stained with blood. Julian closed his eyes and took a deep breath.

As soon as he opened his eyes, he saw it. The tree house was about thirty feet in the air. It stood in the crevice between two redwoods that had grown together at their base and then separated. The wooden beams and planks blended into the shady forest.

They ran to the end of the tree trunk, slid to the ground, and dashed over to the redwoods, peering up at the tree house.

"It's fantastic," Julian said. "Much more houselike than I thought it was going to be." There was an open deck on one side and a small wooden structure on the other.

"I wish we knew how to get up," Robin said.

It was awfully high. Too high for a ladder. And the only branches were above the tree-house roof.

"You can't ask your brothers?"

"They won't be back from Guatemala until July. Anyway, I told you, they won't show me until I turn twelve."

"But we need to get up now. What if I can't come back in August? We've got to be able to get up somehow."

"Maybe we can figure out something on our own. We've got

two more weeks. Then, once we're up, we can start planning Operation Redwood!"

Julian kept staring longingly up at the tree.

"Julian, we're not getting up there today, that's for sure. We don't have a rope or anything. But my dad has a whole book on tree climbing. Or we can use the Internet. If we find anything, we'll come back tomorrow."

They were almost at the house when they saw Bob standing outside the barn, waving to get their attention. "Hey, Julian," he shouted. "You got a message from your friend Danny this morning. He wanted you to call. Said to tell you something about the tide. I didn't quite get it. It's still on the machine."

Robin gave Julian a quizzical look and he tried to suppress a surge of panic. Be calm, he told himself. He began to jog toward the house, then the pain in his knee slowed him to a quick walk. It's probably nothing. Danny's just looking for some excuse to use his stupid code.

When they reached the kitchen, they saw a red "2" flashing on the answering machine. Robin pushed a button and he heard Danny's familiar, husky voice.

"Uh, hello. This is Danny. I'm calling for Julian, who's staying with you." He sounded slightly out of breath. "Um, could you please give him a message. Could you tell him the tide is rising? I really need to talk to him. It's kind of an emergency." His voice was rising higher with every word. "Well, nobody's sick or dead or anything. But . . . if you could just tell him the tide is rising and he should call me that would be great. Um, thank you. And, um, I can't remember if I said that I'm Danny, Julian's friend?"

The machine beeped and immediately a second message began. "Hi, Bob," said a gravelly male voice. "It's Ralph down at the sheriff's. We've got a Daphne Carter from San Francisco on the line who says you've kidnapped her nephew. I'm going to be in the neighborhood. I'd like to drop by and maybe we can clear this thing up. See you soon."

13

CAUGHT

Robin looked at Julian. "Who's Daphne Carter?"

"My aunt," Julian said miserably. "Sibley's wife."

"My dad is going to kill me." Robin's face looked strangely blank. "What does Danny mean, 'The tide is rising'? What tide?"

"That was just his code for an emergency. If Daphne called the sheriff, Danny must have told them I'm here." He took a deep breath. "The sheriff's on his way here to talk to your dad." His mind felt like the inside of a freezer. "What are we going to do?"

"Why would Danny tell, though?"

"I don't know. Daphne probably tortured him."

"Well, don't just stand there. Call him, quick, before my parents walk in."

Julian picked up the phone and quickly dialed Danny's number. He listened for a minute, then hung up. "It's the machine."

Robin started pacing up and down the floor. "We can't stop the sheriff from coming. He's already on his way. Call your aunt."

There was nothing in the world Julian would rather do less than call his aunt. He would rather eat grubs. He would rather run to the Greyhound station and take the first bus that came along.

"What would I tell her?"

Robin's eyes opened wide. "Well, for starters, you could tell her my dad didn't kidnap you!"

He took another deep breath. "You're right. I should call her." He dialed her home phone quickly before he lost his nerve. He would think of what to say when she answered. He heard his uncle's voice on the answering machine and hung up with relief.

"Doesn't she have a cell phone?" Robin asked.

Of course she had a cell phone. The problem with the cell phone was, she'd probably answer it. It was better not to think. He'd started slowly punching in her cell phone number when he heard the sound of a car coming up the driveway.

Robin looked out the window. "It's the sheriff car."

Julian felt like he was going to faint. He had the sickening feeling that all the trouble he'd ever been in before was just a drop compared to the ocean of trouble ahead.

"Come on!" Robin said urgently. Julian just stood watching the patrol car pull up next to Bob's white truck. "Julian! Hurry!"

He followed Robin onto the back deck and down the stairs. There she turned sharply to the right and pulled aside a wooden lattice. They crawled under the deck, then Robin carefully slid the lattice back into place.

The crawl space was dark and musty and filled with old leaves. He could barely see Robin as she crawled up the uneven slope toward the front of the house. He tried to scramble after her without putting any pressure on his sore left knee. As he moved awkwardly forward, he felt the sticky, elastic tangle of a spider web paste itself to his mouth. He sat up to brush it away and hit his head against the cement foundation so hard the pain seemed to ring through his whole body. When the pain had dimmed, he bent down again and slowly crawled next to Robin. She was looking out of a lattice that Julian figured must be just to the left of the front door.

A beefy man in a uniform was standing next to the patrol car, wiping his sunglasses with a handkerchief.

"Hey, Ralph," they heard Bob say.

"Good afternoon," Ralph replied, squinting and holding up the sunglasses for inspection.

"What brings you out here? Did Martha give the green light to our little fishing expedition?"

"I guess you didn't get my message." Ralph put his sunglasses back on and glanced in the side mirror of the car.

"Something wrong?"

"Well, you might say that. We seem to have a little situation, here. I spent a good fifteen minutes on the phone this morning with a woman named Daphne Carter. Ring any bells?"

"No, I don't think so. Why don't you get out of the sun." They both stepped into view, under the shade of the oak trees. "Any relation to Sibley Carter?"

"Now that you mention it, she happens to be his wife."

"Is there some trouble next door?" Bob asked, looking worried.

"She seems to think you're in some trouble. Says you've kidnapped her nephew." Ralph crossed his thick arms. The corners of his mouth were tight.

"Kidnapped her nephew! What in the world?" Bob's face was a picture of amazement.

Ralph gave a low chuckle. "It was worth coming out here just to see the look on your face."

"What? Is she crazy?" Bob said.

"I don't know," Ralph was still chuckling and shaking his head. "She's a piece of work. Misplaced her nephew. Must have run away. I would too if she was my aunt."

"But why would she think I have anything to do with it?"

"Said she had information you'd lured him up here. I couldn't get it straight. Something about Robin too. Kid's name is Julian."

"Julian?" Bob's face crumpled. He put his hand to his forehead and closed his eyes for a moment.

"Wait a minute," Ralph said, his smile fading. "You actually know this kid?"

Julian felt his fingers and toes go numb.

142

"I was afraid of something like this."

"What's going on, Bob?"

"Almost two weeks ago, at lunch, Robin says she's invited a new exchange student up here from San Francisco. Says they were pen pals. Name's Julian Li. Chinese, or half-Chinese, I guess. Good-looking kid. I picked him up at the Greyhound." Bob shook his head ruefully. "I knew something wasn't right."

"He didn't mention the Carters?"

"Not a word. Says his mom's out of town. I left a message. Nancy wanted to keep him. He's been here ever since."

"So how in the world did this kid get hooked up with Robin?"

"I have no idea."

"Well, I guess it is a good thing I dropped by," Ralph said, shaking his head. "I'd better let Ms. Carter know we found the boy." He lumbered over to the car and disappeared inside.

Julian's foot had fallen asleep and his throat itched. He tried to swallow softly to keep from coughing. He glanced at Robin, and she made a silent grimace but stayed perfectly still.

Bob was less than ten feet away. Julian tried to read his expression. He didn't look furious, but it was like a dark shadow had passed over his face.

After an almost unbearable amount of time, Ralph got out of the patrol car. "Well, Bob. Seems like you're going to have the pleasure of meeting Ms. Daphne Carter yourself."

"How's that?"

"Apparently, she couldn't wait for the sheriff's office to clear this up. She's on her way here. She called the office about an hour ago."

"Ralph, I'm sorry about all this," Bob said. "I had a feeling that boy wasn't telling me the whole story."

That boy. Julian thought of the hours he had spent with Bob in the workshop, in the garden, at the table. That Julian, it seemed, no longer existed. He was a stranger again, just some kid off a bus who'd conned Bob into letting him stay.

"Why don't you come inside for now?" Bob said to the sheriff.

Just as their feet banged overhead, a low rumbling began in the distance. The two sets of footsteps stopped, then headed back outside. Julian could see Ralph putting on his sunglasses and staring down the driveway. "Looks like you've got company, Bob," he said.

Daphne's silver SUV rattled up in front of the house in a cloud of dust. Julian took advantage of the noise to shift his position slightly and scratch his nose. Robin started furiously brushing something off her legs. When the engine noise died, they froze again. Julian immediately wished he'd straightened out his legs more. They were already cramping up.

Out of the SUV stepped a man wearing a pink knit shirt and tennis shorts. He looked vigorous and, at the same time, harmless. He loped around to the passenger side and opened the door. Daphne emerged, sporting a pair of cropped black pants and a sleeveless blouse.

"Thank you, Sergei," she said with pointed politeness.

"Ms. Daphne Carter, I presume," said Ralph, stepping toward her.

"Who are you? The sheriff?"

"Deputy sheriff. We chatted on the phone this morning. Ralph O'Brian."

Daphne ignored his extended hand. "Where's my nephew?" she demanded.

Ralph turned toward Bob.

"I'm sure he's in the house, or running around somewhere with my daughter," Bob said.

"Do you mean to tell me you haven't even *located* him yet?" Daphne asked. "This is an outrage! This is unbelievable!"

"Well," said Ralph slowly. "If Bob says your nephew's here, I'm sure he is."

She gave him her coldest stare. "You don't take me seriously, do you? Well, let me tell you something. I'm thinking of pressing charges! My nephew has been missing for almost *two weeks*. Apparently, he was lured up over the Internet by this Bob Elder." She turned to Bob. "That's you, I presume. And when I report this crime, does the sheriff's office even lift a finger to help me?" Daphne paused, finger in the air. "No! If it hadn't been for directory assistance, and Sergei, here," she said, giving him a proprietary glance, "I'd never have found Julian."

Sergei gave a little wave and an apologetic smile.

"Now, ma'am, I can see you're upset," said Ralph.

"Don't you 'now, ma'am' me," Daphne said. "My entire *day* has been ruined. I *wasted* almost four hours driving up here. I had to cancel all my appointments. One of them took me two months to get! If you don't produce Julian this instant"—she paused—"I'm calling the CIA. And the FBI. You'll regret the day you condescended to me!"

"I believe there's been a misunderstanding," said Ralph in a placating tone. "But why don't we get Julian. Maybe that'll help straighten everything out. What do you think, Bob?"

Bob stood still with his arms crossed. Julian remembered that look. It was the same way Bob had watched him when they'd first met in the parking lot.

"Maybe you can clear something up for me," he said. "Julian informed me that his mother is out of the country. Is that correct?"

"His mother!" Daphne rolled her eyes. "She goes off for the entire summer without making *any* arrangements for Julian. No lessons. No camps. I had to set up *everything,* at our expense, I might add. *Then*, when I call to find out about sending Julian a little package I'd prepared for him, the camp says he never showed up! I nearly had a heart attack!"

"You thought he was at camp?" Bob asked.

"Listen," she snapped, "the tuition was paid *in full*. His duffel bag was packed!" Daphne stopped herself. "I don't have to defend myself to *you*." She turned to Ralph with a look of astonishment on her face. "Why am I the one being interrogated here?"

"Well, of course, we have to ensure that you actually are Julian's legal guardian before we turn him over to you," Ralph said calmly.

"You have to ensure what?" Daphne suddenly lowered her voice. "I lived with the boy under my roof for nine weeks. Nine! Weeks!" She stood with her mouth open for a moment, suddenly at a loss for words. "I gave him a room, fed him," she said, picking up steam, "supervised his homework, even threw *parties* for him. If I'm not in charge of him, nobody is!"

Bob studied her another long moment. Then he said, "I'll go fetch him."

Julian could hear the heavy thump of his footsteps above them and then the ringing of the dinner bell.

Robin started sliding down the slope. Julian followed close behind. Somehow, he seemed to be making a lot more noise than she was. His feet had fallen asleep and he felt like he was moving on stumps. He wiggled his toes, trying to make the pins-and-needles feeling go away.

"Do we have to come out?" he whispered. The cobwebby crawl space was starting to seem like the perfect place to spend the afternoon.

"Obviously, we can't stay under here forever," she whispered back. "Those ants were making me crazy! They were crawling all over me."

When the sound of the bell had died away, they heard Bob's footsteps as he crossed back to the front of the house, and they

emerged slowly from underneath the deck. Robin replaced the lattice and gave Julian a critical look.

"You're a mess," she said. Julian wiped his face on his T-shirt, which only served to cover it with grime. The white bandana around his knee was now filthy and spotted red with blood. Robin looked clean and composed, as always.

They walked slowly to the front of the house, where Bob and Ralph were speaking together in muted tones. Julian braced himself as Daphne directed her furious gaze toward him.

"Julian, I could kill you!" she said. "Your uncle is going to have something to say when we get back. There are going to be *serious consequences*."

Julian's knee was still throbbing with pain.

"When I called High Sights Academy to send you a little *package* I'd prepared," Daphne continued, "do you know what they told me?" She came to a halt, eyebrows raised. "They said you were on an *African safari*!"

The outraged look on Daphne's face, coupled with the memory of Danny chatting on about wildebeests, was too much for Julian. His shoulders started shaking with laughter. He tried to maintain a solemn expression, but the more horrified Daphne looked, the less Julian was able to control himself.

Finally, Daphne stopped gaping and shrieked, "Do you think this is funny? Because let me tell you, the humor is lost on me! I nearly killed myself trying to track you down!"

"What in the world is going on here?" At the sound of Nancy's

voice, Julian sobered up instantly. He turned and saw Nancy with Jo-Jo in her arms. Molly was at her side, her face paler than ever.

"Julian's aunt is here to take him home. Daphne Carter. Sibley Carter's wife." Bob's eyes signaled a kind of warning. "Julian, do you have anything to say?"

Julian looked uncertainly around him. He wasn't sure what Bob was asking him for. An apology? His opinion about returning home? An explanation for why his aunt was there, ranting and raving?

He decided that an apology would be the safest route. And he was truly, deeply sorry, now that he saw himself through their eyes—an imposter, an outlaw, taking advantage of their kindness and trust.

"I'm really sorry, Bob." Julian kept his eyes down. "And Nancy," he added, turning to where Nancy was standing.

"You stood there and told us you weren't running away," Bob said. All the warmth had drained from his face.

"I wasn't running away, really, I just . . ." Everything was so complicated. Better to say as little as possible. "I guess I should have told my aunt and uncle where I was going," he continued halfheartedly.

"Perhaps, he has ze bags?" Sergei said helpfully.

"Go get your stuff," Daphne directed. "And clean yourself up!" she shouted as Julian turned and headed inside. "I don't want those filthy clothes inside my car."

Before the front door closed, Robin slipped inside after him. They climbed silently to the loft, then Robin said, "I tried to think of something to say to help, but I couldn't."

"What could you say? It was a nightmare." Julian threw his clothes into his duffel bag. "I guess Operation Redwood is over."

"Maybe a way will open," Robin said doubtfully. "Maybe."

"I better get out of these clothes," he said, and she left. A moment later, he saw the tips of her fingers push a large Band-Aid up from the loft steps. The voices outside were growing louder. Julian could hear his aunt's high, demanding tone and Nancy's voice, low and urgent. Then Jo-Jo started wailing. He's probably tired, Julian thought. It's time for his nap.

". . . wouldn't talk that way to a dog," he heard Nancy saying when he stepped outside again. The voices stopped. Bob had moved over to stand next to Nancy and the children. Nancy and Daphne were glaring at each other and Ralph was standing between them with his arms apart, like a referee.

"I'm ready," Julian said softly.

Without saying a word, Daphne turned, climbed into the SUV, and slammed the door. Julian walked over to where the Elder family had gathered. "Good-bye," he said. Jo-Jo took his thumb out of his mouth and said, "I don't want Julian to say bye."

Julian could barely lift his eyes to meet Nancy's. "Thanks for having me," he said. "Thanks for everything."

She gave him a hug with her free arm. "You take care," she said. "If you need . . . ," she began, but Bob put a cautionary hand on her shoulder. "Thank you for all your help with Jo-Jo," was all she said in the end.

Glancing at Ralph, Julian said again, "Sorry for the trouble." He looked last at Robin, standing barefoot on the front steps. She waved and looked like she was about to cry.

Sergei took his duffel bag and put it in the trunk. "Off ve go!" he said cheerfully.

Julian climbed into the backseat. The car spun around and started down the long driveway, and Julian watched Robin and her family recede through the tinted glass of the rear window.

14
THE VOW OF SILENCE

As Daphne's tirade in the car went on and on, Julian pretended he was a secret agent who'd been captured by the enemy. His mission: to determine how much Danny had revealed. He didn't know when they'd have a chance to talk and he wanted their stories to match. Fortunately, the enemy was more interested in complaining about her ruined day than interrogating him. From what Julian could gather, Daphne and Sibley were still in the dark about two key facts: first, that he'd opened his uncle's e-mails, and second, that Robin's family was connected in any way to the IPX property.

Eventually, Daphne grew tired of craning her neck over her shoulder to make sure that Julian was still listening. Her performance at Huckleberry Ranch had drained her energy. She ordered Sergei to find the nearest latte, then spent the next hour rehashing the story of Julian's rescue on her cell phone. After she had repeated the story four or five times, Daphne called the housekeeper and instructed her to remove the phone and television from Julian's room.

When they finally reached San Francisco, Julian was sent straight upstairs and told to stay in his room until further notice. His bedroom had been stripped bare. There wasn't even a pencil. He sat by the window and listened to the sounds of the house: the garage door opening, the muffled roar of the vacuum cleaner, the click of Daphne's high heels.

Outside, the foghorn sounded its low, rhythmic honk. The gray fog completely hid the Golden Gate Bridge and was so dense that it was impossible to gauge the time of day. When the streetlights came on, Julian jumped.

It was hard to believe that the summer sun was setting far away at Huckleberry Ranch. Julian stood for a long time, staring at the drifting fog. *Had it been worth it?* he asked himself. He was in disgrace, but with his aunt and uncle, that was nothing new. If he hadn't opened Robin's message, he would never have gone to Huckleberry Ranch and he would have missed out on the best weeks of his life. He hadn't known that such a world existed.

He wondered what Robin and her family were doing right now. No doubt Robin was in trouble. Daphne might not have made the connection between his running away and Big Tree Grove. At least not yet. Bob and Nancy, however, certainly wouldn't think it was just a coincidence that he was Sibley Carter's nephew. What would Robin tell them? Would she reveal her secret e-mail to his uncle?

Or make up some story somehow putting the blame on Julian? She might as well, he thought bitterly. He'd probably never see any of them again.

There was a timid knock on the door. Julian opened it, and Preston looked quickly down the hall and slipped inside. He was dressed in his plaid bathrobe and slippers and was holding a paper napkin and two pieces of cheese pizza on a paper plate.

"Julian!" he said, his face bright with pleasure. "I saved two pieces for you. They're still kind of warm, even."

"Thanks. You're a good cousin. You're the best one I've got!" It was an old joke. He was starving. He hadn't eaten anything since breakfast.

Preston sat down cross-legged on his bed. "I can only stay a minute because I'm not allowed to be in here. Mom went out. Helga's on the phone with her boyfriend."

Julian nodded. That should give them ten minutes at least. He sat down and began to devour the pizza.

"So, where did you go?"

Julian sat for a moment, chewing. "Well, I went to visit a friend of mine."

"Who? Danny?"

Julian smiled. Preston had only met Danny twice, but he adored him and was always talking about him.

"No, a girl. Named Robin. She lives kind of far away from here," he said, between bites.

"How did you get there? Did you take an airplane?"

"No," Julian said with regret. It wasn't fair that he'd never even been in an airplane and Preston had practically flown around the world. "A bus. Not like a city bus. A bus that goes to different towns."

"But why didn't you go to camp? I went to camp last summer and it was really fun."

"Well . . ." Julian hesitated. "I wanted to see my friend. And I guess it wasn't really the right camp for me."

Preston shook his head. "Mom and Dad were really mad. When they found out. I don't think it was a very good idea."

"Maybe you're right." Julian finished the crusts of the pizza and wiped his hands on the napkin. "So what have you been up to? Did you finish your redwood report?"

Preston nodded. "I got a five plus out of five. Do you want to see it?"

"Of course."

"I'll see what Helga's doing. Then I'll come back." He leaped to his feet. "If I can," he added seriously. He took the greasy paper plate and napkin, opened the door, and looked both ways. Then he scurried in his silent slippers down the hallway.

A few minutes later, Preston was back, carrying an enormous poster. In the center, he had drawn the outline of a giant redwood tree with crayon and painted it with watercolors. Around the tree were circles of colored construction paper printed with Preston's neat handwriting.

"We had to have eight facts and two opinions," Preston said

with pride. "I did a 'sloppy copy,' and then I did the final draft."
Julian knew how long it took Preston to write a single sentence.
He must have spent hours putting the poster together.

"See, here's fact number one," Preston said. "'More than 95
percent of the original redwood forest has been cut down.'" Next
to this, he had drawn a picture of nineteen stumps and one tree.
"Because 95 percent is the same as nineteen out of twenty," he
explained. "My teacher helped me figure that out.

"Fact number two: 'The oldest recorded redwood tree is more
than 2,200 years old, but the species *Sequoia sempervirens*'—I
don't know if I'm saying it right—'has existed for millions of years.'
I drew a dinosaur here because there were redwoods during the
time of the dinosaurs.

"Fact number three: 'The tallest redwood tree is 379 feet
high.' I didn't need to draw a little picture here. See, I just drew a
ruler along the big tree.

"Fact number four: 'Redwood trees provide shade and
protection for chinook and coho salmon streams.' This is my best
picture. Well, maybe after the big redwood."

The salmon had each scale drawn in pencil and colored in
with blue and green watercolors. The scales looked watery and
shimmery.

"That is a work of art," Julian said. "You'll have to show me
how to make a fish like that."

"I messed up on the green, so I put blue on top, and see, it
turned out great," Preston said happily. "OK, here's my first opin-

ion. Well, it's not exactly an opinion. It's more like a wish but my teacher said it was OK: 'I wish I could live in a redwood forest.'"

Julian thought of Big Tree with a sudden pang. "I'd like to live in a redwood *tree*."

"Oh, that would be even cooler, like a tree house. I didn't think of that. Well, actually, I kind of have something about that later. You'll see. OK, here's fact number five: 'Some animals that live in the redwood forest are salamanders, banana slugs, spotted owls, marbled murrelets, elk, deer, flying squirrels, fishers, and bats.' A fisher is actually not a fish, like I thought. It's cute—like an otter. See? Here's my flying squirrel. It didn't really turn out."

Julian had to admit that it looked a little like a rat. "But squirrels and rats are both in the rodent family," he added gently.

"Fact number six: 'In 1999, the government protected thousands of acres of land in Humboldt County in the Headwaters deal. It is mostly old-growth, which means trees that were not planted by people but have been there a long time.' I didn't know what to draw for this one," Preston said. "You see, finally I decided to draw this girl in the top of a tree. I can't remember her name, but she lived in a tree for two years to keep them from cutting it down and after that they saved the Headwaters."

"Julia Butterfly Hill?" Julian asked, and Preston nodded. Julian wondered why it was that as soon as he learned something new, he would suddenly realize that everybody else already knew it. He'd ask Danny if he knew who Julia Butterfly Hill was.

"Fact number seven," Preston was saying, "is here: 'Trees are measured in board feet. One board foot equals a piece of wood one foot long, one foot wide, and one inch thick.'" Next to this fact, he'd drawn a little wooden board with two tiny rulers along each side.

"I like your knothole," Julian said.

"Here's my last fact: 'One old-growth redwood tree can be worth $150,000.' My dad told me that one. You were allowed to interview people, and my teacher said he counted." The last picture showed a tree with a $150,000 price tag attached.

"Here's my last opinion. 'If I had a million dollars, I would buy six redwood trees so that nobody could cut them down.' You see, I had to figure out the math. My teacher helped me because I was trying to figure out how many redwood trees I could buy with a million dollars. I thought it would be a lot, but it turned out it was only six, plus a remainder, which isn't that many."

Julian wished he could tell Preston about Big Tree Grove, and the tree house, but it was too risky. Instead, he said, "You did a great job on your poster. It's amazing. It looks like a fifth-grader did it." Preston flushed with pleasure.

"Now you better get out of here," Julian added reluctantly. "I'm already in enough trouble for both of us."

Julian woke up the next day with a curious empty feeling. A morning of waiting turned into an afternoon of waiting, which turned into a blank, dull evening. His meals were brought to him on a tray by the housekeeper, and he was permitted to leave his room only to go to the bathroom. He was tempted to use his pocket knife to carve his initials into the baseboard, like the immigrant prisoners on Angel Island, but was sure that not even the tiniest defacement would escape Daphne's eagle eyes. After spending a whole day alone, Julian began to feel as though he didn't even exist. He began to understand why solitary confinement was considered a punishment even for people who were already in prison.

As soon as it was dark, Julian tried to go to sleep, but since he'd spent the day doing nothing, he wasn't at all tired, and he tossed and turned for what felt like hours before finally drifting into sleep. He woke up feeling heavy and groggy and unsettled.

Julian had finished the cereal from his breakfast tray and was drinking his orange juice as slowly as possible when he heard a quick knock. Immediately, his uncle walked in and sat down in the wooden chair across from his bed.

"Good morning, Julian." As always, Sibley's hair was neatly parted on the side and his steely eyes were humorless.

"Good morning." Julian's voice was rusty with disuse.

"You've had some time now to think about what you've done," his uncle said. "I have several issues to discuss with you. First, your behavior has been inexcusable. We gave you a good home for two months. Daphne went out of her way to arrange your summer vacation—and how do you pay us back? By running away. By disrupting our entire household. You have no idea the trouble your little escapade caused."

Julian waited silently for him to finish.

"We're trying to contact your mother. Given your behavior, we think it's best that she return immediately."

It hadn't occurred to Julian that his mother might have to cut short her trip to China. He lowered his gaze and shifted uneasily.

"I would also like some explanation for your behavior. Why would you go up to that place? Were those people friends of your mother's? What were you thinking?"

Sibley stopped, waiting for a response, while Julian stared at the hole in his blue jeans. Was his uncle trying to trap him, or was it possible that he hadn't yet made the connection between Big Tree Grove and the Elders? Either way, Julian could see no advantage in telling his uncle the truth about his escape. The intercepted e-mails, Danny's inspired invention of the Plan, all the plotting they had done to make it work—these were all wrapped together in his mind with his days at Huckleberry Ranch. These were things to keep close to the heart.

On the other hand, he didn't have the energy, or the wits, to come up with another plausible explanation for his actions. If there was one thing he'd learned, it was that plans did not always work out exactly as you'd imagined. Whatever story he made up, Sibley could double check by interrogating Danny or, worse, contacting the Elders.

To speak the truth was impossible. To disguise the truth under a web of new lies would just lead him back in a circle to where he was now.

Julian said nothing.

His uncle waited a long time, until the silence became almost unbearable. Finally, very slowly and without ever dropping his gaze from Julian's face, he said, "Julian, I asked you a question. I would like an explanation of what's going on here."

A strange calm came over Julian. His uncle's pale eyes were boring into him, as if they were trying to access the data hidden in his mind, but Julian felt cool and detached.

"For the last time, Julian," his uncle said, "answer me."

Julian felt like he was floating high above the room. He saw that, really, his uncle's anger was not so important. It was not as important as Big Tree Grove. The circle of redwoods was still there, hidden deep in the forest, cool and shady and quiet. It would be there long after his uncle's anger had died away. Or it should be. It should be there forever.

Sibley stood up. "I'm sorry that you have made this decision, Julian. I don't have to tell you that there are going to be consequences, serious consequences." He stared at Julian for a long time, shook his head, and walked out, closing the door angrily behind him.

15

QUANTUM

When he looked in the bathroom mirror the next morning, Julian was surprised to see his own familiar face staring back at him—the unruly black hair, the dark uptilted eyes. He had survived another empty, endless day and dream-filled night, and he felt that the solitary weekend should have transformed him, made him look somehow older, wiser, and more gaunt, but his face was disappointingly the same.

Almost as soon as he returned to his bedroom, he heard a sharp rap on the door and his aunt appeared before him in her tennis outfit.

"Julian," she said, her voice already registering her distaste. "Your uncle and I have discussed your consequences." She stopped, waiting for Julian to look her in the eye. "We still haven't been able to contact your mother." Daphne gave him a severe look, as though this was somehow Julian's fault. "But obviously we can't have you moping around *here* all day. Especially if you won't even *talk*. So until she returns, we've enrolled you in the Quantum Childcare Center.

"These are the rules: The Center is open from nine to six. When it closes, you'll return here immediately and go straight to your room. You will not go over to friends' houses, and you will not receive friends here. *When* you've provided us with a written explanation of your actions, *and* an apology, we will reconsider the rules and determine any appropriate changes."

Daphne's voice had taken on some of the steely inflection of her husband's. Julian could imagine the two of them coolly discussing the terms of his imprisonment with the same seriousness they brought to any domestic issue, like a bathroom remodel or a dinner party.

"Do you understand me?"

Julian nodded.

"I suppose a 'thank you' would be too much to ask," Daphne added disagreeably, and walked out the door.

Quantum Childcare Center was located in the basement of an old church. When Julian arrived, two little boys with blank faces were playing math games on the computer and a few girls from school were milling about. There was Grace Wu, whom he'd known since first grade, now long-haired and with an inch of bare skin showing above her jeans. She came toward him and started asking him about his summer. But her questions only reminded Julian of Huckleberry Ranch, and he couldn't bring himself to say more than a few words. Finally, she gave up and walked away.

Most of the morning was "free time." Julian persuaded a glum fourth-grader named Gus to play Chinese chess with him. They used a bottle cap and a piece of broken crayon to replace the missing pieces. Julian won two games and let Gus win the third, which seemed to cheer him up a little. Later, the counselors set out dirty tubs of paint for "art." Julian slumped on his stool for a long time, staring at the blank paper. Then he dipped his paintbrush in silver and painted a shining river. Around it, he painted two dark mountains and a black sky with silver stars.

Julian spent the next afternoon on the Quantum playground, shooting baskets by himself under the sun's gray glare. The wind had blown over the trash can, and crumpled papers, soda cups, and plastic bags were scattered everywhere. He was trying to make his fifth basket in a row when somebody slammed into his side and knocked his ball to the ground. Julian looked up angrily.

"Danny!" he cried in surprise.

"Julian!" Danny gave him a hug that lifted Julian off the ground. "I was afraid I'd never see you alive again!" He stepped back, his black eyes shining. "I tried to call you a hundred times over the weekend. My mom even tried. All we'd get was the machine, and then finally we got your aunt but she kept saying you were unavailable, like she was holding you down in the dungeon or something."

Julian laughed. "Well, not quite, but almost."

"It was scary. She kept saying, 'I'm sorry, but Julian is un-available.'" Danny pinched his face up sourly and spoke in a high, whiny voice. "No matter what I asked her—'Julian is unavailable.' Even my mom was worried. I almost talked her into a plan where she'd distract your aunt and uncle, and I'd slip into the house and rescue you. But she chickened out."

"You should have. I was basically in solitary all weekend," Julian said with the casualness of a seasoned spy.

"I tried to warn you! Did you get my message at Robin's?"

"Yes," Julian said, laughing. "'The tide is rising! The tide is rising!'"

"OK. You were right about that one. It wasn't the best thing to have to say in an emergency. I mean, what's the big deal? The tide is rising? So what? It rises every day! Twice!"

"I told you it was a stupid code!" Julian said.

"I've been thinking—for next time the code will be 'It's about Martinez.' Isn't that good? You could slip that into any message. 'Give me a call. It's about Martinez.' Or 'There's a meeting tonight—it's about Martinez.'"

"Yeah, much better." The boys looked at each other and burst out laughing. "What are you doing here?" Julian said. "How'd you find me?"

"Grace Wu told Joey Spitoni. He's in basketball camp with me." Danny glanced around at the trash-covered playground in disgust. "What a mess! Hey, there's Spacey Gracie now!" He turned to the swing set and gave Grace and the other girls a friendly wave, and they put their heads together and whispered, then smiled back.

Julian waved his hand in front of Danny's face. "Come on, Danny. Focus! I've been dying to talk to you, but my aunt took away my phone." They walked to the corner of the blacktop, where no one could overhear them, and sat down on a brown bench covered in graffiti. "What happened with Daphne?"

"It was ugly. Thursday night she calls. She found your old sneakers," Danny snorted, "and was going to send them to you, but when she calls math camp, they say you never showed up. So she calls me. At first, I say I don't know where you are. But then everyone's totally freaking out. They were going to call the police, the FBI. My mom's crying. She thinks you've been abducted. So I had to tell them. I gave them Robin's name and told them she lived near Willits. My dad was ready to skin me alive. I lost my allowance for the entire summer!"

"What else did you tell them?"

"Nothing! They wanted to know who Robin was. I said I thought she was some kind of family friend. I was trying to think what to say, but everyone's asking me questions, cross-examining me. Your aunt threatened to send me to juvenile hall!"

"Conspiracy to aid a runaway! Is running away a crime? Is lying a crime?"

"A terrible sin," Danny said with a Mafia accent, "but not a crime." He shook his head. "Anyway, Daphne obviously found you!"

"Yeah. One minute, I'm trying to explain to Robin why you're talking about the stupid tide rising, the next thing the sheriff's there, then Daphne's driving up."

"The sheriff?"

"Daphne told them Bob *kidnapped* me. Bob is Robin's dad. Luckily, the sheriff was a friend of his." Julian tried to shut out the image of Bob's angry face. "So nobody knows about Big Tree Grove or anything? Or the e-mails?"

"No, I didn't tell them anything about that. What about you? They must have given you a major grilling."

"You know Daphne," Julian said. "She was too busy ranting and raving to ask questions. But then my uncle started asking me who Robin was and why I went up there."

"What did you tell him?"

"Nothing. What could I say?"

"You just sat there and said nothing?" Danny gave him a look of admiration. "Wasn't he mad?"

"He was beyond mad. That's why they kept me in solitary all weekend. Now I'm seriously grounded."

"For how long?"

"For life, I guess. Or until my mom gets back. They're trying to get hold of her." Julian had been trying to avoid thinking about how his mom would react to having to come back early from China, and he continued quickly, "Daphne read me the riot act! No friends allowed! I think she means you."

"What?" Danny said, with a wounded expression. "She

doesn't like me? Now my feelings are hurt." He put his hand on his heart and sobbed dramatically.

Danny wanted to hear every detail about Huckleberry Ranch. Julian told him all about the tree house and everything Robin had said about Operation Redwood.

"A tree house! *And* a covert operation!" Danny said admiringly. "You guys are good."

"But it's not going to happen," Julian said. "Even if my mom comes back, Robin's dad will never let us come now." He felt his spirits sinking. "Do you know that it's not illegal to cut down redwood trees?"

Danny frowned. "Sure. I knew that. If it was illegal, how could your uncle get away with it so easily?"

"All right then, who's Julia Butterfly Hill?"

"Uh, I dunno," Danny said in an Elmer Fudd voice. "A wabbit?"

"Wrong. She was a woman who lived in a redwood tree for two years so that the loggers wouldn't cut it down. Here's another one. You can cut down trees in a national forest. True or false?"

"Oh, come on, Julian, school's over!"

"This is the last one, I promise. True or false?"

"False?"

"Wrong again!" said Julian. "It's true. You can cut down redwoods. You can cut down trees in the national forest. Did they ever teach us that in school?"

"Nothing like that. They never teach us anything that really matters. Why?" He fell to his knees and raised his hands to the sky. "Why? Why does nobody care that we are so terribly mis-informed?" Grace Wu and her friends looked over, giggling, but Danny just shouted louder. "Why do they leave us to *wallow* in our ignorance? The laws of our country don't protect us! They're cutting down all our trees and soon there won't be any oxygen left and we're all gonna die!" Then he jumped straight up from his knees to his feet, like a hip-hop dancer.

He sauntered past the smirking girls. "Who are you staring at?" Danny said, and grinned.

The next afternoon, Danny brought an e-mail from Robin. In the middle of the empty blacktop, Huckleberry Ranch suddenly came alive again. Before, Robin had been an imaginary girl living in an imaginary house near an imaginary forest. Now, Julian could hear the words in her breathless, slightly superior voice:

June 29

Dear Julian (and Danny),

Are you all right? I hope you're OK and didn't get into too much trouble. I sure do understand now why you didn't want to live at your aunt's house!

We are fine here but it's a lot harder to get our school work done without you to look after Jo-Jo. I think my mom REALLY misses having you around!

I've been thinking about Operation Redwood. Ariel

thinks I should wait for things to cool down here before bringing up another visit from you and Danny!

My Dad was not happy to find out Sibley Carter was your uncle, TO SAY THE LEAST! By some miracle, I didn't really get in as much trouble as I thought I would. Dad said he couldn't think of a "fitting" punishment.

John and Dave (my brothers) will be home for the last two weeks of July. I will try to find out how they got up in the tree house!

Write back,

Robin

"OK, so what do you want me to say back?" Danny asked, peering over his shoulder.

Julian hesitated. Suddenly, he felt awkward having Danny write back to Robin. After all, they'd never even met.

"I don't know," Julian said. "Maybe I should write her back myself. Maybe I could get my own e-mail account and write her during 'free time.'"

Danny looked at him hard. "You're cutting me out of the loop?"

"No!" Julian felt his face grow warm. "I just thought it might give me something to do. And it might be more convenient that way, you know?"

"This is what *I* know," Danny said, with a sharp edge to his voice. "I'm the one who came up with the Plan. I helped you figure out the whole thing. If it weren't for me, you would never have

met Robin Elder! When your aunt was raving like a maniac and threatening to take me to the police, I covered for you and I got in big trouble. And I came all the way here to give you this stupid e-mail and now you're trying to cut me out of the loop."

He gave Julian a look of contempt, then turned and walked out of the playground.

Julian stood under the gray sky, shaken. For a few moments, he'd thought Danny might be kidding, just playing the part of the Angry Friend. But by the time Danny reached the end of his speech, Julian realized he was serious. He had seen Danny get angry at other boys at school or even yell at total strangers, but the two of them never fought. Luciana would say in amazement, "You boys are such good friends. Always playing, never fighting. I wish I had a friend like that!"

He hadn't been trying to cut Danny out, exactly. He wanted Danny to be part of Operation Redwood, but at the same time, part of him wanted to keep Huckleberry Ranch just for himself. He and Danny had been best friends since kindergarten and they'd shared everything—the same soccer teams, the same friends, the same teachers. Huckleberry Ranch was the only good thing he'd ever had all to himself.

If he went back with Danny, everything would be different. Danny could be so charming; maybe they'd like Danny better than him. Or worse, maybe they *wouldn't* like Danny. And Julian couldn't really picture Danny sitting quietly inside the circle of redwood trees.

171

His orange baseball cap was almost at the end of the block. Julian raced across the blacktop and past the gate and called Danny's name as loud as he could. The Quantum counselor blew his whistle angrily and Julian stepped back inside the gate and called out again. Finally, Danny turned around and sauntered slowly back toward him.

"What?" he said scornfully. "Do you need help setting up your e-mail account?"

"Come on, Danny. Don't be like that. Write Robin back. Please."

"She's your girlfriend. You can write her back in the privacy of your own home. Or wherever."

"She's not my girlfriend, you idiot. Come on. I didn't mean anything. I can't open my own account anyway. Daphne would probably pay someone to hack into it."

He could tell Danny was relenting. "If I'm in, I'm in," Danny said. "I don't want you e-mailing behind my back. Writing little love notes."

"You're in. Come on! You're my best friend. If it weren't for you, I wouldn't even have gone up there. Write her back. Tell her I have to wait until my mom gets home. Then maybe we can figure out Operation Redwood."

"Since you're groveling, *and* since you're stuck with the Evil Ones," Danny said grudgingly, "I will take pity on you and oblige."

Danny returned the next day with a print-out of his e-mail.

June 30

Dear Robin,

I will give you an update on the situation here.

Julian's aunt (aka "the Evil One") took him back to her house and locked him in solitary. They threatened to keep him there until he confessed about Operation Redwood. Julian took a VOW *of* SILENCE and his uncle grounded him for life. Now we're waiting for his crazy mom to get back from the Far East. In the meantime, when your parents cool down, get them to let me and Julian come up there!

Sincerely,

Danny Lopez

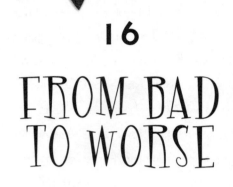

16

FROM BAD TO WORSE

That night, Julian was informed that Sibley would be home for dinner and therefore he would not be eating in his room. Julian arrived at the table promptly at seven o'clock and silently surveyed the spread: creamed spinach, veal chops, quivering salmon mousse, and dinner rolls. Sibley gave him a sour nod, then ate stolidly while Daphne grilled Preston about his day. Every few minutes, she stopped to direct a pointed question at Julian, then stared in mock expectation as he gazed miserably down at his plate.

Julian had already eaten four dinner rolls without attracting Daphne's attention, and he didn't dare try for a fifth. He forced himself to eat a few more bites of spinach and was about to clear his plate when Sibley pulled a piece of paper out of his breast pocket and, with elaborate care, unfolded it onto the polished mahogany table.

"Well, you'll never guess who I finally heard from today," he said.

"Cari! Am I right?" Daphne said immediately.

Sibley simply raised his pale eyebrows. "And you'll never guess what she said."

"Let me guess! She's not coming home!"

"Apparently, she's extremely *immersed* in her work in China." Sibley was now speaking in a tone of such exquisite sarcasm he sounded almost sincere. "She simply can't get away."

"Oh, for crying out loud!" Daphne said. "Didn't you tell her about Julian?"

"I told her it was impossible for Julian to extend his stay with us. She's trying to find somebody else. She asked us to keep him here for now."

"For now? How long is 'now'?"

Sibley gave a disparaging smile. "Undetermined."

"This is the last straw!" Daphne turned to look at Julian. "How can he stay here? He won't even talk to us!"

"Really, Julian," Sibley added. "I think it would be in your best interest to speak up now."

Julian stared mutely at the candles. He knew how his mom was when she was absorbed in something new. Nothing else could get her attention. Not her meals. Not her friends. Not anything. Still, it hadn't occurred to him that he would be stuck with Sibley indefinitely. It hadn't occurred to him that she wouldn't come home.

He had thought things couldn't possibly get any worse. Now he realized he'd been wrong. With a sigh, he stood up and grabbed another dinner roll. Then he picked up his plate, stuffed the roll in his mouth, grabbed his glass and silverware, and walked away from the table.

At Quantum, the counselors had given up even the pretense of entertaining Julian. He sat in the corner, reading old copies of *National Geographic*, while the other kids made bead necklaces. After lunch, he threw seventy-two free throws before Danny wheeled onto the blacktop on his bike.

"Sorry I'm late," he said. "My cousins are here. I can only stay a minute because I'm supposed to babysit, but I wanted to give you this." He leaned his bike against the basketball pole, unzipped his backpack, and thrust a crumpled paper into Julian's hand:

> Dear Julian and Danny,
> My dad showed me this article! Yikes!

Below it was an article from the *San Francisco Chronicle*: RECORD EARNINGS PUT SPOTLIGHT ON LOCAL INVESTMENT FIRMS. It was the kind of dull article that Julian never looked at twice, the type that ran in the Business section. But toward the end, he found the paragraph that had caught Bob's eye:

Among the leaders in profits last quarter was the San Francisco firm IPX Investment Corporation. Led by CEO Sibley Carter, who stepped up to the helm last September, the firm has pursued a strategy of aggressive diversification. "We have our fingers in a lot of pies," Mr. Carter said. "We're always looking for investments on the cutting edge, where the market may be lagging." He said he expects investments in a number of new arenas, from timber to biotechnology, to reap significant gains by next fall.

"'Next fall,' Julian!" Danny said. "It'll all be over by this summer!"

Julian lifted his eyes from the article and looked around the yard. There was the counselor, blowing his whistle, the girls swinging from the monkey bars, a couple of kids playing dodgeball. And in Julian's hand were these dry statements about investments and profits. Nothing in his world or in the article seemed connected with Big Tree Grove. Nothing was sending an alarm that a rare and beautiful place was about to be destroyed.

"Operation Redwood!" Danny said.

Julian shook his head.

"We've got to do it soon," Danny said. "As soon as your mom gets back. She might even help, you know? Take pictures of the redwoods or something."

"My mom's not coming back," Julian said.

"What do you mean?"

"She can't come home. She's too busy." He put the paper in his pocket, picked up the basketball, and threw a perfect three-pointer.

"She's making you stay with the *Evil Ones*?" Danny said incredulously. "That's brutal."

"She's trying to find somebody else."

"Who?"

Julian shrugged. "I don't know."

"You could stay with me! I'll ask my parents."

"Come on! They're not going to let me stay there for a *month*." Julian threw another three-pointer and watched unsmilingly as it whooshed through the rim. "Plus, you've got that journalism camp."

"I'll beg them!" Danny said. The ball bounced toward him and he stilled it with one foot.

"Even if I *could* stay with you, we're never going to get to Robin's," Julian said. "Her dad hates me now. He's never going to let me come back."

"He doesn't hate *me*," Danny said. "Maybe *I'll* go to Robin's this time and *you* can stay home and be the logistical support."

Julian opened his mouth in protest, but Danny punched him in the shoulder. "Just kidding! You're so gullible!" He looked at his watch. "Aaa!" he cried. "I'm late! I gotta go. Once my cousins set our house on fire. They're total pyromaniacs!" He threw the basketball to Julian and climbed onto his bike. "See you tomorrow!"

"Tomorrow's Saturday," Julian said gloomily.

"Oh, sorry." Danny said. "I guess you're stuck with the Dastardly Duo." He gave Julian a look of sympathy. "I'll see you next week. Have a nice Fourth of July."

Julian nodded halfheartedly.

"Adios!" Danny cried, wheeling away. "Good luck!"

Back at Sibley's that evening, Julian just lay on his bed, staring despondently at the empty walls. His mom wasn't coming home. She was halfway around the world, having all sorts of fun without him. She didn't care that he was stuck at his uncle's. Or imprisoned at Quantum. She probably didn't even know what a jerk his uncle really was.

Julian pulled his pillow over his head and breathed his own warm breath. All these silent evenings were getting to him, he thought from inside his black cave. His favorite teacher, Ms. Felicity, had told them that when they were upset, they should try to remember a place where they were happy. Julian tried to imagine himself sitting in the circle of trees at Big Tree Grove. But that just made him feel worse. He was never going to get back to Huckleberry Ranch. Even if he could get away from his uncle, Bob would never forgive him for lying to him. He'd probably never see Robin or her mom again.

Maybe Robin would find a way to save Big Tree on her own. Or was it too late already? He could picture Robin hiding in the forest, watching the giant redwoods crashing down before her eyes.

When he heard a muffled knock on the door, Julian didn't even have the energy to lift the pillow from his head. He wondered dimly if he was getting enough oxygen.

"Hey, Julian." Preston's voice pierced through the haze. "Are you sleeping?"

"No," Julian said, blinking in the light. "You better get out of here. You're going to get in trouble."

Preston closed the door. "What's the matter?" he said. "Are you sick?"

Julian pulled himself up on his elbow. "I'm OK. I'm just . . . I don't know. A little down."

"How come?" Preston's blue eyes were wide beneath the arcs of his pale eyebrows.

Julian had to concentrate to remember what had triggered his cloud of gloom. "Well, you know your redwood project?" he finally began. "I have some friends who have some redwoods. Not their own, but nearby. And somebody's going to cut them down. And my friends don't know how to stop them." Julian knew he was being stupid, talking about Big Tree like this to Preston, but he was too worn out to stop himself.

Preston nodded. "They don't have a million dollars," he said with a knowing air.

Julian couldn't help laughing. "That's right. They don't have a million dollars, and neither do I."

"Some people do, though," Preston said. "Some people are really rich."

"Maybe you shouldn't tell your parents about this," Julian said quickly. "It's kind of a secret."

Preston looked surprised. "Oh, not *them*," he said. "They're not *rich* . . ." but his voice was cut short when the door swung open.

Daphne stood glaring at them, her arms crossed. "Preston, go to your room," she said in her frostiest tone. "Julian. Come downstairs. There's someone to see you."

17

AN UNEXPECTED VISITOR

Julian headed down the stairs uncertainly. Who would be visiting him? Daphne's cool tone gave him no clue. Maybe it was the police. Maybe they *could* send him to juvenile hall for running away. Or maybe his mom had found someone for him to live with. Maybe his old neighbor, Mrs. Petrova, had had enough of Florida and had come back to San Francisco.

But as Julian approached the front door he saw, not the police or Mrs. Petrova, but a small woman, dressed in black, with a purple scarf wrapped around her shoulders. The bright color of the scarf, together with her spiky black-and-white hair, made her look like an exotic little bird.

"Popo!" Julian cried in surprise.

"Julian!" Popo said. She embraced him awkwardly, then looked him up and down through her little round glasses. "Look how tall you are now!"

Either his grandmother had shrunk, or he'd grown over the past several months. They were nearly eye to eye.

"I've spoken with your mother in Beijing," Popo said in a neutral tone. "It seems she can't get away right now. So, the most sensible solution was for me to come stay with you for a while." She said this lightly, as though she were always dropping by unexpectedly. "I need a little vacation anyway. I just got back from a trip to Washington. Very tight deadline."

She studied Julian for a long moment before turning to Daphne with a polite smile. "Thank you for watching my grandson. It was very generous of you and your husband."

Daphne crossed her arms with a petulant frown. "Julian is not free to come and go as he pleases right now," she said. "His behavior has been completely unacceptable. We're still waiting for an apology."

Popo's smile faded. "I'm not sure I've got the full story, yet. I couldn't get hold of Cari until this morning. Something about a camp in Fresno? Or Mendocino?"

"He *ran away*!" Daphne yelped. "We had *no idea* where he was! I had to spend *hours* tracking him down!"

"Julian, why don't you go upstairs and get your things," Popo said. "We can straighten this all out later."

It took a moment for it to dawn on Julian that his confinement was over. He brushed past his aunt and ran up the staircase two steps at a time, as behind him, Daphne's voice wheeled higher and higher. In his room, Julian quickly stuffed his clothes into his duffel bag. He took his toothbrush from the bathroom and jammed a couple of books into his backpack. As he started down the hall, he had the nagging sensation that he was forgetting something. He came to a sudden stop, turned around, and ran back to Preston's room.

Preston was sitting at his desk, drawing sea creatures.

"I'm going home," Julian said softly. "Popo, my grandmother, came to get me." He looked at Preston's picture. "An angler fish," he said. "Very cool . . ."

Preston looked up from his drawing, disappointed. "I thought you were staying here."

"Well, better with Popo than stuck in my room," Julian said. "She's waiting. I'll see you soon, OK? I promise."

"How can I talk to you?" Preston said sadly. "If I do get a million dollars, how will you know?"

"I'm sure you'll find a way," Julian said. "Don't forget, you're my number one cousin." He passed his hand over Preston's soft, blond hair. "I've really gotta go. Take care."

Downstairs, Sibley had joined Daphne, creating a barricade to the door. Julian could just make out the purple of Popo's scarf behind them.

"Eleanor," his uncle was saying. "I see you finally made it back from D.C. Was it a profitable trip?"

"For me, yes. But, of course, how you measure profit depends on what you value."

"Ancient Chinese wisdom?" said his uncle with a fake chuckle.

"I'm getting old, I admit, but not quite ancient. At least not yet." She caught Julian's eye through the doorway. "You're ready?"

"Julian has a little unfinished business with us, as I already informed you," Sibley said, his eyes flat. "He's not leaving here until we get an apology. He put Daphne through hell."

"Hmmm," said Popo. "From what Daphne tells me, it seems as though Julian's been through quite a bit as well. I don't know what Cari would think."

"Well, since his mother is wandering around *China* right now," Daphne said, "her opinions are not really our greatest concern."

"I think it's time we were going," Popo said. She gave Julian a nod, and he ducked under Sibley's arm and stood next to her.

"If he leaves now," Daphne shrieked, "that's it! Next time Cari wants to go traipsing around the world, tell her she's on her own!"

Popo drew herself up to her full height and looked Daphne in the eye. "I don't even know how to begin to respond to that," she said. Then, without another word, she turned and marched down the steps.

As Julian followed Popo down the sidewalk, he felt a surge of energy flow through his body. It was like eating a candy bar on an empty stomach. Not an hour ago, he'd been locked in a solitary room, mute and powerless. Now he felt the rush of freedom.

He climbed into Popo's little blue Toyota and they rode in silence past the monumental homes that lined the streets of Pacific Heights. Finally, Julian asked, "When did you get back?"

"Just this morning. I had to stop in at the *Chronicle* office downtown for a meeting." She came to a stop sign and waved the other driver through. "And I finally got through to your mother. She'd left me a few messages."

"Oh." Julian started picking at the hole in the knee of his pants.

"She seemed to think you needed to get away from Sibley's as soon as possible."

They drove west down Geary Boulevard, the stores and shop fronts gradually giving way to pastel-colored houses. When they turned down his street, Julian could see the white waves breaking on Ocean Beach. They pulled up in front of his shingled gray house.

While Popo prepared the tea, Julian walked from room to room, taking a quick survey of home. From the living-room walls, his mother's masks leered down at him. Everything was in disarray. There were dirty cups in the sink and a vase of dead roses drooped on the dining-room table. His mom must have left in a hurry.

Julian stopped in the hallway and stared at the three black-and-white pictures lining the wall. The first was of his mother when she was about his age, sitting on a park bench in a raincoat. She wore her hair in two long pigtails and she was smiling and leaning her head against the shoulder of a man with sad eyes and a kind face. Julian knew this man was his grandfather, who had died when his mother was a teenager. In the second picture, his mother's face looked slightly puffy and she wore a sleepy smile.

Up against her shoulder, she held a naked infant with a shock of black hair—him. The third picture was of his father, handsome and laughing, his head thrown back, holding a young Julian in his arms.

"I bought this tea in a tea shop in Washington," his grandmother called from the kitchen. "It was very expensive. It's supposed to be good for your memory."

It was disorienting to see Popo standing at the counter instead of his mother. She poured him a cup of tea from a pumpkin-shaped teapot.

"This may turn out to be a good thing in the end," she said, as if she wasn't entirely sure she believed it. "The trip to Washington wore me out. And now we'll have time to catch up." She poured herself a cup of tea and sat down across from him. "Where should we start?"

Julian shifted uncomfortably in his chair.

"To begin with, would you like to tell me why you ran away from Sibley's?" Popo had removed her purple scarf, and with her loose black T-shirt and short hair, she looked like a solemn little monk.

Julian took a sip of the tea. It smelled like earth and honey. Where did his story begin? "Well, Sibley wanted to send me away," he said. "He was sending me to *math camp*. I mean, he never even asked me about it. And it was in Fresno. For four weeks!"

Popo frowned sympathetically.

"And so, I kind of knew this girl named Robin. And her

family had this exchange program in Mendocino County and she said I should come up. At first I wasn't going to, but Danny said it would work. Well . . . it wasn't his fault. I just thought it would be better than math camp. And we thought Sibley wouldn't even know."

"You were planning to come back after the four weeks?" Julian nodded.

"And how did you 'kind of know' this girl, Robin?" Popo asked.

Julian thought he'd been very smooth in glossing over that point, and the question drew him up short. He remembered, with discomfort, that his grandmother was a newspaper reporter.

"Your mother didn't think you would run away from Sibley's without a very good reason," Popo finally said.

"How about, they hated me?" Julian said. All week, he'd kept his excuses for running away dammed up in his mind, and now they burst out uncontrollably. "How about, they hated my dad? And said stupid things about Mom? How about, they couldn't wait to get rid of me? How about, they were sending me to *math camp*?"

Popo took another sip of tea. "What makes you think they hated your father?"

"I don't just *think* it," Julian said angrily. "It's true."

Popo just looked at him.

"I was sick," he began, "and Sibley sent a taxi to pick me up at school." It all felt like a million years ago. "But then he had to go to a meeting and I fell asleep. When I woke up, I found this e-mail Sibley wrote." He took a deep breath. "He said they were sending me away. That I was rude and *sullen*. Just like my father."

Julian felt his voice starting to quaver and he bit his lip. His grandmother looked at him gravely. "I didn't know your father as well as I should have," she began. "But he certainly wasn't rude. Or sullen. Not that I saw, at least." She had a faraway look in her eyes. "He was very good-looking. Very charming. And, of course, he was very young. He wasn't even thirty when he died." She looked away. "It broke your mother's heart."

Julian felt his eyes fill up with tears and he tried not to blink, but it was too late. His grandmother's words had released something inside him. A tear slid down his cheek and he wiped it roughly with the sleeve of his T-shirt. He took another sip of tea.

"And Mom," he said, staring down at his saucer, his voice still shaking. "Sibley wrote stuff about her too. You could tell he didn't like her." He blinked and a tear dripped off his cheek and plopped onto the saucer. Julian smiled and sniffed hard.

Popo handed him a tissue. "Sometimes, it's better not to pry. Whatever Sibley wrote wasn't intended for you."

"There was another e-mail too," Julian said quickly. "From this girl." And, haltingly, Julian began. He told her about Robin's e-mail and about the Plan, about Huckleberry Ranch, about Big Tree Grove and the morning that Deputy Sheriff Ralph O'Brian and Daphne had arrived. He reported briefly on his days in solitary confinement. The only part he left out was Operation

Redwood, because that was a secret and because it probably wouldn't happen anyway.

Popo listened intently, speaking only to clarify something he'd said or ask him if he wanted more tea. When he told her about Danny's message on the answering machine, she raised her eyebrows and laughed.

When he was finished, she said, "You've had quite an adventure. You are a very enterprising young man. It's good to be adventurous and enterprising." Then she added, "However, you should never go visit strangers that you meet by e-mail."

"I know, Popo."

"Something terrible could have happened. Also, you shouldn't disappear without telling people where you're going."

"Danny knew. And I couldn't tell Sibley and Daphne!"

"Well," she said, taking a small sip of tea. "At least you're safe." She searched his face again and smiled, her eyes crinkling happily in the corners. "I took a few weeks off from work. Maybe your mom will be back by then. Or you can come and stay with me in Sacramento."

Ever since Popo appeared at the door, an idea had been forming in the back of Julian's mind. "Popo," he said. "We were supposed to go back to Huckleberry Ranch in August. Danny and me. At least, before the sheriff came. I don't know if her parents will still let me, but if they said it was OK, could I go?"

"We'll cross that bridge when we get to it," Popo said lightly. "I think there's been enough excitement for one day."

They had a late dinner at a restaurant in Japantown. Julian ordered three rolls of cucumber sushi and miso soup, and Popo told him about the museums and beautiful gardens she'd seen in Washington.

It was more time than they'd ever spent alone together before. When his mom and Popo were together, Julian felt like he was watching a play in a language he couldn't completely understand. There would be a warm greeting and an enthusiastic exchange of news. Then, after a while, usually in the middle of lunch, something would go sour. Julian could never figure out what it was, but he could hear it in their voices. By the time Popo said good-bye, everybody would be relieved.

But now Julian found that he was actually enjoying himself. When they finished eating, Popo poured each of them another cup of tea and said, "I'm sorry things didn't work out with your uncle. When your mom told me the plan, I thought it might be"— she hesitated—"interesting for you to meet your father's family."

Julian shrugged. "It wasn't that bad. And I got to know Preston better." He wrapped his hands around the warm teacup. "You know, he did this whole report on redwood trees. I gave him the idea, but he did a really good job. He had all these facts and he said if he had a million dollars, he'd use it to protect redwood trees. He's really nice. Nothing like Sibley and Daphne."

"Well," Popo said thoughtfully, "you gave him the idea to study redwoods, and now he cares about redwoods and he knows a lot about them. That's pretty good. Even with all the news on television and in the papers, a lot of people really don't know what's going on. The people who do know—the ones in charge—sometimes they want to keep it that way. They'll confuse everything, say black is white and white is black."

"But you're a journalist, so you tell people the truth. You tell them what's really going on, right?"

"Well, I try." She sighed. "But sometimes we're just shouting in the dark. Shouting as loud as we can, but nobody's listening."

"That's how Robin feels about Big Tree. Here something so terrible's going to happen. And nobody cares. It's not even against the law. Did you know that?"

"You know, it's ironic," she said. "One of your ancestors, what would it be"—she started counting out on her fingers—"your great-great-great-grandfather actually worked in the logging camps near Mendocino. On the coast, not far from Willits."

Julian stared at her in amazement. "You're kidding me."

"It was my grandmother's father. He was a cook. There's still a Chinese temple in Mendocino from the 1850s. A long time ago, cutting down a redwood with a cross-cut saw was a major accomplishment," Popo said. "People thought there were so many trees, they could never run out."

"But now they're almost all gone and they're still cutting them down."

"That's true." She sighed again. "There was a lot of press coverage of the Headwaters deal, and the government saved thousands of acres of old-growth up in Humboldt County. But not everything. Maybe we should have shouted a little louder."

Julian lay in bed that night, thinking about what his grandmother had said. Over the years, Popo had occasionally shown him one of her newspaper articles, but they were dull and dense, filled with dry language about politicians and committees. He'd certainly never thought of her as shouting in the articles she wrote. Maybe she should actually shout instead, he thought.

He tried to picture his grandmother shouting, but he couldn't. The way she had talked to Sibley and Daphne was as fierce as he'd ever seen her. She was fierce but polite, he decided, like a samurai or a knight. He could picture her in one of those Chinese kung-fu movies, brandishing her sword and deflecting bullets with her bracelets. He drifted off to sleep, imagining his grandmother as a Chinese warrior woman, leaping from treetop to treetop.

On the Fourth of July, Julian called Danny and relayed the story of his escape from Sibley's, which Danny greeted with satisfying hoots of delight. That night, sitting on a cold stone wall overlooking the Bay, the boys watched the firecrackers shoot up into the sky. As the glow of fog changed from blue to pink to green, they raised their cups of hot chocolate and toasted Julian's liberty.

After the holiday weekend was over and Popo had recovered from her jet lag, she set about cleaning the house. With ferocious energy, she mopped and scrubbed and straightened up piles, sending Julian out to empty trash cans and buy sponges and cleaning supplies.

Julian couldn't relax with her sweeping under his feet all the time. He decided to reorganize his room as well. He winnowed down his rock collection, filled an entire trash bag with outgrown clothes for Goodwill, and recycled three boxes of old spelling tests and book reports and drawings he no longer liked. Popo bought him a blue comforter to replace the one he'd had since first grade, a matching beanbag chair to read in, and a small blue lamp to put next to it. His room, when he was finished, looked fit for a seventh-grader.

Danny had started journalism camp, but in the evenings his room still functioned as Operation Redwood Headquarters. He relayed the news of Julian's good fortune to Robin, who wrote back promptly:

July 7

Dear Julian and Danny,

Glad to hear that Julian's grandmother is back. That's GREAT news. I know you must be thrilled. Here, things are not so great. First, our new exchange student is SUPER obnoxious. She actually called Jo-Jo a LITTLE BRAT (when she thought I wasn't listening). Worse, my dad heard a rumor they might start logging in a few weeks. I still haven't brought up your visit with my parents. My mom would be OK but I'm afraid with my dad it's still a SORE SUBJECT. Though I think he felt a little sorry for you after meeting Daphne! (Who wouldn't?)

Maybe you should write him an apology. He's a big believer in apologies. Well, so long for now,

Robin

"A brat!" Julian said, looking over Danny's shoulder at the screen. "They probably wish *her* aunt would come and drag *her* away!"

"Yeah. Now they'll appreciate what an angel you were!" Danny said. "And why should you apologize? You were just trying to *help* them. Robin's father should apologize to *you* for letting Daphne abduct you!"

Julian half agreed with Danny. He *hadn't* been running away. Nobody could have guessed that Daphne would track him down like she did.

But if Bob wouldn't let them back, then they could never do Operation Redwood. And if they didn't do Operation Redwood, Sibley would never change his mind about Big Tree. It would just be business as usual for IPX.

Unless he could figure out some other way to change Sibley's mind. After all, Sibley *was* his uncle. There were a few obstacles—like the fact that Sibley hated him and never wanted to see him again. But think if he somehow succeeded—if he could single-handedly save Big Tree Grove! Then he wouldn't have to apologize. He could return to Huckleberry Ranch a hero.

All week Julian racked his brains, trying to think up a way to convince Sibley not to log Big Tree, until he imagined his mind must look like one of those computers in space movies, beeping and flashing as it crunched all the data. He thought so much his head hurt, and he still hadn't come up with a single good idea.

Over the weekend, he biked to Danny's, hoping he would give him some inspiration, or at least be up for a game of basketball, but Danny was stuck doing a project for journalism camp.

"How did I end up going to a camp that gives *homework*?" he grumbled. "*You* were the one who was supposed to be stuck with the overachievers. My mother must be secretly taking lessons from the Evil Ones."

"Just get it done. Then your brain will be free to help me think."

"I'm trying! I'm trying! It's not so easy."

"Forget the stupid homework, then. Look up 'saving redwoods,'" Julian said.

"You think we're going to find a little handbook?" Danny said. "'Saving Redwoods 101'? In case you weren't listening, I'm supposed to be looking up press releases." Danny shook his head. "Earth to Julian! I have to find three examples. And then write my own."

"OK. 'Saving redwoods' and 'press release.' Search on that. Just to see."

They got 242,000 results.

"Try that." Julian pointed to a link at the bottom of the page, but Danny had already clicked on another link, and then another. Every time Julian saw something interesting, the screen vanished and a new page appeared in its place.

"Danny, stop that!" Julian said. "You're going too fast."

"No ho-ho!" Danny said, clicking away. "I'm in hot pursuit. I'm on the trail. I can smell it." He clicked another link. "How about this baby?"

A photograph of giant redwoods filled the screen. Below it was a press release from the Sierra Club about an old-growth redwood grove in Santa Cruz. The timber company had agreed to protect the trees from logging, permanently, by donating them to the state park system.

"Is this what you're looking for?" Danny said. "What's going on in that tiny little brain of yours?"

"I don't know," Julian said, studying the text. "I mean, it's not like Sibley's going to just give the trees away."

"Let me just print it out. I need it for camp anyway. Then I'm going to try 'press release' and 'San Francisco Giants'—that'll be a little more entertaining."

Julian took the sheet out of the printer and looked at it again. Something about it intrigued him, something to do with his visit to his uncle's office. It was like a little echo in the back of his mind and he was hoping if he just ignored it for a while, it would sound a little clearer and help him figure out what to do.

18

OPERATION BREAK-IN

The following Friday, at six o'clock in the evening, Julian and Danny stood on a corner in downtown San Francisco, trying to make themselves look as inconspicuous as possible. It wasn't difficult. They weren't so old that they looked threatening or so young that they looked lost. The rush-hour commuters streamed past them indifferently, hurrying home for the weekend.

"Have you got the press release?" Julian asked.

Danny pulled a piece of white paper from his back pocket, unfolded it, and held it up in front of Julian's nose. "Yes, for the fourteenth time! Are you satisfied?"

"OK, OK." Julian checked his watch. They were supposed to be at the Metreon, watching a movie.

"We look ridiculous in these clothes. We look like twins. Or like girls—'Jules,'" Danny said in a girlish voice, "'let's wear the blue pants and the white shirt tomorrow. OK?'"

"No. We look perfect. Like private-school kids. Trust me," Julian said, staring at the gold door of the skyscraper in the middle of the block.

Danny leaned against the building and started beating a rhythm against his legs. "We're going to go to jail for sure. Operation Break-In is the worst plan we ever thought up, or *you* ever thought up, I should say."

"Stop calling it that!" Julian frowned and turned his attention momentarily away from the door. Their fake press release was ready. The only tricky part was getting into Sibley's office without anybody seeing them. "You got a better idea?"

"Um, minding our own business? Trying not to get a criminal record?"

Julian suddenly shrank back against the wall. "Look! The guy in the suit! That's Sibley!"

"They're all in suits!" Danny said, craning his neck.

"No, look. The tall one. See—he's hailing a cab."

"Yeah, that's him," Danny said with a distinct lack of enthusiasm. They slunk back against the side of the building. Sibley ducked inside the taxi, and they watched until it pulled into the stream of traffic. "OK, so he's gone. What's next?"

The exodus into the subway stop was slackening. Julian took a deep breath and looked at his watch. "OK. We better go in now. If we wait, it'll be too late. We'll look suspicious. Oh, and take off your sunglasses. We don't want to look like gangsters." He started walking toward the door.

"I've got a bad feeling about this."

"Just look like you know where you're going. The elevators are straight through the door. We're going to the fiftieth floor. Don't look at security. If they stop us, we'll say we're meeting my uncle."

Julian slowed as a middle-aged woman in a gray suit approached the entrance from the opposite direction. She pulled open the heavy, gold door and walked briskly past the security guard. Julian and Danny fell in behind her. Once inside the elevator, Julian waited until the woman pushed button number 37, then pushed 50.

"Back to work?" the woman said with a motherly smile.

"Just meeting my uncle," Julian said.

The elevator whizzed up to the twenty-fifth floor. Then, they all stared mindlessly as the number for each floor lit up, one by one: 34, 35, 36. "Boy!" Danny said, when the woman finally stepped off at the thirty-seventh floor, "I was about to pee in my pants."

"No. It was perfect. The guard probably thought she was our mother."

The elevator started up again. "I'm having a panic attack," Danny said. "When the door opens, what are we going to do? There might still be people around."

"Even my uncle leaves early on Fridays. The bathroom's right by the elevator. Pretend you know where you're going. That's the key."

When the doors opened, Julian saw with relief that the sumptuous reception area was deserted. They walked immediately to the bathroom without seeing a soul and locked themselves in the handicapped stall. A few minutes later, a man came in, used the urinal and stood at the sink for a long time. Through the crack in the bathroom stall, Julian could see him combing his hair, practicing his smile and spraying something in his mouth. After he'd gone, Julian cautiously poked his head out the door of the bathroom.

"There's only a few lights on, but I don't see the cleaning crew yet. I guess we just have to wait."

Danny grabbed his head in despair. "Julian! I can't wait in this bathroom for another hour. I feel like I'm in San Quentin already."

"We've got no choice. You're the one who told me about the motion detectors at your mom's work. We've got to wait for the janitors. With you here, we can actually talk to them."

"We don't want to talk to them! What are we going to say? 'Don't mind us. We're just trying to break into the computer system!'"

Julian frowned. "Relax. Repeat after me: 'My friend left his homework assignment on his uncle's computer. We just need to copy it.'"

Danny mumbled something in Spanish, but since the only word Julian recognized was "*estúpido*," he didn't think it was a translation.

"We'll give it five more minutes," Julian said.

But five minutes passed, and passed again, and he was beginning to wonder if they should forget the whole plan when he heard a low hum. He cracked open the bathroom door. There they were: Victor and Irene, vacuuming the office just up the hall.

"It's them!" He took a deep breath. "Let's go."

As the two boys walked by, Victor and Irene looked up from their work.

"*Hola!*" Julian said with what he hoped was an innocent smile.

Victor turned off the vacuum and said something to Irene in Spanish.

"Tell them I'm just going to use my uncle's computer again for a few minutes," Julian said to Danny.

Danny put on his most charming smile and started speaking rapidly in Spanish. The few words Julian could pick out gave him no clue what they were saying.

Finally, Danny waved good-bye and they started walking down the hallway.

"What were you saying?" Julian asked.

"Nothing much. They remember you from last time you were here."

"That's all? You guys were talking for five minutes!"

"I don't know. Just where they're from, their kids, stuff like that."

A corridor of empty cubicles appeared on their left and Julian hesitated a moment before following it. At the end of the dark hallway was Sibley's office, with his name on a gold plaque by the door. Julian turned on the lights and sat down in front of the computer. The screen was dark.

"It's off," he said.

"Try touching the space bar. Maybe it's just sleeping."

The screen stayed dark.

"How do we turn this thing on?" Julian said, annoyed.

Danny looked at him like he was a bug. "Get out of the chair." They traded places and Danny reached down and pushed several buttons. "It's a good thing I came along. I can't believe you thought you could do this without me!"

The computer started humming and, a minute later, a blue screen came up with the words "ID" followed by "PASSWORD."

Julian watched over Danny's shoulder. "That wasn't there last time," he said. He felt a little wave of panic come over him. "What do we do now?"

"How about you give me the ID and password and I'll type them in."

"Very funny."

"Well, ID's usually your first initial and last name. At least in my mom's office." He typed in SCARTER. "Now for the ten-million-dollar question."

"How many guesses do you think we get?"

"Three? Ten? I think if you try too many times, they get suspicious."

"Who does?"

"I don't know," Danny said in annoyance. "Whoever's keeping track."

"And then what? You can't guess anymore?"

"Maybe. Or else the walls start closing in and daggers start shooting out from all directions."

"Ha–ha." Julian sighed. "If you were Sibley, what would your password be?"

"Beats me."

"How about 'Preston'?"

Danny cocked his head to the side. "That's worth a try. What do you think?" His fingers were poised over the keyboard.

"Go for it."

Danny typed PRESTON. The screen blinked and then a message appeared: YOUR ID/PASSWORD IS NOT VALID. PLEASE TRY AGAIN.

Julian felt a creeping shadow of fear. "OK, that wasn't it."

Danny swiveled the chair around and looked out at the lights of the Bay Bridge. "Nice view."

"Come on, Danny. Concentrate."

"How about 'Death to Redwoods'?"

"Danny! Come on!"

He turned the chair back around. "Julian, I don't know! How about 'IPX CEO'?"

"Why not? Try it."

Danny typed and the computer blinked out the same message.

"It does say 'try again,'" Julian said hopefully.

Danny looked up at him. "I don't think we should try more than three times. Something really could happen."

"OK. One more time." He looked around the room for inspiration. "It's like Rumpelstiltskin."

"We should check his drawers. My mom's always yelling at people for leaving their password taped to their monitors."

Julian tried to open the three side drawers, but they were all locked. The center drawer, however, slid open to reveal three pencils, a pen, and a yellow legal pad. On the pad, a list of phrases was written in Sibley's angular handwriting:

Strategize for success
Understand the market
Communicate power
Compete for the prize
Educate your adversary
Expand your portfolio
Demand allegiance

"So much for that idea," Danny said. "Now what?"

"Maybe it's one of these words."

"But which one?" Danny bent down to stare at the legal pad more closely.

It was their last chance. Julian stared at the strange phrases. What were they? Some kind of business tips, he figured.

"Let's just pick one," Danny said. "I want to get out of here."

"No, wait." Julian tried to concentrate. It was stupid to assume these phrases contained the password. It could be anything—

the name of Sibley's street or his first pet or just some random combination of numbers. He placed the list back inside the drawer and was gliding it shut when he reached out and grabbed the pad again.

"Danny, I just realized something. Read it," he said, thrusting the pad in front of Danny's face.

"'Strategize for success, Understand—'"

"No. The other way."

"What other way?"

"Read the letters. The first letters of each line. From top to bottom. Look. S-U-C-C—"

"Succeed!" Danny said.

They looked at each other.

"The perfect password for Mr. CEO," Danny said in a villainous voice. "Do we try it?"

Julian let out a deep sigh. "Try it."

"Here it goes." Danny put his hands on the keyboard. "Capitals or small letters?"

"Let's try capitals."

Danny typed SUCCEED into the password box. The screen blinked and dozens of icons appeared.

"It worked!" Danny cried. "It's a miracle! You're a genius!"

Julian felt his confidence return. "It's a sign. A sign that it'll all work out." They were doing the right thing. The plan was fool-proof.

The noise of the vacuum cleaner, which had disappeared

without them noticing, suddenly came closer. Danny clicked on the e-mail icon and the screen blinked.

"What are we looking for?" he said.

"Anything about publicity or press releases. I know I saw something like that before. We need the e-mail list."

Danny scrolled down screen after screen. There were dozens of e-mails just from the last few days.

"Look around the time that last article came out," Julian said. "The one Robin sent us."

Danny scrolled down and down.

"Look! There!" Julian pointed to the screen. The subject line read "Press Release re IPX Profit Margins."

Danny clicked and a list of e-mail addresses filled the screen.

Julian bent down to examine them. "This is what we need. This is all the reporters. See, the LA *Times*. That one—sfchron.com— that's the same as Popo. It must be somebody at the *Chronicle*. We'll send our press release to everyone on the list. And it'll look like it came from Sibley."

"How about the IPX addresses?" Danny asked. "See—there are three or four of them."

"Delete them all," Julian said. "The longer we can keep this going without anybody at IPX knowing about it, the better."

Danny hit a few buttons. In the subject line, he typed, "FOR IMMEDIATE RELEASE: IPX TO SAVE REDWOODS."

"OK, good," Julian said. "Now, where's the draft?"

Danny pulled the folded white paper from his back pocket and began to retype it into the e-mail. Julian watched the words materialize on the screen. They'd gone over it together so many times he'd almost memorized it.

Several acres of old-growth redwood in Mendocino County known as Big Tree Grove will be protected forever, the San Francisco firm of IPX Investment Corporation announced today.

Prior to being bought by IPX, the 120-acre property was previously owned by the Greeley family. Ed Greeley, who passed away several years ago, never logged in Big Tree Grove and used sustainable timber harvesting on the remainder of the property. IPX's new policies will continue these practices.

"A number of neighbors and environmental groups were opposed to the timber harvest," said Sibley Carter, the CEO of IPX. "When we considered their arguments, we realized they were winners. Even though we got a timber harvest plan approved, we're not going to log. We want to do the right thing. These redwoods are very old and it would be a crime to cut them down."

Under the new IPX policy, the former Greeley property will continue to provide important habitat for deer, bear, and fishers.

The new policy is effective immediately.

When Danny had typed out the last word, they both read it over carefully. It was good, Julian thought. Better than good. Professional.

"It's as good as that other press release," Danny said.

Julian nodded. "You think it'll work? It sounds official enough?"

"I think it's pretty close." Danny frowned. "Maybe not a hundred percent perfect. What do you think?"

"I'm not sure about fishers. Maybe they live in the river. Maybe we should say 'other wildlife.'"

"Yeah. That's good." Danny typed in the new language. "Anything else?"

Julian looked down at the traffic crawling along the streets, the lights shining in the purplish sky. "We better just send it now. We might make it worse without realizing it. It's like those multiple-choice tests. Sometimes your first answer is the right answer."

"It's perfect," Danny agreed. "We shouldn't change it under stress."

"Right."

"Send it now?"

Don't think, Julian said to himself. "Yes. Send it."

"No regrets?" Danny asked, finger poised over the mouse.

"It's a good plan. Once this comes out, they'll look bad if they change their policy again."

"What's the worst that can happen?" Danny said.

"Exactly."

"Now?"

"Go!"

Danny pressed Send. "All right," he said. "I'm outta here."

"Shut it down."

Danny pressed a few more buttons. The screen flashed and then died out.

On their way out, Danny stopped and said something earnestly to Victor and Irene. They laughed and Irene made a quick remark that made Danny open his eyes wide and grin.

When the boys were inside the elevator, Julian said, "What did you say? To Victor and Irene?"

"Nothing much."

"You always say that!"

Danny shrugged. "Learn Spanish. You'll be a better spy."

The lobby door opened. The security guard was glued to his chair, reading a newspaper.

"OK. Don't run, but be quick," Julian whispered.

They walked heel-to-toe, gliding by as quickly as they could. When they reached the glass doors, the fat guard looked up. "Hey! You guys need to sign out!"

They rushed through the door and down the subway stairs. With their bus passes, they slipped easily through the turnstile. The rush-hour jam was over and the station smelled like sweat and grime and exhaust. The lights were flashing for an outward-bound train, and the boys raced down the escalator and managed to jump inside just before the doors closed behind them.

As the train rattled away from the station, Julian looked over at Danny, sweating and still breathing hard, and his spirits started to rise like a helium balloon. They had invented the perfect plan to save Big Tree Grove, and it had gone off without a hitch.

19
STUMPED

Julian woke up early the next morning to beat Popo to the *Chronicle*. He checked the main news section and the Bay Area section, but there was nothing about IPX or Big Tree Grove. Sunday's paper had nothing either.

He called Danny at home.

"Do you think the story will run tomorrow?" he asked.

"Stop worrying about it," said Danny. "I, personally, am trying to block the entire incident from my mind. That way, I won't fail the lie-detector test."

"Maybe somehow the e-mail was never sent."

"Could be. Maybe there was some other level of security we didn't get by. Or maybe it just didn't make the news."

"I'll check again tomorrow." Julian couldn't hide his disappointment.

"Hey, look on the bright side! At least we're not in jail."

But Monday, there was nothing either, and by Tuesday, Julian had given up. When he got to the breakfast table, Popo was already in her regular spot, sipping her coffee and flipping through the paper. She'd set a place for him with a glass of orange juice and his favorite kind of bagel, sesame with cream cheese. Julian sat down sleepily.

"All's quiet in the world," she said, turning a page. "Oh, this is interesting. A story about IPX."

Julian dropped his bagel so fast it skidded off the plate and onto the floor. Popo gave him a look, and he bent down and tossed it back onto his plate, while she lay the newspaper flat for him to read.

On page A8, near the bottom of the page, the headline read IPX TO HACKERS: NO CHANGE IN LOGGING POLICIES. Julian felt his heart start to sink.

Last Friday evening, unidentified hackers issued a fake press release purporting to signal a change in logging policies for the San Francisco–based IPX Investment Corp. Controversy over IPX's plan to clear-cut a rare stand of old-growth redwood in Mendocino County seemed to be over when formal appeals by neighbors and environmental groups failed. Apparently, however, the environmental community has not lost interest. The fake press release, purportedly issuing from IPX headquarters, declared that IPX would preserve the stand of redwood permanently.

Skeptical reporters immediately contacted IPX spokeswoman Myrna Gonzalez, who stated that the document was a hoax. "Our proposed timber plan has been reviewed by all relevant state and local agencies," she said in an interview yesterday morning. "It has their stamp of approval. It helps meet the enormous demand for valuable timber and complies with all applicable environmental laws."

No suspects in the hoax have yet been identified, although Gonzalez suggested that radical ecoterrorism groups could be responsible.

———————

Julian felt his insides turn hollow. He had failed. He had thought up the most brilliant scheme possible to convince IPX not to log Big Tree, and they hadn't even come close. Nobody had been fooled for a minute.

Big Tree Grove was doomed. His dream of returning in triumph was shattered.

When Julian told Danny the terrible news, he wasn't even that upset, just relieved that IPX had placed the blame on eco-terrorists.

Julian, on the other hand, felt like he was under a dark cloud. Why couldn't something turn out right for a change? Some invisible mechanism seemed to keep him rooted in his own life, while Huckleberry Ranch receded farther and farther into the distance.

At journalism camp, Danny had moved on from press releases to restaurant reviews. Julian lay sprawled on Danny's bed while Danny considered the most diplomatic way to critique a new Vietnamese café Popo had taken them to.

"How's this?" Danny finished typing and read with a flourish, "'Fried tofu on French bread, while not for everyone, has an East-meets-West appeal perfect for San Francisco.'"

"How about 'Fried tofu on French bread, while not as horrible as it sounds, is pretty horrible,'" Julian suggested.

The computer beeped and Danny clicked on his e-mail. "Robin Hood's back!"

Julian sat up to see the screen:

July 21

Dear Julian and Danny,

I told my mom Julian was staying with his grandmother now. Since seeing Daphne she's been calling Julian "that poor boy." This is a GOOD sign. Snowball started out as "that poor kitten." Dad still hasn't mentioned Julian. No new news about Big Tree here but did you see that article about the hackers?????? Weird. My brothers showed it to me (they're sleeping in the loft, so if you don't hear from me it's because I can't get any PRIVACY).

The only good news is, that horrible exchange student FINALLY left. She was getting on EVERYONE's nerves!

We were all THRILLED to say goodbye to her and her HAIR DRYER!!!!

Robin

"Even Robin doesn't suspect us," Danny said with a sigh of relief.

"We should tell her it was us," Julian said. "At least *somebody* would appreciate all our hard work."

"Of course! What we need's a written confession!" Danny turned away from the screen and glared at Julian. "You know, the police can confiscate your computer and find out everything you ever wrote. Even if you erase it." He leaned back in his chair. "At least Robin hasn't given up hope."

"Danny, Operation Redwood is not going to happen."

"Aww, don't be such a pessimist. Operation Break-In was a long shot! It would have been a miracle if it worked!" Danny started typing:

July 21

Dear Robin Hood,

We saw the article! I must say, those hackers were brilliant! However, **THE FORCES OF DARKNESS** are always on the alert . . .

What do you have against hair dryers? I have two packed for my visit already!!!!

Speaking of which, keep working on your mom!

You've got to get us up there or Julian will go into a deep depression! And you'll break our hearts! Speaking of hearts, does your dad have a heart of steel? I thought it was only Mr. CEO! Get us up there and together we'll work to vanquish . . . **THE FORCES OF DARKNESS!**

Sincerely,

Your future operative, D. Lopez

P.S. Ask your brothers how to get up in the tree!

Julian glanced at the e-mail and said, "Robin's not going to change her father's mind. You should have seen his face. He basically called me a liar. He called me *that boy*. He didn't even say good-bye."

"That doesn't sound too good," Danny agreed. "What if you did apologize? I mean, not that you did anything wrong, but maybe it would soften him up."

"What am I going to say? 'Sorry I lied to you. Please let me and my friend come back because we have this plan to do more things behind your back. That you definitely wouldn't approve of. If you knew about them. Which you don't.'"

"Jeez! You don't have to say it like that! Don't you remember when we had to write 'the persuasive essay'? Mr. Orlovsky? 'Poot your best foot forward'?"

"Forget it, Danny. Finish your review."

"Julian! Two weeks ago you were a *prisoner*. You were at

Quantum. You didn't even have a *phone*. Now you're with Popo, free as a bird." Danny gave Julian a searching look. "Operation Redwood is going to happen. Have a little faith!"

The fog never seemed to lift now. The whole city was socked in, but out near the ocean, it was especially damp and windy. It was like living inside a giant cloud. In the mornings, Popo would tighten her bathrobe and turn up the heat. "I told your mom not to move out here," she grumbled over breakfast. "I grew up in this neighborhood. It's cold all summer long."

"I like it by the ocean," Julian said. "Especially with global warming. I think we're better off here."

"Maybe you're right." She looked at him fondly. "You know, I only have another week of vacation left," she said, pouring them both another cup of tea. "Whatever happened to that plan you were telling me about? To go back to Huckleberry Ranch?"

"Nothing," Julian said. "Robin's dad was pretty angry. With the sheriff coming and everything. It's not going to happen."

She gave him a searching look, then said, "I'm afraid you'll get bored just hanging around with me all day. Though I'm enjoying it so much, I'm starting to think I should retire early!"

"Mom said you'll never retire," Julian said. "She said you'll work 'til you drop."

Popo set her cup carefully in the saucer. "All my life, I've worked hard. There weren't so many women journalists when I was starting out. Or Chinese reporters. You *had* to work hard."

Her eyes looked sad. "I made mistakes, maybe. When Cari was little . . ." She paused. "I can see things now I couldn't see back then."

Julian pulled out the comics section from the newspaper.

"You know, your mom just sent me an e-mail. She'll be back before school starts. She can't wait to see you."

He looked over at her doubtfully.

"When you were a baby," Popo said, "your mother carried you everywhere in a beautiful flowered sling. She sang to you all the time." She stared into her cup. "It hasn't been easy for her. Losing her father, and then Will. And she had you before she was really grown up herself." Popo seemed absorbed in her tea leaves, then looked up and scrutinized Julian through her little round glasses. "She needed some time on her own. But you know she loves you more than anything. And she's not the only one."

Then she laughed and started to clear the dishes. "What a sentimental old lady I'm becoming!" she said. "Soon I'll be crying at the commercials on TV!"

20

GOOD NEWS

Dear Julian and Danny,

I have the most AMAZING news! My parents said you guys can come up to Huckleberry Ranch when Ariel's here! !!

I can't BELIEVE it!! HONESTLY, I thought my dad would never EVER let you come. I was sitting at dinner and OUT OF THE BLUE he brought it up HIMSELF! I never even asked him (well, I did ask my mom like 100 times so maybe she worked on him).

So, can you come????? It would be the first two weeks of August (that's ONE WEEK FROM TODAY!). And we can start work on You Know What!! My dad's going to call Julian's grandmother but let me know ASAP!

Robin

July 24

Dear Robin Hood,

I'm calling Julian now . . .

I just told him the news and I'm pleased to report he's totally psyched!

Glad to hear Pop has seen the light!

D

July 25

Dear Robin,

Danny and I can't wait to go up there! My grandmother already said it would be OK. She's got to go back to work anyway (she's a reporter for the San Francisco Chronicle). We're still working on Danny's parents. They don't want Danny to live with strangers. Plus, they're still a little upset about the whole running away/Daphne/kidnapping thing. His mom wants to send him to stay with his cousins in Fresno. Here's Danny:

Fresno is about the most boring place on earth. My cousins spend all their time chasing me around the pool. I don't even get to relax for a single minute. I am BEGGING my parents to let me come!!!

—D

July 25

Robin,

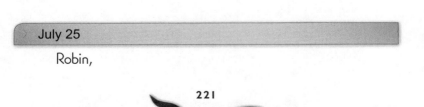

Danny's mom has been on the phone with your dad for about an hour. Any news on getting into the tree house??

Julian

July 26

Dear Julian & Danny,

My dad says you're coming!!!!!!!!!! HOORAY!!!!!!!!!!!!!

Robin

July 26

Robin,

Now that we're coming, we want to make sure we can get up in that tree house!! What's the news from your brothers? Are you up yet?

Operation Redwood Headquarters

July 27

Operative Robin,

May the fleas of a thousand camels infest your armpits if you do not respond to this e-mail ASAP.

Operation Redwood Headquarters

July 28

Operative Robin,

Operation Redwood Headquarters will be forced to terminate you if you do not report for duty immediately.

GOOD NEWS

Because we cannot permit our agents to continue to operate when their loyalty and commitment are in question, this termination will be LETHAL. Please provide the name of your next of kin so that we may notify them in a timely fashion.

O.R.H.

Dear Fellow Operatives,

Please do not TERMINATE me as I have been working undercover. John and Dave absolutely REFUSE to take me up to the tree house until I'm ACTUALLY 12, which is TOMORROW!! They're coming up the stairs so—gotta go.

R

Robin Hood,

Forget about your stupid brothers. I already figured out how to get into the tree. Do the words "triple auto-locking carabiners" mean anything to you?? How about slingshot? Throwline? Children's BUTT-strap harness????

Danny the Tree Climbing Expert

Dear Danny,
SLINGSHOT????
Robin

Robin Hood the Ignorant,

You need it to get the rope into the tree. Plus, we could use it to hunt wild game. We're not all vegetarians you know. Here's Julian:

Danny did an article for journalism camp on tree climbing. You wouldn't believe all the stuff that's on the internet. Now he thinks he knows everything. As you can probably tell, he's got a big head. He's hitting me now so here he is:

My head is just fine. Julian's the one who wanted to look for the gear at Goodwill. I was like, JUST WHAT WE WANT—A WELL-USED ROPE! After all, we're only using it to dangle from a branch 30 feet off the ground!!! Julian's CHEAP. That's something you should know about him. Even when your life is at stake, he'll be trying to pinch pennies!

—Danny

Danny says I'm cheap but he always wants me to pay for everything!

—J

Julian's cheap but he has a big bank account (or maybe he has a big bank account BECAUSE he's so cheap!). Sadly, my family has not fully embraced multiculturalism, especially the Chinese custom of giving children money on New Year's. Can you tell we're bored and have nothing better to do than write this stupid e-mail?????? OK. We're signing off before we bore you to death.

Signing off,

The S.F. Special Forces

P.S. Happy Birthday!

Dear S.F. Special Forces:

I have GOOD NEWS!!!!

The Initiation is Complete! It was kind of dumb but I did learn how to get up, which is a good thing because my brothers are leaving TODAY. The only hard part is getting the first person up to send the pulley seat down, but they showed me exactly how to do everything and where they keep all the gear! So WE'RE UP!!

Can't wait to see you! Ariel's SUPER excited too!

Operative Robin

Operative Robin,

Pulley seat! This is going to be awesome! As a wise sage once said: "Our pathetic little lives will not be in vain any longer."

SFSF

P.S. Make Danny show you his song and dance number to "Lean on Me." He's doing it for his church talent show!

July 30

Dear SFSF,

I can't believe you'll be here TOMORROW! My brothers just left, but Ariel's coming this afternoon. Bring anything you think might be useful. And, obviously, this is all TOP SECRET!!

Robin

July 30

Dear Robin,

I packed everything I could think of: compass, binoculars, lighter, PowerBars. My grandmother gave me an emergency kit with a space blanket and Band-Aids and stuff. Unfortunately, I can't find my pocketknife. Write back by tomorrow a.m. if you want us to bring anything else.

Julian

July 31

Dear Operatives:

I am so excited I can't STAND it!!! Ariel and I already set up your tent! You've probably left already and so I'm writing to nobody. If you've left, then I'm even MORE excited! OPERATION REDWOOD IS ABOUT TO BEGIN!!

Robin

21

THE REDWOOD CLIMBER

After the long, rattling ride on the dirt road, Robin's house came into view, just as Julian remembered it. The chickens were pecking at the dirt in front of the lattice where he and Robin had hidden. The window boxes were blooming with new flowers and Molly was pushing Jo-Jo on the tire swing.

By the time the engine stopped, Jo-Jo was running to the car shouting, "Julian! Julian!" and Robin had appeared on the front steps with another girl who Julian figured must be Ariel. Her thin legs stuck out from a pair of cut-off overalls. She had a dreamy, crooked smile. White-blond bangs nearly covered her brown eyes, and a long braid hung down her back.

The girl squinted at the two boys as they climbed out of the backseat. "You must be Julian," she said as Jo-Jo climbed into his arms.

"And you're Danny, right?" the girl said, pointing.

Danny bowed. "At your service. You must be R.E.L." he said. "And *you*, madam, must be Robin Hood."

Robin linked her arm through her friend's. "It's AIR-ee-ul, not R.E.L." She looked Danny over thoughtfully. "You know what? You're exactly what I thought you'd be like."

"I'm famous!" Danny cried. "My reputation precedes me!"

Nancy came out of the house, smiling like it was the best day of her life. She hugged Julian, holding him tight until Jo-Jo climbed out of his arms and into hers.

Popo, who had been looking about with a reserved air, stepped forward. "I want to thank you so much for taking the boys. I know Julian's been looking forward to this so much. You made quite an impression on him."

"And he made quite an impression on us," Nancy said warmly. "You must be very proud of your grandson."

Out of the corner of his eye, Julian saw Bob ambling over from the work shed, his expression friendly and open; there was no trace of the angry mask he'd worn when Julian had last seen him. "I've been looking forward to meeting Julian's loyal friend," Bob said, shaking Danny's hand. Then he put an arm around Julian's shoulder and said, "Welcome back. We're glad to have you."

Julian looked down and watched the patterns of dappled light flutter across the dry grass. He was himself again, not *that boy*. Not a stranger.

When Popo's blue Toyota had rattled down the road and out of sight, Danny turned to Julian with a huge grin. "We're here! You happy now?"

In reply, Julian gave him a sunny smile.

"Mom," Robin said, "can we show Julian and Danny the tent? We got it all set up and they can put their stuff there."

"I don't see why not. You two have earned the afternoon off."

The boys grabbed their bags and Robin and Ariel led them around to the back, where a bright yellow tent with a gray rain tarp had been set up under the oak trees. Molly and Jo-Jo traipsed behind them.

Glancing back, Robin shouted, "Molly, you're supposed to be watching Jo-Jo. Ariel and I watched him all morning." She turned to Jo-Jo and said sweetly, "Don't you want Molly to push you on the tire swing?"

Jo-Jo nodded.

Molly glared at her sister indignantly. She bent down next to Jo-Jo and said, with equal sweetness, "Don't you want to go with Julian? Don't you want to go in his tent?"

"I wanna go with Julian. I wanna see the tent!" Jo-Jo cried.

Molly looked disdainfully at Robin.

"You think you're so smart!" Robin said. Turning to Julian, she whispered, "We'll show Danny Big Tree instead. We can plan there." She unzipped the tent flap and threw the boys' bags inside. Then they all set off down the trail to Big Tree.

"You are so mean, Robin Elder!" Molly cried, standing by the tent with Jo-Jo's hand in hers. "You're the meanest person on earth!"

"Is she mean?" Julian could hear Jo-Jo saying. "Is she mean to you? Is she not your friend?"

Julian felt bad leaving them behind. But maybe Robin was right. They couldn't take the chance that Molly would report everything back to her parents.

Mercifully, Robin showed no inclination to race that day, and Ariel dawdled along, stopping every few minutes to pick up a pinecone off the forest floor, examine a banana slug, or just watch the river where it ran along the trail.

"I love being back here," she said, sniffing the forest air. "Oh, look at that cute little chipmunk!"

"Where?" said Danny.

"Over there. On that log." Julian looked, but all he saw was a log. "They don't have any chipmunks in Phoenix. It's all roads and houses and cats and ugly little dogs."

At the river, the girls crossed first. Julian watched Danny hesitate just a moment before walking nonchalantly across the tree trunk bridge.

"Look," Ariel said. "There's that big burned-out tree we used to play in. Remember, Robin? We'd pretend it was our house and your mom would make us a picnic and we'd bring the bunnies and feed them little carrots?"

"And then one of them ran away and we spent the whole day looking for it?"

"We had so much fun." Ariel sighed. "I'd give anything to move back here."

"Look! See those redwood saplings?" Robin pointed to a group of small trees, the tops bent down and broken. "That's a bear marking its territory."

"Great! That means we're in its territory!" Danny said.

"Lions and tigers and bears, oh my!" The girls linked arms and started skipping along the path.

The broken saplings were higher than their heads. Danny picked up a stout stick and they hurried to catch up to the girls. There was safety in numbers.

Julian was just glad to be back on the path to Big Tree again, bears or no bears. He walked confidently up the switchbacks that had seemed so steep when he'd first raced Robin. At the spring, the girls put their heads under the faucet and drank the sweet water.

Danny looked on dubiously. "Do you know where that water comes from? How do you know it's not toxic?"

"It's a mountain spring," Julian said. "In a bottle, it'd cost you two bucks."

"Doesn't it have dirt in it? And who knows what else. Squirrel pee?"

"Suit yourself." Robin wiped her wet chin with the back of her hand. "This is what you're drinking all week."

Danny took a long drink, then grabbed his throat and keeled over. Robin raised her eyebrows, and they all started off down the trail, leaving Danny sprawled along the path.

A moment later, they heard his footsteps racing after them.

"Hey! I could have been dead back there!"

"Hah!" Robin said.

"It's possible! An allergic reaction to some rare mineral." Danny shook his head. "This is one tough crowd!"

After about fifteen minutes, they crossed the river again and hiked down the trail to the heart of Big Tree Grove. They were all quiet for a moment. The giant redwoods stood silent. The afternoon sun barely filtered through to the forest floor.

"I can't believe anybody would cut down these trees," Ariel said at last. "This *is* the best forest in the world. It's what every forest would be if it could."

"Wow! This place is awesome!" Danny walked up to one of the largest trees. "All four of us together couldn't reach around this tree! It's like Muir Woods without the little fences."

"That's what I thought!" Julian said.

Danny grinned. "You're glad we're here, huh?"

Of course he was glad, Julian thought. "Aren't you?"

"Come on! Let's show Danny and Ariel the tree house!" Robin said impatiently.

They tramped through the forest, across the fallen tree, and then stopped, peering at the tree house. "So, tell me how we're going to get up there again?" Danny asked skeptically.

"I've got everything in the shed," Robin said. "Ropes, carabiners, a halter. My brothers got it all organized. Then once *I'm* up, I set up the pulley seat and we're ready to go. Tomorrow afternoon, if we can get away from Molly, we'll carry everything out here."

"So, what's the plan? What else do we need for Operation Redwood?" Danny asked.

"Mainly food, I think. We've got to have supplies. Julian said he was bringing PowerBars. Did you guys bring anything?"

"I brought dried apricots," Ariel said.

"Candy bars!" Danny shouted.

"That's good. We've got boxes of cereal in the pantry. And apples in the basement. We could live for a long time on that."

Ariel was wandering all around, examining every tree and plant. "Look at all these ferns. There's not a single fern in Phoenix. I can bike from my mom's house to my dad's house and there's not one single pretty thing to look at."

"Well, that's why we're here. To try to save this place, right?" said Robin. "OK, Operatives! Here's the plan of action. The next task is to get the equipment out here tomorrow. Once we're up, we'll start collecting food and other supplies. Operation Redwood has officially begun."

But they had no time to go to Big Tree the next afternoon, or the next. True to their word, Bob and Nancy had a long to-do list for the children to work on. And even the regular chores—feeding the goats and chickens, weeding the gardens, and harvesting the fruits and vegetables for meals—took a big chunk of each day.

Julian found his box where he'd left it on the workshop shelf.

He was pleased by his tomato plants, which were as tall as his waist and covered with small green tomatoes. Bunny the goat was twice as big as she had been before, a feisty kid who wouldn't sit on Julian's lap anymore. Julian was put in charge of training Danny to milk Aphrodite. Danny, however, refused to cooperate. "I am *not* touching those things," he said, inspecting the goat's underside. "Anything else, but no goats." Julian eventually gave up and did the milking himself.

But Danny was happy to help with repairs and building projects. Bob had never gotten around to completing the deer fence he and Julian had begun in June. With the three of them working, it was done in two days. As Danny put the finishing touches on the gate latch, he actually began to whistle. It was almost like he was putting on a show.

The children had almost given up hope of ever returning to the tree house when Nancy announced after lunch on Tuesday, "I'm taking Molly and Jo-Jo into town to buy new shoes and pick up some groceries. If you all would just clear up the dishes, you can have the rest of the afternoon off. We've been working you pretty hard."

The Operatives exchanged quick glances and sprang into action. Robin jumped up and offered to braid Molly's hair. Danny cleared the table, and Julian found Jo-Jo's striped shirt on the bathroom floor and coaxed him into it.

Nancy watched her daughters affectionately. "You see, Molly, it's not true that Robin is *always* mean to you."

Molly, who was studying her hair in the mirror, said nothing.

"She only notices when I'm mean," Robin complained. "The ninety-nine percent of the time I'm nice, she's oblivious."

"See, even you admit you're mean," Molly said.

"One percent of the time! Tops!" Robin twisted the last hair tie around Molly's braid. "You look gorgeous. Note: a compliment."

When the truck reached the end of the long driveway and pulled out of sight, Robin led the operatives to the shed. Five minutes later, loaded down with supplies, the four operatives were on their way to Big Tree Grove.

The tree house looked a lot higher than Julian had remembered.

"You're going to get all the way up by yourself?" Danny asked dubiously.

"Well, the only really tricky part is getting the rope up over that beam, the one sticking out." Robin grabbed a length of thin, black cord out of their equipment bag and tied it to a stick. She threw the stick high into the air, where it made a graceful arc, then banged into the trunk several feet below the beam.

"Let me try," Danny said.

"No, give me another chance." Robin picked the stick off the ground and untangled the cord. "My brothers did it easy." But this time, the stick was even farther off the mark. Julian tried, and Danny tried twice, coming within a few feet of the beam on the second try. Ariel's attempt went several feet wide of the tree.

Robin threw the stick up two more times, and then they all sat down, discouraged. "Anyone got any other ideas?" she asked.

"Let's just kidnap Preston instead and hold him for ransom. 'You leave these trees alone,'" Danny said in his Mafia voice, "'or your boy's wearing concrete shoes.'"

Julian glared at him and Robin scowled. "We can't throw away the whole plan because of one little obstacle. We almost got it."

"Well," said Danny, "there are other ways to get a rope over a tree."

"Like what?" Robin asked.

"Slingshot. Bow and arrow." Danny was enjoying displaying the fruits of his tree–climbing obsession. "Crossbow—now, that would be the ultimate. Or a throw weight."

"What's a throw weight?" Robin asked.

"It's like a beanbag," Julian said.

"I've got a plain old beanbag. Only it's back at the house."

Danny tried the stick again, and again it fell several feet below the beam. "Well, it looks like we're never going to get the rope up this way. Maybe somebody should go get the beanbag."

Robin pointed her chin at Ariel. "She's the fastest."

Danny almost choked. "You've got to be kidding me! There's no way Ariel's faster than me. Or Julian."

Robin shrugged. "How much do you want to bet?"

"A candy bar to the winner!" Danny said jubilantly.

Ariel leaned against the tree to stretch her legs. "Where is the beanbag exactly?"

"It's in the dresser in my bedroom. Inside the top right-hand drawer."

"All right. Let's go," said Ariel and she sprang away from the tree and up the slope, with Danny close behind. Julian watched in astonishment. Danny loped along with his usual athletic grace, but Ariel looked like she was running in fast forward. They disappeared over the top of the ridge, and he could hear Danny calling out, "I'm going to get you! There's no way you're getting my Snickers!"

Robin sat with her back against the tree. "She's going to win. She's the fastest girl on earth."

Julian laughed. "It'll be good for Danny. Keep him humble." He paused. Here, in the warm afternoon light, the forest was so silent—silent a thousand years ago, silent a hundred years ago, silent a month ago when he was sitting alone in his uncle's house.

"Can you believe we're all here?" Robin said at last. "I thought it would never happen."

"How'd you get your parents to let us come? You know, when I saw the sheriff car, I thought it was all over. I thought your dad would never want to see me again. Ever."

"Yeah, me too. I don't really know what changed his mind. Maybe it was your aunt! She didn't win any popularity contests here! I think my dad felt sorry for you. It's not your fault Sibley Carter's your uncle."

"So you told your dad you sent him that e-mail?"

"I had to. I mean, once they knew you were Sibley Carter's nephew. I had to explain that!"

"And you told them I was in his office? And how I opened Sibley's e-mail?"

"I just told him you found the e-mail by accident. Dad didn't really ask for details."

Julian felt himself breathe a little easier. At least Bob wouldn't think he was some kind of sneak.

"You must've been glad to see your grandmother," Robin said. "When's your mom coming home, anyway?"

The sound of a woodpecker rang out like a distant jackhammer. "Later this month," Julian said. "I'm not sure exactly when. I haven't really talked to her."

"What do you mean? You haven't talked to her since you were here in *June*?"

Julian looked up, surprised at the outrage in her voice.

"There aren't any telephones in China?" she asked.

"Well, she sent me some postcards. She and my grandmother have talked a few times."

Robin just stared at him in bewilderment.

"She's busy," Julian said.

It was true, he couldn't imagine Nancy heading off to China for the summer and not calling home once. Or Danny's mom. But they were in a whole different category of mothers: normal mothers who gave you chores and made you do your schoolwork and sit down to dinner.

His mother was not like them. She was young and beautiful. A free spirit. In fact, she was always joking to her friends about how he was more responsible than she was.

"She'll be back soon," he said. "That's just the way she is."

Robin's dubious expression made Julian uncomfortable, and he decided to close the curtains on this conversation. There was something else he'd been waiting to tell Robin. "You know the article about the IPX hackers?"

"Yeah. What a weird story."

"Well, you know who the hackers were?"

Robin shook her head.

"It was us. Me and Danny."

"You're lying!" Robin said. "You and Danny couldn't do that!"

"No, we did. We waited until everybody was gone and Danny spoke Spanish to the cleaning crew so they wouldn't suspect anything and we wrote the fake press release and everything. It was the perfect plan. Too bad it didn't actually work."

The look he'd been waiting to see on her face finally appeared: awe. She was impressed. "I can't believe you guys did that!" she said. "I didn't think you had the guts."

"We have more guts than you think." Not exactly the best retort, Julian realized, after the words came out. "But don't tell Danny I told you. Because he really wants to keep it a secret. He's worried about his parents finding out."

He felt a thud on the side of his head and looked down to see a beanbag about as big as his fist, made out of a blue bandana. Danny and Ariel were laughing.

"You guys need to be on your guard," Danny yelled. "An entire army could sneak up on you and you wouldn't notice."

"Who gets the candy?" Robin said.

Danny kowtowed before Ariel. "What can I say? She's amazing. If I hadn't seen it, I wouldn't have believed it. She's like the Road Runner." He grabbed the beanbag and quickly tied it to the thin rope. "OK, eef I make eet dees time," he said in a Spanish accent, "I weel be a man again." He did an exaggerated windup. The beanbag sailed up and soared over the beam and down the other side. "Oh, yeah!" Danny cried, doing a touchdown dance.

Robin waited for Danny to regain his composure before handing out directions. They tied the black cord to the thick, white climbing rope and pulled until the rope was over the beam and its two ends were dangling in front of them. Robin pulled the harness up to her waist and stepped forward with a shorter piece of blue cord in her hand.

"First, you need to tie the climbing rope to the harness with a Blake's hitch. Like this, see? Then you tie a foot loop."

She labored at the knots. Julian and Danny tried to follow the movement of the ropes but she was too fast.

"John and Dave made me practice these two knots all week." She checked all the knots again. "OK, now you put one foot in the lower knot and that kind of scoots you up." As she said this, she rose about a foot into the air. "Now you pull up here," she said grabbing the higher knot, "and you just keep going."

She looked like a caterpillar, bending in the middle and then stretching out again. With each stretch she went higher and higher until her bare feet were dangling above their heads.

"We've got to learn how to do that," Danny said to Julian. "We could climb the TransAmerica Building."

"How's the weather up there?" Ariel shouted.

"It's nice. Nice and breezy!" Robin kept inching her way up while the others made encouraging comments. Finally, she was level with the platform. She stepped into the tree house and threw her arms in the air. "Ta-da!"

They gave Robin a round of applause and watched as she unhooked her halter from the rope and walked to the opposite end of the platform. In the distance, they heard the dull gong of the dinner bell.

"I'm not going to be able to set this up today," Robin called down. "But it's all ready to go."

"Are you serious?" Danny said. "We don't get to see the tree house?"

"Well, at least we got Robin up," Ariel said.

"Yeah! Good job, Robin! See ya later!" Danny turned and walked away jauntily.

"Don't worry! I can get down no problem. That's the fun part." Robin clipped herself back to the rope and placed her foot inside the loop again. Then, stepping off the platform, she pulled against the upper knot and whizzed down in little fits and starts. Julian watched her graceful legs and bare feet stretched out below her cutoffs, and for a fleeting moment he had the same sensation he'd had the first night at Huckleberry Ranch. Life was full of surprises. This girl, this tree-climbing, knot-tying girl, had been here all the time. He'd discovered her out of six billion people, and now they were friends.

22

INTO THE TREETOPS

The next morning, Bob put the boys to work extending an old trail going along the creek—clearing underbrush and building steps from old railroad ties. By the second day, they could anticipate some of Bob's orders, and they fell into an easy rhythm. When the lunch bell rang, Julian was surprised it was already noon. They walked back to the house, chatting amiably about Bob's next big project: converting his equipment from gasoline to biodiesel. Julian listened with half an ear, but Danny asked question after question until Bob, in exasperation, sent Julian to the loft to find an article explaining the process in detail.

Several stacks of neat papers were piled on top of the computer desk. Julian hesitated, then began leafing methodically through the papers. He finished one stack—bills, invoices, articles clipped from magazines and newspapers—and was halfway through the next when he saw a flash of familiar writing. At first,

Julian thought he'd found one of the exchange-student forms they'd faked, but he'd seen all the forms and there'd been nothing like this: a long letter, in Danny's best handwriting, addressed to "Mr. and Mrs. Elder."

Julian pulled the paper from the stack and stood, skimming the unfamiliar words.

Dear Mr. and Mrs. Elder,

I am writing to beg you to not be angry at Julian anymore. He wants to go back to your house more than anything. Sometimes it's hard to tell with Julian but trust me—I'm his best friend. If he did anything wrong, it was due to circumstances beyond his control or I put him up to it. It wasn't his fault his mom took off. His aunt and uncle treated him like dirt—which you probably already know if you met his aunt! It was Robin's and my idea for him to run away. We didn't know the sheriff would come. Now you're hitting him when he's already down. His mom's still not back and he doesn't have a dad and he's really nice and smart and he's never been in trouble ever (outside the sheriff). So I think you should give him another chance out of basic human decency.

Sincerely,
Danny Lopez
P.S. Julian doesn't know I'm writing this so please don't tell him.
P.P.S. You don't have to invite me up, either.

When he got to the end of the letter, Julian felt a little dizzy. Everything that had happened in the past few weeks he now saw in a new light—Robin's excited e-mail, Bob's friendly greeting, Danny's cheerful demeanor. And somehow, knowing that Bob and Nancy—and maybe even Robin—had read Danny's letter made him feel exposed, like he'd been walking around in his underwear.

Julian heard Danny bellowing his name from the deck. The last thing he wanted was to be caught snooping. Julian carefully stacked the papers back on top of Danny's letter and found the biodiesel article in the last pile on the desk.

He started down the spiral stairs, then stopped midway. What would he have done if he were in Danny's shoes? Probably nothing. But Danny had written the letter in his best handwriting and found the Elders' address and sent it off. And the letter *had* worked—it had changed Bob's mind. He was back at Huckleberry Ranch and he was Julian again, not *that boy*, and he owed it all to Danny. With a flush of shame, Julian remembered that day at Quantum, when he'd wanted to keep Huckleberry Ranch all to himself.

He stood on the step, his mind turning. He didn't know what to do with this new information he'd stumbled across. He certainly didn't want to discuss it with the Elders and he didn't know what to say to Danny, so Julian simply filed it away in his mind, like a rock in his rock collection that nobody would ever look at but him.

On Friday afternoon, the operatives were finally able to return to Big Tree Grove. Within a few minutes, Robin was up in the tree house. She hung the pulley seat from a metal hook screwed into a thick beam and lowered it jerkily to the forest floor. It was made of weather-beaten green canvas and attached to a complicated system of ropes and pulleys. When it bounded to a stop, Danny made a little bow and swept his hand toward Julian. "After you?"

Julian took a step toward the chair, then stopped himself. "No, you go ahead," he said. He'd been doing Danny little favors all day—giving him the extra cookie, carrying the heavier tools from the trail. But he still couldn't shake the feeling that he was somehow in his debt.

Danny gave him a perplexed smile, then climbed into the chair. Julian watched impatiently as he pulled himself up hand over hand. After Ariel had made it to the top and sent the chair back down, Julian finally took his turn. The canvas was rough and smelled faintly of mildew.

Julian reached for a rope.

"No, pull the other one," Robin shouted down.

Julian pulled with two hands until his feet were dangling in the air.

"That's it!" Robin said.

Julian rose and rose until he hung slightly above the floor of the tree house. Robin smiled happily. "Do you like it? Isn't it great?"

Julian grabbed her outstretched hand and climbed onto the deck. Robin wrapped the pulley–seat rope around a metal cleat to secure it while Julian looked about curiously. The front side of the tree house was a deck, about six feet square. Along the side of the deck were long benches with hinged tops that doubled as storage bins. Everything was dusty and covered with leaves and redwood needles and little redwood cones. In the middle of the tree house, the floor narrowed where it was cut around the two giant redwood trunks that jutted up from below. Then the back of the tree house widened out again, like an hourglass, and there was a little cabin with a pointed roof.

Ariel and Danny were walking around the deck, peering in all the storage bins.

"They're all empty," Ariel said. "We can put our food and stuff in there."

"And if it rains, we can go in the cabin," Julian said.

"You see," said Robin. "We're totally safe up here. Nobody can get us."

"Look here!" Ariel ran her finger along the wooden railing. "Look at all these initials. A.G. T.C.G. R.W.G. F.C.G."

Robin studied the letters. "Those must be from the Greeleys.

One of the boys was named Tom, I think. Maybe that's him—T.C.G."

Julian traced his fingers over the smooth letters. "Here's more. J.R.E. D.A.E."

"That's my brothers!" Robin said. "John Robert Elder. David Armi Elder."

Danny was looking down at them from the roof. "This is so cool. We can carve our initials too."

With a pang, Julian remembered his ivory pocketknife. He hadn't realized it was missing until he began packing for Huckleberry Ranch, and then he couldn't remember the last time he'd seen it.

"Let's try to get back tomorrow night. For a test run," Robin said.

"There's plenty of room for all of us to sleep here." Danny hopped down off the roof. "Too bad there's not a little fireplace. A fireplace and a little DVD player. Then this place would be perfect."

It's already perfect, Julian thought to himself. And at the same moment, Ariel said, "It's already perfect."

"There actually is an old fire ring down on the ground," Robin said. "But I don't think we can arrange the DVD." She suddenly turned businesslike and clapped her hands together. "OK, everyone! Here's the plan. We'll ask my parents if we can all camp out tomorrow night. We'll bring our sleeping bags and supplies and as much extra as we can. It'll be a trial run for Operation Redwood."

"Does your dad know about the tree house?" Julian asked.

"Obviously, the answer is no!" Robin said. "That's why it's a secret, remember?"

"What are you going to tell him, then?" Julian didn't think he could stand being *that boy* again. He looked at Danny. After all, hadn't Danny begged Bob to let him come back? Hadn't he basically promised he wouldn't cause trouble again? But Danny looked unperturbed.

"I'll tell him we're camping in Big Tree, OK? That's true, right? It's not even a half-truth, it's entirely true!" She looked at Julian's worried face. "We're not doing anything wrong. Come on, Julian, don't chicken out on us now!"

That night, for dessert, Nancy barbequed peaches over the coals. She handed Danny and Julian each a heaping bowl topped with vanilla ice cream. "It's so nice to have you boys around. It reminds me of when John and Dave were your age."

"The new fence looks great. And we've finished a good chunk of that trail too," Bob said. "It would have taken me weeks to do by myself."

"I'm helping too," Molly said, stirring her ice cream around to make a pinkish soup.

"Sure you are, bean sprout. You're a big help."

"I'm helping too!" Jo-Jo said. Bob picked him up and started spooning ice cream into his mouth.

Julian ate slowly, matching each bite of warm, sticky peach

with a bit of cold ice cream. He was perfectly happy eating his dessert and listening to the pleasant hum of the conversation when he heard Robin's voice, urgent as always, saying, "Mom, can we camp out in Big Tree tomorrow night?"

Julian ate another bite of ice cream. Everything was so pleasant. Nobody was mad at him. And, if you thought about it, wasn't Operation Redwood bound to be a failure, like Operation Break-In? They could just spend their last week having fun instead: picking berries and swimming in the river and hanging out in the tree house.

He saw a glance pass between Nancy and Bob. "I don't see why not," Nancy said.

"Can I go too?" Molly asked. "Please, Mom?"

"No!" Robin cried. "She's too little. We want it to be just the four of us!"

Nancy sighed and studied her daughters' faces, but before she could speak, Bob said, "Now, I don't see why Molly can't go with them. She's been working hard too."

"Dad! Please! She's going to ruin everything!"

"Robin, that's enough," Bob said sharply. "Molly can join you and you're going to include her and that's that. We've let you have your friends up here for two weeks, and she doesn't have anyone. And I don't want to hear that you're not being nice to her. Do you understand?" He looked hard at Robin and gave a warning glance to Ariel and the boys.

Robin looked down. Even in the waning light, Julian could see tears in her eyes. She stood up and started grabbing the dishes off the picnic table and taking them inside. Ariel jumped up to help her and Julian and Danny sat awkwardly in the silence.

"Maybe tonight would be a good night for a campfire," Nancy said with a forced cheeriness. "Why don't you gather some kindling."

Danny, Julian, and Molly started scouring the ground for twigs and dry sticks. Jo-Jo followed them around saying, "What are you looking for? Sticks? Are you looking for sticks? Are you gonna start a fire?"

By the time Robin came out with marshmallows, the fire was burning cheerfully. They had a contest for the most perfectly toasted marshmallow. Julian, who had patiently turned his over the coals until it was an even tan, won hands down.

"Your marshmallow's on fire," Ariel pointed out to Danny.

"I don't care. I like them burnt." He held the flaming marshmallow under his face and made a zombie face. "Tonight the moon is full," he said in a zombie tone, "and I am hungry."

Jo-Jo started crying and hid his face in his mother's shirt.

"Shame on you," Robin said. "Scaring a little child."

Danny blew out the marshmallow torch with a sheepish grin. "For my penance, I vill eat it." He stuck the blackened marshmallow into his mouth and pulled it off the stick with his teeth.

As the fire died down, Bob brought out his guitar and Nancy and the girls began singing. They seemed to know an endless number of songs: rounds, nonsense songs, songs about hiking and canoeing and mountains and flowers. Julian and Danny didn't know any of the words. Finally, at Julian's insistence, Danny agreed to sing "Lean on Me." Julian stumbled along with the refrain, and at the end everyone applauded. Later, as the boys crawled into the cold tent, they could still hear Bob picking out the melody to Danny's song on his guitar.

The following evening, the four operatives, with Molly in tow, began their march toward Big Tree. Their backpacks were loaded down with as much food as they could carry: sandwiches, granola bars, pistachios, beef jerky, carrot sticks, cheese, apples, bottles of juice, and a double batch of chocolate chip cookies. In addition, they were each lugging their own water bottles, sleeping bags, and flashlights. Julian watched Molly's backpack droop lower and lower. Finally, as they started up the switchbacks, he unhooked her water bottle from her backpack and attached it to his own. Molly gave him a grateful smile.

At the faucet, they caught their breath and refilled their water bottles. It was all downhill from there. Once they crossed the creek, Robin pointed to a peeling wooden shack almost hidden behind a giant redwood. "Take note: the outhouse," she said with a meaningful grin. When they reached the fairy ring, Robin turned to her sister and said sternly, "OK, Molly, we didn't want to bring you into this, but we have no choice. We're going to show you something secret, but you have to promise, cross your heart and hope to die, no crossies, that you won't tell until we say it's OK.

You can't tell Mom or Dad unless I specifically say it's OK or you'll ruin everything. Do you understand?"

Molly's pale face glowed in the shade of the trees. She opened her eyes wide and nodded solemnly.

"OK, everyone! Let's go!" Robin commanded. "We're almost there." The others groaned, then readjusted their backpacks and trudged forward. When they reached the fallen tree, they clambered up unsteadily, weighed down by the heavy packs. Molly gave a little cry of surprise as the tree house came into view. "Hey, what's that?"

Robin ignored her sister until they'd all reached the base of the two giant redwoods and thrown their packs on the ground. "This is our tree house," Robin finally said. "You weren't supposed to know about it until you were twelve and then there was supposed to be this really cool initiation with me and John and Dave, but since you *insisted* on coming, you're going to miss all that, OK?" Robin looked down at her sister intently. "But the important thing is we have a plan. A secret plan. Do you understand?"

Molly nodded.

"You know how they want to cut down Big Tree Grove?"

Molly nodded again.

"Well, we're going to stay up in the tree house to protest. Like Julia Butterfly Hill. Remember her?"

"For two years?" Molly's orange eyebrows shot up in astonishment.

"Not for that long. But as long as we can. That's *us*. Not *you*. You're too little."

Molly started to object but Robin cut her off with a fierce stare. "You're lucky we let you come with us tonight. And this is a secret, remember?"

In a few minutes, Robin was at the top, lowering down the pulley seat. They let Molly have the first ride. She clenched the rope so tightly her knuckles turned white, but the pulley system was foolproof and soon she'd scrambled into the tree house and was waving down at the others.

For dinner that night they had cheese and crackers and carrot sticks and peanut butter and jelly sandwiches, all tasting mildly of bug spray. Robin parceled out two cookies each for dessert. Then, because there were no grown-ups around, she handed out two more. When they were done, the girls spread out their sleeping bags inside the cabin. The boys set up on the deck under the open sky.

Julian looked at his watch. It was just after eight. "What are we going to do now?"

"It's too early to sleep," Robin said. "It's not even dark yet."

"It will be soon," Julian said. "The days are getting shorter." As soon as he said it, he felt a little sad. It made him feel like summer was almost over.

They decided to play hide and seek. They played, searching and tagging and racing through the forest, until they could barely see each other's faces. Julian was the last one to be It. He found

Robin and Ariel hiding together behind a rotting, moss-covered log and Danny inside a burned-out redwood cavity, but Molly was nowhere to be found.

"Help me find Molly," he said to the others. "I've looked everywhere. She's not under that big fern like the last two times."

In the vanishing light, they called for her and searched behind every tree and stump. When Molly didn't answer, the forest seemed to grow a shade darker. Even the sound of her name, ringing out over and over, began to sound ominous. Julian felt like he was in the opening scene of a horror film.

They gathered under the tree house.

"I'm getting worried," said Ariel. "Maybe she wandered off somewhere."

The children stood peering into the gloom. A few minutes earlier they had been running around laughing, but now they could barely make out the shapes of the giant trees against the dark sky. An owl hooted and then there was silence. Julian suddenly remembered the bears.

"Let's get our flashlights," Robin said. "Come on. We better start a search party." She turned toward the pulley seat. Only then did they notice that it was not suspended above the ground where they'd left it, but was dangling just above their heads.

"Boo!" cried Molly, her pale face peering over the edge of the seat.

Ariel shrieked. Danny laughed. Julian started breathing again and Robin yelled, "You are crazy, Molly Elizabeth Elder! You scared me to death. Here I was worried sick about you and you're playing tricks on us!" She gave the chair a shove and sent Molly swinging above their heads.

Molly started giggling. With her legs tucked up and her head bent down she was invisible again.

"That was awesome!" Danny said with admiration. "That was a brilliant hiding place."

"Go up in the tree house and brush your teeth and send the chair down for the rest of us," Robin said. "And if you pull another stunt like that, you're sleeping on the ground tonight, where the salamanders will crawl all over you."

"I'm going up after Molly. My heart is beating so fast I think I'm going to die," Ariel said.

Danny was the last one up. He climbed out of the pulley seat and secured the rope around the metal cleat so they would be safe from wild animals, serial killers, or other predators. Molly kept saying, "Were you scared? Did I surprise you? You didn't see me up there?"

They brushed their teeth, spitting their toothpaste over the railings, and the girls changed into their nightgowns inside the cabin. Finally, everyone settled down in their sleeping bags. When they turned off their flashlights, they were enveloped by the dark night. Julian heard a steady chirping noise and then something scuffling through the dry leaves. A raccoon? A bear? Didn't mountain lions climb trees?

"Hey! Don't bears and mountain lions climb trees?" he asked into the night.

"Not *redwood* trees!" Robin's voice answered him. "There's no branches! Where do you guys come up with this stuff!"

It was a clear night. Julian looked up at the millions of stars, so dense and dazzling here. Their light took millions of years to reach Earth. Some of the stars might already be gone, he thought. And by the time they see us, we might be gone too.

The tree creaked softly in the breeze. An owl hooted. He thought of Popo, alone in her house in Sacramento. On the other side of the Earth, in China, the sun would be shining. Star shine and sunshine, somehow he'd never realized they were the same, he thought dreamily, and then he drifted off to sleep.

23

INTRUDERS

The sound of the birds woke the children early. In the sunshine, the forest looked bright and ordinary again. For breakfast, they ate the apples and the rest of the chocolate-chip cookies and passed around a box of cereal. Danny and Julian started a game of crazy eights and Robin and Ariel joined in after the first round. Molly lay down with her chin in her hands, looking into the forest.

"Somebody's coming," she said so softly that only Julian heard. He craned forward and saw two men, dressed in jeans and T-shirts, walking slowly from tree to tree. One had a mustache and was carrying a can of spray paint. The other was older and wore glasses and a camouflage cap.

"Everybody down," Julian whispered loudly.

Danny and the girls looked up from their cards, and Julian pointed at the two men. Robin crouched down behind one of the storage bins and the others quickly flattened themselves on top of the sleeping bags and peered through the railings.

Nobody spoke a word. They watched as the man with the paint can sprayed a blue slash on a giant redwood about twenty feet away.

"Boy, you don't see trees like this anymore," said the older man. He gave the tree an appreciative look and jotted a note on his clipboard.

"This place is a gold mine. My granddaddy's place used to look just like this when I was a kid. If he hadn't sold it, I'd be a rich man."

"The rest of the property's not bad either. There must be half a million dollars' worth of fir back on that northern slope."

"Yeah, but this here's the real treasure."

The spray-painter was standing right underneath them. They could see his brown mustache and the glint of his blue eyes through the cracks in the floorboards. "Hey, look up here," he said. "There's a tree house!"

"You better watch out, there might be somebody living up there."

Julian felt a sharp poke in his side. Robin was motioning for everyone to stand up. When nobody moved, she gave them a dirty look and stood up tall, her chin thrust out. Julian and Danny jumped up next to her, and Ariel and Molly reluctantly followed.

The spray-painter made a long blue streak on one of the trunks below them.

"Hey, this is our tree house," Robin yelled down. "What do you think you're doing?"

The spray-painter grabbed his chest and pantomimed having a heart attack. "Holy smokes!" he cried. "What are you doing up there?"

"What are *you* doing spray-painting our tree?" Robin demanded.

"The trees you're marking," Julian said, "are those the ones you're cutting down?"

"That's the way it goes, kids," said the man with glasses. "Sorry. You're going to have to build your tree house someplace else."

"We don't want to build it someplace else," Danny said. "We like it right here. Why don't you go cut down trees someplace else?"

"Because we've got a THP for these trees, that's how come," the spray-painter said.

Ariel stepped forward. "But these trees are so beautiful. You guys just said there's not many of them left."

"Listen, kids," the older man said. "The harvest plan's already approved. These trees are worth a bundle. They're coming down."

"Well, we're not leaving," said Robin.

The spray-painter grinned and glanced back over his shoulder. "Looks like we've got some juvenile tree sitters here."

"OK, we'll make a note of that in our report to Mr. Carter," the older man responded with mock seriousness, writing something on the clipboard.

"You better! You better make a note of it, because Sibley Carter is his uncle!" Robin said, pointing at Julian.

The men stared up at them, confused. "What in the world are you talking about?" the older man said.

"This boy," Robin grabbed Julian by the arm, "is the nephew of Sibley Carter. *The* Sibley Carter. The CEO of IPX." She pulled Julian forward a little. "And he's not leaving either. Not until you guys agree not to cut down any of these trees."

"Are you kidding me?"

"No, it's true," Julian said. The squeak in his voice made him wince and he tried again, in a lower tone. "He's my father's brother."

"If Sibley Carter was my uncle, I sure wouldn't be living in a tree house," the spray-painter said.

"What's your name?" the older man asked.

"Julian." And a little louder, "Julian Carter-Li."

He started scribbling in his clipboard. "Any of the rest of you claiming to be Mr. Carter's relatives?"

They shook their heads. Molly said, "My daddy's Bob Elder."

"Oh, you're Bob's kids." The man made another note on his clipboard. "Did your daddy tell you to trespass on this property?"

Molly shook her head solemnly.

"I didn't think so. You tell him Pete came by." He stepped back and adjusted his cap. "Come on, let's finish up here," he said to the spray-painter. "We better make sure there's no other kids hiding up in the trees."

Robin watched them walk away, dismayed. "Tell Carter we're not coming down!" she yelled. "We're serious! He'll have to chop us down!"

The spray-painter gave her a thumbs-up. Then the two men walked off into the forest, stopping every so often to mark another tree.

"Well, we showed them," Danny said sourly. "They were shakin' in their boots. I'm sure they're going to go back and call the whole project off."

Ariel was craning over the side of the railing. "Our beautiful trees," she wailed. "They've put graffiti all over them. Look at that!"

They all stared down at the blue marks. The men were now nowhere to be seen.

"Maybe we can erase all the marks. So they won't know which trees to cut," Danny suggested.

"I don't think you can erase spray paint," Robin said.

"Well, paint over it, then," Danny said. "With bark-colored paint."

Nobody responded.

Ariel began gathering up the scattered cards from their game of crazy eights. "We need to do something else. Just sitting in this tree isn't going to be enough. Not even close."

"We could tie ourselves to the trees," Robin said. "When the chain saws come."

"Danny will be up for that," Julian volunteered.

"Danny will be up for what?" Danny said. He'd crossed to the other side of the tree house to inspect the damage.

"For the giant chain saws to hack you to pieces to save Big Tree," Robin said.

"Sure." Danny nodded cheerfully. "I'll be a martyr for the cause! 'He was such a good boy. So noble! So brave! So handsome!'"

"Such a good-looking corpse!" Ariel said.

"Once they put him back together," Robin added.

Julian sat picking at a little redwood cone. "What we need is more publicity."

"Too bad we don't know any journalists," Danny said pointedly, and then when Julian didn't respond he said, "Too bad none of our grandmothers works for a major newspaper."

Robin stared at Julian. "Your grandmother works for the *Chronicle*. We can call her!"

"I don't know," Julian said. "You can't just go and write stories about your grandson and his friends and call it news."

"This *is* news," Robin said. "'Small family ranch bought by investment firm. Rare old-growth destroyed.' It's gotten plenty of coverage up here. Come on, you've got to at least try."

Julian could picture Popo frowning on the other end of the line, in a hurry, on a deadline. She would worry he would fall out of the tree house or end up in trouble. And what would Sibley do if the *Chronicle* really did publish a story about them? Somehow, all the time he'd spent thinking about Operation Redwood, it hadn't occurred to him that Sibley might somehow get involved. And what about Bob? But he didn't have time to puzzle everything out. Robin's eyes were locked on his face.

"OK, I'll call her," he said, hesitantly. "The worst she can say is no. Or," he added, "'You're coming home right now.'"

"Ariel and Danny, you stay here in case the men come back. Julian and I are going back to the house to call his grandmother. Molly, are you staying or coming?"

"Staying," Molly said firmly.

Robin and Julian sprinted back toward the house. Julian noted with satisfaction that he kept right behind Robin, even on the switchbacks. When they finally burst into the living room, they found Nancy reading a book to Jo-Jo.

"Mom!" Robin stood inside the glass door, trying to catch her breath. "The men are coming to Big Tree Grove and they're marking all the trees to cut them down and we told them we're not leaving the tree house and Ariel and Molly and Danny are there guarding it and we have to call Julian's grandmother and tell her."

She had obviously decided that full confession was the best strategy, Julian noted with a certain feeling of relief.

"Slow down," Nancy said. "What are you talking about?"

"There's an old tree house in Big Tree," Robin said, still panting. "And that's where we had the campout. That's why I didn't want to bring Molly, because I was afraid she was too little. But everything was going great and then we saw the men."

"What men?" Nancy knit her eyebrows together. Jo-Jo stuck his thumb in his mouth and started turning the pages of his book.

"The men who are going to cut down the trees! They're marking all the trees they're going to log, even the ones for our tree house. We told them to stop, but they weren't listening to us at all. We had to do something! So we told them we're not coming down from the tree house until they agree not to cut down a single tree in Big Tree Grove."

"I see." Julian couldn't read Nancy's expression. She sighed and pushed her hair behind her ears. "And what's this about Julian's grandmother?"

Robin turned to Julian.

"Well," he said, "we thought maybe my grandmother could get the *San Francisco Chronicle* to write a story about Big Tree Grove. And that might help. Since you guys lost the THP appeal and everything." He was glad he remembered about the appeal.

"Please, Mom!" Robin got down on her knees and clasped her hands together. "We *have* to do this. Don't say we can't. Please?"

"I'm not saying that yet." Nancy's face was unreadable, like she was doing arithmetic in her head. "I need to talk this over with your father. I'll be right back." She swung Jo-Jo up on her hip and walked toward the open sliding doors. Jo-Jo started wailing, "I don't wanna go out! I want the choo-choo book!"

"Wait just a minute, honey," Nancy said to Jo-Jo. She stopped at the door. "They didn't threaten you or anything?"

"Threaten us? No! They gave us a thumbs-up," Robin said in disgust. "And tell Dad the guy's name is Pete."

"Pete?" Bob came in through the front door, carrying the day's mail. "Where did you see Pete?"

Robin repeated the whole story to her father.

"Absolutely not!" he said. "I am not having you turn into one of those crazy tree-sitters. It's not safe, for one thing. And it's trespassing. Ed Greeley was always a good neighbor to me."

"But Dad, it's not Ed Greeley anymore. That's the whole problem. Do you think IPX is a good neighbor? And it's not dangerous. John and Dave were just up there. And the Greeley boys played in the tree house for years. I bet you even played in it!"

Bob pressed his lips together and turned his face aside, reaching up to adjust his wide-brimmed hat.

Robin smiled slightly. "It's super sturdy—not a single loose board! Very well-constructed. Very nice craftsmanship!"

"You're breaking the law," Bob said, but his voice had lost some of its edge. "I don't want the sheriff out here again." He looked pointedly at Julian. Julian lowered his eyes and shifted nervously.

"Daddy, we're not!" Robin said. "We're just up in our tree house! Ed Greeley let the boys play there. And if the laws don't protect Big Tree, then they're not good laws anyway."

"What good is it going to do for you kids to sit up in a tree house? I don't see how that's going to accomplish anything."

"It might. Nothing else is working. It's worth a try. Especially if the *Chronicle* writes a story about us."

"I want a story!" Jo-Jo called out. Nancy whispered in his ear and shifted him to her other hip.

Bob shook his head. "The whole thing's going to turn into a circus. I can see it already."

Julian's mind was reeling from all the back and forth, but Robin answered right away. "No, it won't. There's already been stories about it up here. Everybody knows about it. But a story in the *Chronicle* would be different. Then all those San Francisco people would read it and maybe IPX cares more about them. If they even wrote a story, which they probably won't anyway."

Bob's face softened ever so slightly as he watched Robin. He crossed his arms. "How long were you planning on staying up there?"

It was a chink in his armor and Julian saw Robin take heart. "Not that long. It's a tree house. We can't stay up there forever! Ariel and Julian and Danny have to leave Sunday anyway. Remember, Daddy, you and Mom said it was really, really important to save Big Tree! You said we should try everything we could!"

Bob looked at Nancy. "What do you think?"

Robin clasped her hands again and stared silently at her mother.

"Well, I don't see how it could do any harm, really," Nancy said. "And they *are* working for something they believe in. 'Speak truth to power'—that's what we've taught them."

Bob looked back and forth between his wife and his daughter. "If anything happens, if we say it's time to come down, you all come down."

"I promise," Robin said.

"I mean right away."

"OK, Daddy."

"You too, Julian."

"Yes, sir." Julian had never said "sir" in his life, but somehow it seemed called for.

"Where's Molly?" he asked.

"In the tree house," Robin said. "With Danny and Ariel."

"Molly stays here. And I don't want you getting out of your chores. I want to get more of that trail done."

"Every morning two of us will come and two can stay in the tree house. We'll come first thing when you ring the bell. We'll work extra hard."

Bob sighed. "I don't know how I ended up with you. Always getting into scrapes and causing trouble. John and Dave were never like this."

Robin smiled sweetly. "Nature or nurture. Either way, it's not my fault."

Bob drank a glass of water and walked back toward the door. "In one hour, I want two kids out at the trail ready to work. No slackers. I expect instant obedience, unstinting labor, hours of uncomplaining toil."

"On your orders, Dad."

Bob smiled wryly and walked out of the house, shaking his head. Nancy smiled at her daughter. "Looks like your prayers have been answered." Her eyes were still worried. "I hope this all turns out OK."

"It will," Robin said confidently. She came just to her mother's chin and Julian looked at her and wondered how she could be so certain everything would turn out right, when it seemed to him entirely possible that everything would turn out completely wrong.

24

THE STORM

The following afternoon, Ariel and Robin were on watch, perched on the roof with their binoculars. Danny sat on the deck, chiseling his initials into the railing with his pocketknife, while Julian put the last layer of varnish on his little box. They were discussing the best way to construct a zip line to the ground when they heard Robin's whistle. Looking into the forest, they saw Molly standing on the fallen log, dwarfed by a tall man with dark, wild hair. She pointed to the tree house, then turned and ran toward home.

"Hello, tree-sitters!" the man called up when he'd reached the base of the trees. "I'm Bruce, from the *Chronicle*."

Robin grinned. They hadn't been certain he would come. "Do you want to come up?" she asked.

"You'd better not be one of Carter's spies," Danny shouted.

Bruce burst into laughter. "Trust me! I'm a bona fide journalist. Eleanor Li sent me."

"Those are the magic words." Danny lowered the pulley seat down.

Bruce squeezed into the chair and, without waiting for instruction, started pulling on the rope. Soon, he was lurching toward the tree house, his long hairy legs dangling below him. He extricated himself with some difficulty from the chair, then stood looking about him with a bemused expression.

The tree house was now fortified for their stay. The sleeping bags were neatly rolled up and baskets of walnuts and apples and a large water jug were set out on top of the storage bins. Inside the bins were even more supplies: peanut butter, several loaves of bread, a pound of cheese, boxes of cereal and crackers, a container of powdered milk, and two jars of jam.

Ariel offered Bruce two chocolate-chip cookies, then he sat down on one of the storage bins and began firing off questions. He wanted to know their names, their ages, what they studied in school, the history of Big Tree Grove and the Greeley family, how they'd found the tree house, how long they'd been there, what they ate, and whether they were scared to sleep up in the tree at night. Occasionally, he would grab another cookie and jot down a note on his yellow legal pad.

After they had talked for nearly an hour, he turned and said, "So, Julian Carter-Li, how does a nice guy like you end up butting heads with your own uncle? Are you two still on speaking terms?"

"Well," Julian stammered, "we haven't really spoken for a while."

"I'll bet!" Bruce said, laughing. "So here he is, the new CEO of this hot-shot investment firm and you start a protest."

Julian blushed. "I wasn't really thinking so much about my uncle. I was just thinking about Big Tree and how it's been here for so long—practically forever—and that it would be a terrible thing to cut down all these trees."

Bruce jotted some notes down in his legal pad. "Where did you guys all meet, anyway? We're pretty far from San Francisco."

Julian glanced nervously at Robin.

"What?" Bruce's dark eyes darted quickly between the two of them. "Did I say something wrong? What's the big secret?"

"We're old friends," Julian said.

"What—how old? Since you were six or something?"

"We were pen pals," Robin said with a false smile. "Part of the home-schooling curriculum."

Bruce gave them both a hard stare, then shook his head. "I can tell when I'm being stonewalled," he said. "But I'm glad your grandmother called. Eleanor Li's the best journalist I know. And you guys have added a nice human-interest angle. Nobody cares about all these THPs and departments-of-this and boards-of-that." He flipped through the pages of his legal pad. "OK, just one last question: What's your message to the world?"

"This THP is terrible," Robin said. "The Greeley property was harvested sustainably for years and it still should be. They should preserve Big Tree Grove and any other old-growth. Forever."

Bruce raised his eyebrows and jotted down a few notes.

"There's a bunch of bigwigs getting rich off of trashing this place," Danny said. "They should go to jail instead!"

"It should be against the law," Julian said.

Ariel, who had said only a few words during the interview, suddenly broke in. "My mother used to play in Big Tree when she was a little girl. And Robin and I played here when we were little. The clear-cuts, they're the ugliest thing you've ever seen. The ground all ripped up and slash all over the place. Look around here. There's nothing half as beautiful as this in San Francisco or Los Angeles or Phoenix. If they keep cutting down the trees, nobody will even remember what a forest is supposed to look like."

Julian looked at her in surprise. It was like the running. She dawdled around and then suddenly she was moving like lightning.

Bruce finished scribbling, then put away his notepad. "If I don't get lazy, the story should run on Wednesday." He took several photos from up in the tree house and then lowered himself, hooting and laughing, to the ground. Holding up his camera, he told them to look serious, then angry, then cracked jokes to make them smile. Robin threw him an apple for the road, and he caught it with a flourish and headed down the path.

The next afternoon was hot and muggy, and by evening, the heat still hadn't broken. It made everyone listless and took away their appetites. The girls lounged in the cabin, reading. Danny started chiseling his initials deeper into the side railing. Julian watched him, wondering how he could have been so stupid as to lose his father's knife and thinking he would never again have anything half so cool and perfect.

Finally, Ariel roused herself to cut up some cheese and tomatoes and they all ate sandwiches and granola bars under the colorless sky.

"Wouldn't you love to climb to the top of these trees?" Robin said when dinner was done. She was lying on the storage bins, staring up at the treetops.

"We could do it," Ariel said. "I bet John and Dave could teach us."

"John has a friend who climbs redwoods," Robin said. "It's his *life*. John said he saw all sorts of cool things up there. There's huckleberry bushes—growing right out of the tree trunks. There's rhododendrons blooming. There's little miniature bonsais growing in the crooks of the trees. They're growing in *dirt* two hundred feet up. These *little* trees are more than a hundred years old and they're growing out of the branch of a thousand-year-old redwood."

"Trees *in* the trees?" Ariel said.

"That's what he said." Robin crossed her ankles and wiggled her bare toes. "These trees are so old. They're *older* than the dinosaurs. When all the continents in the world were still smushed together, there were redwood trees, or something like them. The asteroid that wiped out the dinosaurs—the redwoods were fine. John said they covered half of the world. Then they shrank down to just California. And then the loggers came along and cut them all down."

"The end," Danny said. "That was a cheery little story."

"Well, Big Tree's still here," Ariel said. "That's kind of amazing, when you think about it."

Robin got to her feet and poured lemonade from a canteen into her tin cup. "I can't wait until the story comes out."

They rinsed the dishes in the creek and the girls ran off to the outhouse. When they returned, it was nearly dark. Julian helped them out of the pulley seat and cleated the rope. Now that he was used to the tree house, it felt like the safest place on earth, safer than the city. Any decent burglar could break a window, he figured, but it would be almost impossible to break into the tree house in the dark.

It was still too hot to get inside their sleeping bags. Julian was just looking for his flashlight when the sky flickered, casting a momentary gray light over the tree-house deck.

"Lightning!" Ariel cried.

The sky flashed again. This time, they heard a low, angry rumble in the distance. A feeling of dread stirred inside Julian. He'd never seen lightning in San Francisco.

"I love storms!" Robin shouted, looking up at the sky.

Julian could hear the wind coming before he felt it—warm and damp and smelling of salt and sap. The branches above them bowed and swayed.

"Correct me if I'm wrong," Danny said, "but is it possible that a tree house is not exactly the safest place to be in the middle of a lightning storm?"

As if in answer, a brilliant fork of lightning ripped across the sky. Julian stood transfixed. The trees shifted uneasily, and soon the sound of the wind sweeping over the forest was like the roar of the ocean. A few heavy raindrops blew onto Julian's face. A tin cup went rattling off the storage bins and across the floor.

"We better get our stuff inside!" Robin called. "Before it's too dark to see." Her alarm stirred them to action. Julian and Danny grabbed their backpacks and pillows and sleeping bags and threw them into the cabin while the girls stuffed everything else on the deck—dishes and canteens, notebooks, two candles, a box of crackers—into the storage bins and slammed the lids shut. When they were done, the deck looked strangely bare and abandoned in the dim light.

The sky flickered again and Robin started counting aloud—"one thousand, two thousand, three thousand, four thousand . . ." There was another low rumble.

"Five seconds!" Robin said. "That means the storm is still a mile away."

Danny looked up at the sky, his face tense. "Let's get out of here! I'm serious. Let's go back to the house while we still can!"

"We're safer here," Robin said. "Besides, it's too late. It's already dark."

There was another bolt of lightning, then a low crescendo of sound that exploded into an earsplitting clap of thunder.

Ariel gave a little shriek and Danny cried, "We're going to die!" They ducked into the cabin. It was even darker inside than out, and Julian had to blink a few times before he could see a thing. Finally, Danny, who'd been fumbling through the bags, turned on his flashlight. In its eerie white glow, he crossed himself quickly. "Oh, God, don't strike this tree house!" he muttered. "I promise to be good for the rest of my life!"

Robin was still standing near the doorway, peering into the forest. "That was a big one," she said. "But I don't see any flames. I don't think it hit anything."

"Remember that tree in town?" Ariel said. "It was hit by lightning and burned to the ground."

A forest fire. Or a lightning strike. They weren't so uncommon. At the Monterey Aquarium, Julian had learned you were more likely to be struck by lightning than attacked by a shark and he'd always found that reassuring when he was swimming in the Bay. But, now, sitting thirty feet up in a tree in the middle of a lightning storm, Julian didn't find it so comforting.

There was another crash of thunder. Danny's flashlight dimmed and went out.

"Oh, great!" he said in a pained voice. "Doesn't anybody else have a flashlight?"

Julian fumbled around, but the bags were all jumbled together, and it was almost completely dark.

The tree house trembled, and all at once the rustling sound of the trees seemed to expand until it was as loud as a rushing waterfall. Dense rain descended on the forest. With the rain, the last traces of light vanished.

"I can't see you guys. I can't even see my own hand," Danny said with a note of panic in his voice.

Ariel's voice came out of the blackness. "I'm right here, Danny."

"Me too. I'm here," came Robin's voice.

"I'm right next to you," Julian said. He scooted a little to the right until his knee hit what he thought was Danny's leg. "See?"

The next clap of thunder was so loud that Julian jumped. Danny made a small whimper. A flash of lightning electrified the sky and revealed, for an instant, the inside of the cabin, and Julian could see that, underneath the darkness, they were all still there.

Then it was pitch black again. They sat silently, listening to the heavy drone of the rain. Each neon flash in the sky, punctuated by a crack like a shotgun, was like a warning that they were in mortal danger. But it was too late to go back. Robin was right. They were better off in the tree house than stumbling blindly through the forest.

The floorboards creaked beneath their feet. Whether I'm going to die now, Julian thought, is out of my control. In the terrible blackness, he felt half dead already. He shifted his knee against Danny's leg just to reassure himself that they were both still alive.

The trees shuddered. Surely, they had been through worse than this, Julian reasoned. After all those years, what was the chance that the trees would be struck by lightning tonight? What was the chance that lightning would strike down the four of them, when they had lived such a short time?

On and on went the storm—a flash, a crack of thunder, and then the sound of rain gusting through the darkness.

Each time the wind rose, Julian could feel the tree trunks tensing and bending beneath them. He knew, of course, that, technically, trees were alive. He'd studied biology in school. He'd learned about photosynthesis and respiration and cell division. But now, for the first time, he understood that a tree was an actual living thing—unseeing, unhearing, unconscious, but alive and perhaps aware in some other way, swaying with the wind, absorbing the rain, breathing. Their tree house was anchored to a living thing. And all around them, a whole forest of living things bowed under the forces of wind and rain and electricity.

Nobody said a word. Then, as suddenly as it had come, the rain stopped.

The rustling of the trees rose up again through the darkness. The trees swayed back and forth, but stayed rooted in place. They had stood there, Julian thought, for a thousand summers and a thousand winters. And each year would have had at least ten bad storms, he figured, storms where the rain pelted down and the wind howled. Ten thousand storms. And somehow the trees had survived. And even when these trees died, the forest would still be there. After all, for a tree to die wasn't the same as a person, was it? A tree lived for hundreds of years, and how could you even say when it died? Old logs lay on the forest floor, slowly turning to dirt, and little saplings grew right out of their trunks.

Through the windows, Julian could see the brilliant flashes lighting up the sky. He breathed in and out in the blackness, listening to the hushed whispering of the trees. And slowly, the periods of silence grew longer and longer. The growl of the thunder and the flickers of lightning grew fainter. An owl hooted, and hooted again. The storm had passed.

"It's over," Julian said at last.

They sat without speaking for another minute. "I guess we should try to find our sleeping bags," Robin finally said, yawning loudly. Julian could hear her rummaging around. There was a clank and, finally, the glare of her electric lantern lit up the small cabin.

Julian walked outside and touched the floor of the deck. It was barely damp. The trees had acted as a kind of leaky umbrella over them. Danny was still slumped against the cabin wall. Julian grabbed their sleeping bags and pillows from the cabin and lay them out on the floorboards.

"Come on, Danny," he said. "It's all set up." Without saying a word, Danny crawled out onto the deck and into his sleeping bag. Between the branches, Julian could see the stars blinking into view again.

"That was not fun," Danny said in a low, rough voice. "You really shouldn't be in a tree during a lightning storm."

"All's well that ends well," Julian said.

"Fortunately, we're not dead," Danny said. "Unfortunately, now I have to be good for the rest of my life."

Julian smiled in the darkness. "You know what, Danny?" he said after a moment.

"What?"

"I found that letter you wrote to Bob." Julian paused. "I didn't mean to, but—it was a good idea."

"What are you? An actual undercover agent?" Danny said. "Jeez."

Every minute it seemed like more stars filled up the black spaces in the night sky. It was like the storm had swept the air clean. Julian wasn't tired now. He was wide awake and filled up with something like happiness.

Danny sighed and gave a little sniff.

"Lean on me," Julian sang out suddenly in the darkness, *"when you're not strong."*

There was a pause and Danny bellowed at the top of his lungs, *"I'll be your friend, I'll help you carry on!"*

"Oh! Our poor ears!" yelled Robin.

"Have some consideration!" Ariel said. "We're trying to get a little sleep over here."

"Well, you don't hear me complaining about your snoring!" Danny said. "Mercy! The two of you are like a pair of elephants over there. Here we've been suffering in silence every night and you jump down our throats just for singing you a little lullaby."

Julian heard muffled whispers and then the two girls started singing a round. It had only one verse and they sang it over and over.

"Stop! Stop!" the boys shouted.

"Truce," said Julian. "No more singing!"

Robin stopped and Ariel finished out the verse in her thin soprano. After her last note, the only sound was the soft shush of the redwood canopy, far above them.

25

THE CONFRONTATION

The next morning, the forest looked scrubbed and fresh. The rain had washed away a summer's worth of dust. The girls went off to work duty, promising to check the paper to see if Bruce's story had run. Just before noon, Julian heard a triumphant shout. Robin was running up the path, waving a newspaper in her hand, with Ariel and Molly close behind.

"Quick!" Danny yelled down. "Send up the paper in the pulley seat. We want to read it!"

"*We* haven't even read it yet!" Robin called back indignantly. "We saved it so we could all read the story together."

When all the girls were up, Robin spread the paper on the floor of the deck, turned a few pages, and there they all were, leaning over the tree-house railing and smiling. Page A6, not the best, Julian thought. But the headline was good: ANCIENT REDWOOD STANDS VANISH AS DEMAND FOR OLD-GROWTH CONTINUES.

Underneath their picture it said "Julian Carter-Li, Danny Lopez, Ariel Glasser, and Robin Elder stage a tree-house protest of IPX's plan to clear-cut Big Tree Grove in Mendocino County."

Julian's eyes went up to the top of the story:

While most kids are still in camp, four children in the heart of Mendocino County have found a different summertime activity: protesting the logging of ancient redwoods. Big Tree Grove is part of a 120-acre parcel recently acquired by San Francisco investment firm IPX Investment Corp. In April, the state approved a timber harvest plan that would permit logging of the parcel's rare old-growth redwoods, as well as a number of younger stands.

"Big Tree Grove has been here so long. It would be a terrible thing to see it destroyed," said Julian Carter-Li. Julian, a student at Filbert Middle School in San Francisco, also happens to be the nephew of Sibley Carter, who stepped up as the new CEO of IPX last September. Coincidentally, he says he met Robin Elder, 12, who lives next door to Big Tree Grove, through a pen-pal program.

"No more logging of old-growth," Robin declared, looking like a future forest activist.

Much of the original redwood forest in this area was

logged by the 1920s and timber harvesting continued to dominate the economy through most of the twentieth century. Today, while logging still brings in tens of millions of dollars a year, the volume of logs from Mendocino County is a fraction of historic levels. Local mill closures, increasing government regulation, and competition from overseas logging are leading to a change in the timber culture of the region.

Less than five percent of the original redwood forest remains today, most protected in state and federal parks. The most recent major governmental acquisition was the joint state and federal purchase of 7,500 acres of the Headwaters Forest in Humboldt County in 1999, which preserved the largest tracts of old-growth then in private hands. The few pockets of unprotected old-growth remaining today are subject to harvesting under the state's forestry laws.

The article continued with interviews with state employees, wildlife biologists, and an IPX spokeswoman. Julian skimmed to the last paragraph, which read:

Ariel Glasser, 11, who grew up not far from Big Tree Grove, says she plans to stay in the tree house as long as she can. "My mother used to play in Big Tree Grove when she was a little girl," she said. "Look at all this beauty. If they keep cutting down the trees, nobody will even remember what a forest is supposed to look like."

Julian watched Ariel smile as she came to the end of the article. "So, what do you guys think?" he said.

"Here I thought I was being so articulate and witty," Danny said in an injured tone, "and I didn't even get a quote."

Julian frowned and looked at the page more closely. "Well, you got the photo op. You're the only one who looks halfway decent." It was true. Robin was squinting, Ariel's crooked smile was crookeder than usual, and Julian was staring slightly off to the side. Danny grinned at the camera like a movie star.

"Do you think people are reading it?" Ariel said.

"Sure they're reading it." Robin looked up at last from the paper. "Thousands and thousands of people. It's exactly what we needed. This article is going to put Big Tree Grove on the map."

But the forest was so quiet for the next two days that it was hard to believe their story was being broadcast to the world. The children continued to work on the trail in the morning and prepare their meals in the evening. They read and reread the article until they practically had it memorized. And all the time, they kept waiting for something to happen, but Big Tree Grove remained as still as ever.

Friday afternoon, Molly, Ariel, and the boys were playing

poker on the deck while Robin sat brooding in the corner. "You know," she said, "even after you leave on Sunday, I can still do Operation Redwood. I mean, Julia Butterfly Hill lived by herself for two whole years."

"I could stay too." Molly put down two pairs.

"After all, we can't just abandon Operation Redwood. We've only been here six nights. That's nothing. We can't expect over-night success."

"What do you want? A big battle with IPX, with armed guards and everything?" Danny said. Julian was in the middle of dealing the next hand, but something in Danny's tone made him look up.

"I don't know," Robin said. "Anything's better than this."

"Well," Danny said, shifting his gaze. "Be careful what you wish for, because there's something big and ugly coming toward us. And it's not in a good mood."

Julian whipped around and saw two men who looked like security guards clomping through the forest. Pete, the man with the clipboard, was close behind. And following purposefully after them, his face set in stone, was Sibley.

Robin bolted up, leaped over to the pulley seat, and tied the rope to the cleat. "Remember, there's nothing they can do to us. We're safe up here."

The four men stopped, and Pete pointed up at the tree house. Sibley gave a sharp nod, then strode forward alone. He was dressed in a dark blue suit, a gold tie, and shiny black shoes. He looked,

Julian thought, like an executive who'd been kidnapped and released in the middle of the wilderness to find his way home.

"Where are these guys coming from?" Julian asked in a low voice.

"Greeley Road isn't far," Robin whispered. "It's an easy walk from the road to here."

They watched in silence as Sibley crunched toward them. When he was directly below the tree house, he stopped and stood looking up at them with a grim expression. "Julian. Danny. Girls," he finally said.

"Hi, Uncle Sibley," Julian said.

"Hey, Mr. Car-ter!" Danny was looking forward to this, Julian could tell.

Sibley's expression didn't change. "I knew you were hiding something, Julian," he said at last. "I knew you came up here for some reason. No wonder you wouldn't talk." He stared at Julian as if he were trying to calculate what other schemes he might have cooked up. "Look, you've had your fun. It's time to come down now."

The children were silent.

"We can't come down," Julian finally said. "We can't come down until you promise to save Big Tree Grove."

"Julian, this isn't a game. You need to come down immediately."

Nobody spoke. A cloud suddenly shifted so that the sun was shining directly into Sibley's face. He squinted and loosened his necktie.

"This land doesn't belong to me, Julian," Sibley began in a more conciliatory tone. "It's IPX property. That tree house is IPX property. It's not safe. You could break your necks."

"Kids have been playing up here for years and years," Robin said. "Nobody's ever gotten hurt."

"But you have to admit, it could happen."

"We're not admitting it!" Danny yelled down.

"Listen, you kids are trespassing on private property. That's against the law. If you come down now, we won't have to press charges."

"We're not coming down," Robin said.

Sibley didn't even look at Robin. His eyes were focused on Julian. "I know you probably thought we were too tough on you after you ran away. I was your age once. We were doing what we thought was best."

Julian considered. "Uncle Sibley, I didn't come up here because of that. Or because of you. We're doing this for Big Tree Grove. We just want people to know what's happening so you won't cut it down. We want you to change your mind."

"Julian, I am not the bad guy here." Sibley took out a hand-kerchief and wiped his gleaming brow. "This was a done deal before I even came on board. I tried to explain that to Preston this morning. It's bad enough you're giving IPX all this negative publicity. Now my own son thinks I'm the bad guy."

"Preston read the article?" Julian couldn't help smiling.

Sibley glared at him. "And of course, somebody gave him the

idea to do a report on redwoods. You must think you're pretty clever."

"Preston did that whole report himself. I didn't help him at all," Julian said. "You shouldn't cut down Big Tree. Even Preston knows that. Everything isn't about making money."

"IPX is about making money," Sibley said in a low voice. "That's what we do."

"But there must be another way," Julian protested.

"There's always costs. There's always risk. That's the way the world works. Money doesn't just grow on trees." Sibley attempted a strained smile.

"There's only four percent left," Julian said.

"We'll plant new trees."

"It's not enough. We can't come down. Please, don't cut down Big Tree Grove. Please."

"There are ways to make you come down," Sibley said. "Though we'd rather not."

"I've got a pinecone in my pocket and I'm not afraid to use it," Danny shouted.

Sibley ignored Danny. He made a motion as if turning to go, then stopped, and pulled something from his jacket. He weighed it in his hand a moment, then held it up. "Julian, I believe you left this at my house."

The smile faded from Julian's face. There, in Sibley's hand, was the ivory pocketknife.

Sibley turned it over in his hands. "It's a nice little knife. Two blades. Dad's initials—J.S.C. John Sibley Carter. I remember the day Billy got it. There was a race on Buzzards Bay. We sailed all day and your father came in first by a boat length. He won the cup. Youngest winner ever." Sibley opened one blade and closed it with a click. "Dad was so proud, he gave him this too."

Robin glanced worriedly at Julian. "Hey, that's not fair. He got that from his father and you won't give it back?"

"All I'm asking him to do is respect the law and come down from the tree house." Sibley's voice was calm now, in charge. "Let's go, Julian. The show's over."

"That's from his *father* and you're holding it hostage?" Danny said. "That's pretty mean, you big Grinch!"

"You're holding our property hostage," Sibley said. "That's not so nice either."

Julian stood almost hypnotized by the glare of the sun on the ivory handle. It was just a thing, he reminded himself. It had just belonged to his father, it wasn't part of him.

"You can't stay up there forever." Sibley checked his watch impatiently.

"My father gave me that knife," Julian finally said.

"That's why I brought it. I respect your rights, and I'm asking you to respect mine. And IPX's."

A breeze stirred and the branches high above the tree house began to whisper. Julian took a deep breath. "I'm not coming down. Not even for the knife." He could feel Robin's eyes on him. "I never thought you'd come here. But now that you have, you see what it's like. You could tell IPX not to cut down these trees. You could save Big Tree Grove."

His uncle's expression didn't change. "What exactly *do* you kids want?"

"We want Big Tree Grove to be protected," Julian said. "Forever."

"And outside Big Tree," Robin added, "we want sustainable timber harvesting. Like Ed Greeley did before."

"Give Julian his pocketknife!" Danny shouted. "And for the rest of us, a million dollars in unmarked bills!" Robin glared and Danny held up his hands. "Just kidding!"

Sibley wiped his brow again. He put the knife back in his jacket and walked away toward the three men. Molly tugged at her sister's shirt and started whispering in her ear. Robin nodded, then bent down and murmured a few low words.

After a few minutes of somber conversation, Sibley returned.

"We're willing to compromise," he said loudly up to them. "I think you're going to be pleased. It's a little late to make changes, with the THP approved already, but Pete says we can spare the tree house and still break even. If you all come down right now."

"The tree house!" Ariel said. "What's the point of having a tree house in the middle of a clear-cut?"

"We didn't come up in the *trees* to save the *tree house*, we went in the *tree house* to save the *trees*," Danny said. "Capisce?"

"That's my final offer," Sibley said. "If you don't come down now, saving the tree house is off the table."

"You know," Robin said, "I think Julian deserves his dad's pocketknife. What if only he came down?"

"What?" Julian spun around and stared at Robin. He couldn't believe she was offering him up on the negotiating table.

"If he came down, you'd give him the knife, right?" She grabbed an apple from the basket and started polishing it on her shirt.

"That's right," Sibley said. "He comes down, he gets the knife."

"Here, are you hungry?" she said, throwing the apple down toward him. It slipped through his fingers and rolled a few feet along the forest floor. Sibley bent down awkwardly to pick it up.

"Um, thanks." He dusted off the apple and looked as if he might take a bite, but didn't.

"What are you doing?" Julian said to Robin in a low voice. "I don't need the knife. It's not that important. I'm staying with you guys."

"Julian's with us! Forget the knife," Danny whispered loudly. "And why are you feeding him?"

Robin ignored them. "How do we know it's really Julian's knife?" she shouted down.

"Julian knows."

It was true. Julian had recognized the knife immediately. He'd never seen another one like it.

Robin paced along the deck with her hands in her pockets, then turned quickly to Sibley. "Show me again."

Sibley took the knife out of his jacket and held it up.

Robin lay down on the floor of the tree house and stuck her head between the railings. "I don't see the initials," she said. "Hold it up higher."

Sibley glanced back at the men, then held the knife high into the air. Nearly as high as the pulley seat. That was funny, Julian thought. He knew he'd seen Robin cleat the chair at the top, and now it was halfway to the ground.

Suddenly, a pale hand reached over the top of the chair and snatched the pocketknife from Sibley's grasp. Robin leaped to her feet and started pulling furiously on the rope. As the seat lurched into the air, Molly sat upright, her thin cheeks flushed and her eyes shining brightly.

"Special delivery!" she cried in a trembling voice, unable to stop grinning. She handed the knife off to Danny, who presented it with a flourish to Julian.

"Thanks, Molly," Julian stammered, too stunned to say more. He ran his thumb along the smooth ivory handle and the silver initials, his grandfather's initials, then put the knife in his pocket. When he turned back to Sibley, he thought he saw a flash of desperation on his uncle's face.

"Is this just a game to you all?" Sibley said. "Because, let me tell you, IPX doesn't think it's funny. I don't think it's funny."

"I, personally, thought that was pretty funny," Danny said. "Come on, weren't you surprised? I know I was."

"For the last time, I'm asking you to come down. Please. As the head of IPX, and as your uncle."

Julian could sense the others holding back, watching him. His uncle stood below, sweating and squinting, but Julian was beyond his reach. The ivory knife was in his pocket. He was surrounded by his best friend, two fast-running local girls, and an intrepid eight-year-old. And he was thirty feet in the air.

"We're not coming down. Please, don't cut down Big Tree Grove. Please. You could save it. You could bring Preston here."

Sibley's face hardened. "This conversation is going nowhere. I have to tell you, you're making the wrong decision. You're going to regret this." And, giving Julian a spiteful look, he turned and stumbled on a tree root, barely catching himself.

"Have a nice *trip*?" Danny called out. "See you next *fall*!"

Sibley approached the three men and motioned to the tree house. After a minute, Sibley and Pete turned and walked off in the direction they'd come. The two security officers hitched up their belts, crossed their arms, and settled into position.

26

REMEMBERING

Robin threw up her arms. "We did it! We actually came face-to-face with Sibley Carter! And he couldn't make us come down! Not even close! And he's angry about the publicity, so that must mean it's working! It's all working even better than we thought it would!"

"He must think we're stupid," Ariel said. "Saying he would save the tree house. Like that was such a big deal. One poor little tree house surrounded by a bunch of stumps."

"Mr. CEO!" Danny said with contempt. "Mr. Negotiator! It's so *dangerous* up here, huh? Like he would care if we broke our necks!"

Julian took the knife out of his pocket and held it up with a smile. "You guys were amazing. How did you figure it all out? How did you know it would work?"

"It was my idea. I thought of it," Molly said. "I knew it would work and it did!"

"You were the hero!" Robin bent down and placed her hands on Molly's shoulders. "You were fearless!" She looked around at the others. "As soon as she told me her idea, I started thinking and thinking. Trying to figure out how to distract Sibley so he wouldn't notice the pulley seat coming down and how to get him to hold up the knife."

Danny started to hum the theme song to *Mission Impossible*.

"I saw her climb in the pulley seat," Ariel said. "When your uncle went back to talk to those other men. But I thought she was just scared."

"Hah!" Molly crowed. "I wasn't scared. It was all part of the plan." She was still so excited, she was hugging herself and jumping around the tree house.

"I don't like the looks of those two brutes, though," Danny said, eyeing the security guards.

"Do they have guns?" Molly said, suddenly serious.

"Don't be silly." Robin put her arm around Molly. "They're not going to shoot us."

Molly made a terrified face. "Now I *am* scared."

"I think Molly should go home," Ariel said with a frown. "She's done enough."

"If I go down, those men will get me," Molly said.

"I'll go down with you," Robin said. "Then you run home. Those two guys could never catch you. They're like Tweedledum and Tweedledee."

When Molly was a safe distance away, Robin pulled herself

quickly back up to the tree house. The guards didn't move. The children ate their lunch in a state of high alert, keeping an eye open for any sign that the guards might turn violent. But the two men just stood in the shade, occasionally bending their heads toward each other and crossing and uncrossing their arms.

Danny watched them through the binoculars. "No guns," he said. "Definitely not armed. So, can we go down or are we stuck up here?"

"What do you want to go down for?" Robin said.

"A human being cannot stay in a tree indefinitely. Nature calls."

"Julia Butterfly Hill used a bucket."

Danny looked at her in disbelief. "Absolutely not. No buckets. That's where I draw the line. That old outhouse is bad enough."

They glanced over at the motionless guards.

"Well," Robin said, "I guess you might as well give it a try. Even if they caught you, there'd still be three of us left."

"I'll be back in a flash. Come on, Julian, I need you for backup." Julian waited until Danny had jumped out of the pulley seat, then quickly raised it to the top.

The guards didn't even turn their heads.

A few minutes later, a pebble hit Julian in the arm. Danny was waving from behind a giant stump. Julian cautiously lowered the pulley seat and Danny dashed forward, hurled himself into the chair, and pulled himself up at top speed.

Julian whistled and glanced over at the two guards, still rooted in place. "Boy, you made it just in time!"

"Better safe than sorry!"

"I guess we should be grateful they're *not* doing anything," Robin said. "I wonder why they're even here."

"They're spies," said Danny, looking at them through the binoculars again.

"They're just here to intimidate us," Julian said. "And to keep track of when we come down," he added glumly. After the exchange with his uncle, he'd almost convinced himself that they were never coming down. At least, not until Sibley agreed to protect Big Tree Grove forever. They'd been invincible. It was a shock to remember that Popo would be coming to pick them up in two days.

"Even if we have to go down eventually, we still did pretty well," Robin said. "We got the newspaper article and Sibley Carter actually came up here to negotiate with us. Maybe a way will open. It feels a lot closer to opening than it did before."

The security guards made the children feel like prisoners. The air was hot and heavy and the long afternoon stretched before them like an endless chore. They spoke in hushed voices and played cards until nobody cared who won or lost. Finally, Danny was left playing solitaire. Ariel started writing in her diary, and Robin just lay on her back, looking into the sky.

Julian took out his pocketknife and opened the smaller blade. He found Danny's initials on the railing and, next to them, scratched the outline to his own: J.C.L. When he'd carved out a passable version of his initials, he took out his wooden box and placed the knife inside. Now it had a safe home. He'd never lose it again.

As Julian returned the box to the storage bin, he heard a loud "hello" and looked down to see Nancy and Jo-Jo lugging a huge picnic basket through the forest. When they reached the base of the tree, Robin lowered the pulley seat and Nancy placed the heavy basket into it. Then she took out two foil-wrapped packages, two paper cups, two napkins, and a canteen and put them in a paper bag.

"I thought I'd better check on you all. I heard there was a lot of excitement this afternoon," she said as Robin hauled the basket up.

"You're feeding the enemy?" Danny said, eyeing the paper bag. "You should be setting up a blockade! What kind of ally are you?"

"A 'love your enemies' sort of ally," Nancy said with a smile.

Jo-Jo, who had been waving frantically up at them, cried, "I wanna go in the tree house!" Julian brought him up in the pulley seat, and the little boy walked around importantly, inspecting the storage bins and peering out through the rails.

Nancy began chatting with the guards. She handed them the paper bag and, for the first time, they sat down on the ground, digging into their sandwiches and taking swigs from their paper cups.

After a few minutes, Nancy returned and shouted up, "Do you

all need anything? Molly told me Mr. Carter came by. Is everything OK, Julian?"

Julian nodded.

"We're great!" Robin said loudly, glancing at the guards. "Never better. We could stay here forever!"

"Thanks for the chow!" Danny shouted down.

"Well, I should probably head back," Nancy said, obviously reluctant to leave. "You all be careful." She swept her hair behind her ears and looked up at them with a worried smile. "Robin, can you get Jo-Jo back down here?"

Jo-Jo dove into Robin's sleeping bag like a ground squirrel. Robin had to dig him out, squirming and crying, and wrestle him into the chair. "I'll bring you up another day," she said soothingly, and an image came to Julian of Jo-Jo at their age, running through a sun-baked clearing where Big Tree Grove had once stood.

Nancy headed off with Jo-Jo on her shoulders. By the time the children had unpacked the picnic basket, his distant wails had subsided.

Ariel spread a red-checked tablecloth and laid out spaghetti in a metal tin, a green salad, peaches, a small chocolate cake, and four bottles of lemon soda.

"We should make it really nice," she said softly, "to celebrate the successful capture of Julian's pocketknife!" She took a small purple candle out of her backpack and Julian pulled the lighter from his emergency kit and lit it. They ate their candlelight feast in near silence, then lay back against the storage bins, full and happy.

They had just started to clean up when Robin peered through the railing and whispered, "Hey, guys! They're coming over here." The guards lumbered over and set down the paper bag at the base of the trees.

"Tell your mom thanks again for the dinner," one announced. "The canteen's in the bag."

"We're going home!" said the other. "Sleep well!" They waved and trudged away into the forest.

"They're leaving?" Robin stood with her mouth half open.

"This could be a trick," Danny said. "They might come back armed."

"I don't know. They seem pretty harmless," Julian said. "They probably don't want to be here either. It must be pretty boring to sit there watching us all day."

Ariel climbed up and straddled her legs over the edge of one of the railings. "Maybe it was your mom's peace offering." She took a deep breath and looked out into the forest. "Anyway, it's ours again. We should make a mental snapshot so we never forget this night."

"What's that?" Julian said.

"You know how grown-ups can never remember what it was like being a kid?"

He nodded.

"I'm not going to be that way. I remember everything. I

remember standing in my crib. I remember our old house, when I lived here with my mom and dad. And if I think I might forget something, I write it in my diary or I take a mental snapshot. I concentrate really hard and tell myself that I'm going to remember every single thing about that moment."

She sat down on a storage bin. "Come on. I'll show you how. You have to be very, very quiet." She took a deep breath. "First, shut your eyes." They sat down and Julian closed his eyes. "You start with smelling," she said, sniffing hard. "Right now, I can smell spaghetti and lavender from the candle. And trees. The smell of the forest," she said in a low, breathless voice. "Now, listen."

Julian listened to the river, murmuring in the language of water on stone. The birds sang their evening songs. A mosquito whined in his ear and he swatted it away. He could hear his own breathing and Danny, sniffing loudly.

"Now," said Ariel, "concentrate on what you feel."

"I feel something coiling around my leg!" Danny cried. "A rattlesnake! Help!"

"Be quiet, Danny!" Robin ordered.

A light breeze stirred against Julian's face. The wood under his hands was rough and hard.

"OK, now open your eyes. Look all around and remember what you see."

Their faces, in the twilight, looked new to Julian for a moment: Ariel's smile, crooked and mysterious; Danny's look of skeptical good-humor; Robin's steady gaze. The redwoods rose up all around them and they floated among the trunks as if they were riding on a magic carpet. The white sky showed between the treetops.

"Finally," Ariel's voice was hushed, "you have to look in your heart and remember what you're feeling. Like if you're angry or sad . . ."

"Or if you're filled with glee because you defeated your enemy," Danny said.

"Hush!" Robin frowned. "If you don't want to participate, Danny, nobody's making you."

Danny crossed himself. "Forgive me," he said in his Mafia accent.

Julian's stomach told him he was full of spaghetti and his mind told him he was secure in a tree house in a redwood forest, a place unimaginable just a few months before. His new friends had undertaken a brave quest on his behalf, and his father's knife was safely in its wooden box. He had looked down on his uncle and spoken the truth.

"OK, now," Ariel said, looking intently from one to the other, "you will never, ever, ever forget this moment. Even when you're sixteen or twenty-seven or sixty-five. You will always remember it exactly this way, the way it really was."

Was this true? Julian tried to narrow down the moment to its essence: candle smoke, bird song, a soft breeze, his friends' faces, contentment. "I am Julian Carter-Li," he said to himself, "in a tree house in Big Tree Grove with Danny, Robin, and Ariel, having

stood up to Uncle Sibley, and outlasted two security guards."
Certainly he would remember everything in a day, a month, a
year. Why not forever? All he had to do was remember to keep
remembering.

Later, when they'd settled down into their sleeping bags for
the night, Julian lay awake, staring up at the stars. He imagined
Big Tree Grove filled with tree houses. One for each of them. They
would build zip-lines and complicated pulley systems for moving
people, messages, and supplies from one house to the other. They
would never have to touch the ground.

27

UNDER ATTACK

Julian was jolted awake the next morning by something slippery snaking across his face. He reached for it half–asleep and found himself clutching the end of a smooth white climbing rope. There was a tug on the other end.

"Now our rope's stuck!" a voice rang out. "What are we gonna do?"

"Stuck? What'd you get it stuck on?"

"I don't know."

"Aww, you bumbler!"

Julian froze. Maybe his uncle had sent these goons. He looked quickly around. The girls were quiet and Danny was snoring slightly, his mouth slack. Julian gave him a small kick and said in his ear, "Somebody's trying to break in to the tree house."

Danny grasped the danger immediately. He crawled stealthily

306

over to the girls and squeezed their noses until they woke up, sputtering. "We're under attack! Wake up!" he whispered.

Maybe he could catch the intruders off guard, Julian thought, and disarm them. He yanked the rope with all his strength, but whoever was holding the other end had a firm grip. Danny sneezed three times.

"Hey! Somebody up there?" a voice called out.

Robin was sitting up, wide awake, while Ariel blinked and stretched sleepily. They were both in their nightgowns. Julian crawled over to the railing, where the intruders' rope went up and over the beam, and motioned to the others.

Below them stood two disheveled young men wearing enormous, stuffed backpacks. Tied to the backpacks with odd bits of string were pieces of clothing, water bottles, a battered guitar case, and pots and pans of various sizes.

"Go away," said Robin. "You can't make us come down!"

"It's those kids! They're still here!" said the one holding the rope. He wore a tie-dyed bandana and had a scruffy blond beard. "In their jammies!"

"Why wouldn't we be here?" Danny said. "Who are you, anyway?"

"I'm Trout." He nodded at his friend. "And he's Crow."

Crow smiled broadly and touched a hand to his red knit hat in greeting. Beneath his hat, his brown hair hung lankly around his round face and his nose stuck out like a small potato.

"Why are you attacking us?" Danny said.

"Whoa! Slow down. Slow down. We're not the enemy," Crow said. "We're on your side!"

"We're here to join you in the fight for our redwood friends," Trout continued. "We're gonna continue the sacred vigil."

"Well, we're still here," Robin said. "Go away. This is our tree house."

"You're Robin, right? I'm Crow. You're Robin. That's kind of funny. Crow. Robin. Birds of a feather and all that." He reached under his red hat and scratched his head.

"How do you know my name?"

Crow turned to his friend in amazement, then stared back up at them. "Come on—you're famous! Old-growth forever! Yes!"

Robin turned to Julian. "Hey! They read the article!"

"Oh, yes, the article has been read," Trout said, pulling on his scraggly beard. "Read deeply, and digested. By us. By others. Others in high places."

"Let's just say I don't think Mr. Sibley Carter got his forty winks last night," Crow added. And unexpectedly, he closed one round brown eye and gave them a wink.

"What do you mean?" Julian asked.

"Some of our acquaintances were in the neighborhood," Crow said. "With signs."

"Signs and songs," Trout intoned. "Don't forget songs."

"They're *picketing* Carter?" Robin asked in amazement. "I can't believe it! This is fantastic!"

"Are they still there?" Julian could picture Preston staring in consternation at a bunch of noisy protestors outside his window.

"Who knows?" Crow said with an air of mystery.

"Do you hear what they're saying?" Robin shouted. "It's working!"

"If we're so famous, who am I?" Danny called down.

Crow looked at him blankly. "Who's he?" he whispered.

Trout frowned and pulled at his scruffy bead. "D something," he muttered. "Dick, Duck, Dirk . . . no. Darwin? Davey?"

"Lo-pez!" Crow shouted out with a huge grin.

Danny looked down at them severely. "Danny. Danny Lopez."

"And you're Carter's nephew," Trout said, pointing to Julian. "And you!" He pointed to Ariel. "You're that sweet little Earth-lovin' girl."

Ariel frowned. They all stood in silence, staring at each other.

"Maybe you could lower that chair thing down, so we could come up and get acquainted," Trout said at last.

"This could be one of Sibley's tactics," Danny warned.

Robin narrowed her eyes. "No way," she shouted down. "Go find your own tree house."

Their faces fell. "You dumb bumbler," Crow muttered. "I told you this wasn't gonna work."

"I didn't say it *was* going to work, I said it *might* work. I said *if* it worked *then* it would be a good idea."

"No way. You said, 'It'll work. It'll work. We'll scale the tree house!'"

The children glanced quickly at one another.

"We need to talk," Julian said. "Privately."

"No problemo," Trout said, and the two of them ambled over to a nearby tree.

Robin and Ariel went into the cabin and changed into shorts and T-shirts. Then the children gathered together on the deck.

"Maybe we should tell them to come back another day," Julian said. "After we're gone."

"We can't leave our tree house to those guys." Robin looked at him in disbelief. "Look at them!"

They were lying on their backs with their packs still on, like upside-down turtles.

"Whoa!" Trout cried out. "The tree house is below me now. The kids are all upside-down."

Robin had a point, Julian thought. "OK, we won't let them up for now. But what about when we leave? We couldn't stop them even if we wanted to."

"We could set booby traps," Danny said. "They trip the wire, a boulder lands on their heads. Something like that."

The children began discussing the pros and cons of various protection and surveillance devices. Trout and Crow slipped out of their packs and found a seat on an old log, where Trout began picking out songs on his guitar. After a few minutes, a high, nasal voice called out from below, "Excuse me, do you know where the children are?"

They glanced down. A slight, balding man was peering through his glasses at Trout and Crow.

"Children, children, there are children everywhere," Trout sang.

"I've come to see Julian Carter-Li. And the others," the man yelled over the sound of the guitar.

"Children in the bushes, children in the trees, listen to them giggle, listen to them sneeze," Trout wailed.

The man followed Trout's gaze to the tree house. "I'm a reporter from the *Willits News*," he shouted up.

"What can we do for you?" Robin said.

"It's a little hard to talk over this music! Couldn't you come down to make a statement"

"We can't come down," Robin said. "We're protesting!"

"Robin's in the treetops, Trout's stuck on the ground, itty bitty feller's looking all around," Trout sang out.

"Listen, I'm not going to grab you."

Robin sighed. "OK. I guess it's safe enough." She climbed into the pulley-seat and zoomed down to the ground.

"Look at the little robin!" Crow said. "She's flying back to Earth!"

"Wait! I'm coming too!" Danny cried, hauling up the pulley seat. "I've got my sound bites all ready this time!" He lowered himself down and Julian heard him say confidently, "Danny Lopez, that's L-O-P-E-Z."

There was a shout from the direction of the river. Julian

turned and saw a small group making its way through the woods. Most were dressed in hiking clothes. A few were barefoot. A young woman with a pierced belly button called out to Trout and he raised a hand in greeting. Julian felt trouble gnawing at his stomach. Bob wasn't going to like this. Well, Julian thought, what could he do? He hadn't invited them.

Robin reappeared on the tree-house deck. Julian frowned at the newcomers, but she just grinned with excitement and said, "Julian, it's your turn. The reporter wants you to make a statement."

Reluctantly, Julian let himself down in the pulley seat. As soon as his feet hit the ground, Crow grabbed him by the shoulder and pulled him and Danny into a giant embrace. "You guys," he said with feeling. "You're an inspiration to us all!"

Julian smiled weakly.

"Whoo!" Danny said with a shake, "Raise your arm, lose your charm." And he made a quick turn and ducked away.

Julian managed to extricate himself from Crow's other armpit, only to find himself bombarded with questions from the waiting reporter. "Are you and your uncle close? Do you have a good relationship?"

"It's not about my uncle," Julian repeated for the third time. He noticed a few more stragglers crashing their way through the woods from Greeley Road. "We just want to protect Big Tree Grove."

When the reporter finally ran out of questions, Julian returned with relief to the tree house. But when he stepped out onto the deck, he found a serious-looking man in glasses and an earnest young woman sitting on the storage bins, deep in discussion with Robin and the others. He gave them a little wave, then climbed onto the cabin roof. At least there he wouldn't have to answer any more questions.

"Those two know a lot of people," Robin said happily, when the couple finally said good-bye. "They're in touch with all the big environmental groups. They talked to the scientists who spoke at the THP appeal. They said the protests in San Francisco are serious."

"Now we've hit the big time!" Danny shouted.

At ten o'clock, the security guards reappeared. They sized up the crowd nervously, one barking into his radio, the other standing with his jaw open.

The four children huddled together on the deck, looking down at the scene below.

"This is great!" Robin said.

Trout gave a shout and the singing suddenly swelled.

Ariel frowned. "I don't like it."

"Me neither," Julian said.

"I want it to be the way it was before. Just the four of us."

Candle smoke, the evening breeze, the three faces in the tree house, contentment, Julian thought. And most important, except for the calling of the birds, quiet.

Julian was the first to see Sibley coming along the path, dressed now in his weekend wear. Filing resolutely behind him were three officers in uniform, wearing helmets with protective shields. And behind them strode some sort of living action hero, with a black crew cut, heavy boots, and a faded blue T-shirt that fit snugly over his enormous chest.

"All right, everyone, party's over," said the first officer. His voice came out loudly through some kind of hidden microphone.

"This is private property, everybody go home," said another.

The crowd stopped singing and started to chant, *"Save the redwoods, save the redwoods, save the redwoods."*

"If you do not immediately vacate the premises," the first officer repeated, "you will be arrested for trespassing on private property."

The reporter leaned in to take a picture and the officer said, "That goes for you too."

The chanting continued, growing louder and more riotous. The police circled about, batons in hand. Suddenly, the first officer nodded, and the two others grabbed the girl sitting closest to them. She screamed. Ariel reached for Julian's arm and they watched as the two officers half-dragged and half-carried the girl's limp body down the trail.

"Enough!" Trout shouted. "There is no place for violence in the sacred redwood grove!" He stood up, banged out a few chords and started singing, "Let her go, let her go, la di da, la di do." Crow grabbed their backpacks and hoisted one over each shoulder. The earnest couple gave Robin a small salute. The crowd rose slowly to their feet, chanting, "Let her go! Let her go!" Then, like some lost and tattered marching band, they all began to follow Trout down the path. The remaining officer trailed behind them, fingering his baton. The reporter was taking pictures. And gradually, they disappeared into the forest. The sound of chanting grew fainter and fainter. Julian heard another shout, distant this time, and the grove was quiet again.

It was just the children, up in the tree and, down below, Sibley and the giant.

"Children," Sibley said at last, "it's time to come down."

Nobody spoke.

"This man," Sibley said, "is here to help you come down. That's his job. He's a professional. Nobody's going to get hurt."

Julian could feel Ariel's nails digging into his arm.

"The name's Ivan," the huge man said in a tremendously deep voice. "I see you've got a nice little chair hanging there. I think that's the way to go. It's a lot easier for everyone."

"Do you want to go down?" Julian whispered to Robin.

"No way," Robin whispered back. "I'm not leaving."

"Children, this is your last warning," Sibley said.

They watched nervously as Ivan wrapped some kind of strap around the trunk of the tree and adjusted it around his torso. He gave a sudden heave, and pulled himself several feet up the trunk.

"Holy guacamole!" Danny said. "He's climbing straight up the freakin' tree."

They stared mutely as he came higher and higher toward them.

"How's he *doing* that?" Julian finally said.

Robin scowled. "He's got some kind of nails in his boots."

"Jeez-o-man!" Danny said, in awe. "We're being attacked by Paul Bunyan!"

"He's down below us. I don't see how he can get up into the tree house—" Robin began, but before she could finish, a green rope looped up and over a branch and Ivan's slightly bug-eyed face appeared above the railing. They could see each short black hair sticking out of his pale scalp. Within moments, he had swung his huge body over the railing and onto the deck.

"Hello, kids!" Ivan's voice boomed out like a tuba. "Now, what'll it be?" He held out an enormous, muscled arm toward Ariel. "What about you, blondie? Ladies first?"

Ariel shook her head almost imperceptibly.

"Freckles?" He held out his hands appealingly to Robin, but she just crossed her arms and didn't budge.

"Come on, boys. This is going to be a lot easier if you cooperate."

"But we don't *want* to come down," Julian said.

"How much do you weigh?" Ivan asked, appraisingly, his head to the side. "I don't think more than a hundred pounds." Without warning, he lunged toward Julian. He almost grabbed him, but Julian took a step to the side, ran along the storage bins, and scrambled up onto the roof. He crouched down on the sloped shingles, his heart racing. Everything around him seemed to have a hard, bright edge around it.

Ivan looked down at Sibley and lifted his gorilla hands in a questioning gesture.

"Leave the others," Sibley said. "But get Julian. We can't let this go on any longer."

Julian looked around for an escape route, but before he knew it, Ivan had bounded up on the roof next to him.

"Jump, Julian!" Robin cried, and Julian jumped free just in time. He ran to the far side of the tree house and climbed up and over the railing. His toes were on the tree-house floor and his hands were clinging tightly to the wooden rails, but he felt precariously balanced, hanging from the outside of the wooden structure that had always safely enclosed him.

Ivan came to the edge of the railing. Julian could see the pale blue of his buggy eyes and smell the detergent from his T-shirt.

The only sound was his heart pounding. Then, with a loud "Hi-*ya*!" Danny made a flying leap onto Ivan's back and began punching him on the shoulders.

Ivan's enormous bulk barely quivered. Slowly, with Danny still clinging to his back and pounding furiously, he reached out and gripped Julian's wrist. With his free hand, he grabbed the green rope, and clipped it to the belt loop of Julian's jeans.

Julian felt helpless and, at the same time, overcome by a

wave of rage so powerful it completely filled his head. "No!" he screamed, louder than he'd ever screamed before. "Let go of me! Let go! It's not fair!" He couldn't stop himself. It was almost as if his voice were coming from somebody else.

And then, from far below, in a commanding tone that broke through the sound of his own screaming, Julian heard a raspy voice cry out, "Young man, let go of the boy immediately. This has gone far enough."

28

THE INTERROGATION

Ivan obeyed, dropping Julian's wrist instantly. Danny slith-
ered off Ivan's back to the ground. Julian clung to the
tree-house railing, breathing hard, filled with a hot energy.
The voice had been low and aristocratic, like some grande dame
from an old black-and-white movie. Julian craned his neck to
see who had spoken, but his view was blocked by Ivan's enormous
chest.

Sibley cleared his throat. "I don't know what you're up to, but
trust me, this is not the time or the place—"

"It's a good thing I came when I did and not some camera
crew. Can you imagine how that scene would have played on the
evening news?"

"What *are* you doing here?"

"The board is not pleased, Sibley. Witherspoon is apoplectic.
The controversy is driving away clients."

"What controversy?" Sibley's face was an angry red. "A bunch of tree huggers? It'll all die down in a matter of days."

"Sibley, you've lost your perspective," the voice continued, with an air of hypnotic authority. "IPX against four children in a tree house? You must realize this has become a public-relations fiasco. And the protests are only going to get bigger."

"Then they'll be quashed," Sibley said in an ugly tone.

Ivan shifted slightly, and Julian could make out below him a formidable-looking woman with gleaming white hair, dressed in a red jacket and skirt. She was looking up at Sibley with unflinching eyes. Behind them both stood Bob, his arms crossed, his face stern.

"I appreciate your intentions," Sibley continued in a more ingratiating tone. "But you're not on the board anymore. I'm taking care of this. The protestors have been removed. The children are coming down."

"Sibley, you simply do not appreciate the magnitude of the problem. You can't just go on ignoring the board's directives. They want this incident ended—the article was the last straw. The only question remaining is what to do with the property? And to resolve that," she lifted her head and Julian felt her search out his face and study it with unwarranted intensity, "we need to bring these children down from the tree house and give them a seat at the table."

There had been no question of obeying the Lady, as the children dubbed her. Ivan, chastened, dropped quietly down on his rope.

Bob gave Sibley a dark glance, then watched over the children as they descended one by one on the pulley seat. He instructed them to return to the house, then turned and followed Sibley and the Lady down the trail toward Greeley Road.

It was only when they had crossed the river that the children realized they had abandoned their protest. But somehow, Julian thought, they had all understood, without discussing it, that they had no real choice. They didn't feel defeated. To the contrary, they were elated, too excited to talk clearly, unsure of what would happen next.

Before they even entered the house, they could hear Bob's voice, low and angry. When they reached the kitchen, he stopped talking abruptly. The Lady was seated at the table, next to a sleek laptop and a pad of legal paper. Sibley shifted uncomfortably in his seat.

"You see, they're here now," the Lady said without smiling. "Children, please have a seat." Julian sat down as far away from Sibley as possible, with Danny and Robin on either side of him.

"Hello, Julian," the Lady said. Julian wondered again why she had singled him out from the others. "Do you have any idea who I am?"

To simply say no seemed rude. And the more Julian looked at her, the more he felt as though he had seen her before. Maybe she was in the news. Somebody famous, like a senator or an ambassador. He glanced at Robin, but she seemed just as perplexed as he was.

"I'm sorry," he finally mumbled.

"Let's just say, for now, that I know who you are. I've been watching you, and I have a number of questions I would like you to answer for me." She didn't wait for him to respond, but continued briskly. "To begin with, could you tell me how is it that you came to be interested in Big Tree Grove?"

Julian blanched. "Um," he said after a moment. "It's next door to Robin's house."

"Of course." She gave a nod in Robin's direction. "And you and Miss Elder were pen pals, if I remember correctly. And that precipitated your sudden departure from Sibley's home." Her gray eyes gave him no hint of what was coming. "Is that correct?"

Julian nodded.

"And how do you explain the amazing coincidence that your pen pal, Miss Elder, just happens to live next door to the IPX timber holdings?"

The moment Julian had dreaded had finally arrived. Perhaps they had been tricked after all. Perhaps the whole conversation with Sibley had merely been a ruse to get them down from the tree house.

"I can't really explain it," Julian said at last.

"Then perhaps I can shed some light on the matter." She pressed a button on her laptop and an image appeared on the opposite wall. "Ah, the wonders of modern technology," she said in a pleased voice. "Tell me, do you recognize this e-mail?"

There, on the wall, appeared his name, "JULIAN," and beneath it, the terrible phrases that still haunted him—"lacks even the most basic social graces," "mother's lifestyle," "Julian does resemble his father," "the sullenness, etc.," "intensive math." Julian felt his heart start to beat faster. Sibley was studying the projection with narrowed eyes.

Julian searched the face of the white-haired Lady for some clue as to how to answer. She was looking at him with an intensity that he took at first for anger, but then decided was simply curiosity.

"Yes," he finally stammered.

"Of course, you do," she said, sounding pleased. "And this one?"

At the top, it said "SIBLEY CARTER IS A MORON AND A WORLD-CLASS JERK!!!"

Sibley's face flushed to a bright pink. Robin squirmed in her chair and glanced nervously at her father. "You recognize it as well?"

"Yes." Julian's stomach was starting to churn. He was afraid he was going to throw up.

"But you erased the e-mails so your uncle wouldn't know you'd seen them."

"Well, yes." Julian didn't dare look in Sibley's direction.

"And yet here they are! You're surprised, I see, but I've learned that a computer never forgets." She carefully pressed a few buttons, and the images disappeared.

"You see, I'm a great fan of mysteries, and when I saw your face in the paper, I knew this was my chance. Coincidence is the stuff of fiction, not real life. Something more than coincidence brought you to Robin Elder's house, and I came all the way here to find out what. And, now, I believe I have succeeded. It was Sibley's letter, followed by Miss Elder's e-mail, which actually triggered your departure from Sibley's home. Am I correct?"

"I guess so," Julian said. "Well, they were already sending me away."

"Indeed. And prior to erasing the letter from Miss Elder, you relayed it to your good friend, Mr. Danny Lopez."

Julian nodded mutely. Danny, for once, had nothing clever to say.

"You were able to manage all this while Sibley was away at a meeting, when you were alone, ill, in his office. For hours, so I understand. Is that true?"

"Well, the first e-mail had my name on it," Julian ventured as a sort of apology.

"And the other was quite irresistible, I'm sure." She stared in an amused way at Sibley. "You subsequently made contact with Miss Elder. And ran away to her house."

Julian nodded.

"You were, however, apprehended by Daphne and returned to San Francisco and, ultimately, to your maternal grandmother. And then, a press release was issued."

Julian nodded warily.

"A heartwarming press release. All about how IPX would do the right thing and save Big Tree Grove." She pressed another key and the press release appeared on the wall.

Seeing it, Julian couldn't help but feel a surge of pride. He glanced at Danny, who was watching the woman warily. Bob scanned the text against the wall.

"Unfortunately," the Lady continued, "the *Chronicle* didn't print the press release in full, or even in part. Sibley had to provide me with a copy. But still, the grandeur of your vision! And the attention to detail!" For the first time, she looked truly happy. "At first, I thought you must have had help. But the more closely I investigated, the more I was certain that you acted alone. With the assistance, of course, of your partner in crime, Mr. Lopez."

Partner in crime? Danny looked worried.

"And then of course, there was the password! Tell me, how did you manage to puzzle that out?"

"Just a lucky guess." Julian wasn't about to admit going through Sibley's drawers.

"'If at first you don't *succeed*, try, try, again,'" the Lady said archly. "I used to tell your uncle that long ago. I suppose it sunk in. But, in any case, the faux press release did *not* succeed. There was no change in IPX policy. No noble gesture from Sibley. Just pabulum spit out by a corporate spokeswoman."

Julian wasn't sure what pabulum was, but he nodded.

"And then," she said, eyes shining, "you began your protest. And you got quite a bit of press coverage, thanks, no doubt, to Mrs. Li. But really, did you ever actually believe," she asked in her cool tone, "that you would succeed? That you could save Big Tree Grove?"

Julian didn't know what to say. They had thought, walking

back to the house in such high spirits, that they *had* succeeded. He had the sensation that the Lady was hiding something, holding something back. And, yet, the Lady's curiosity was disarming. Her fascination with the subject seemed to mirror his own.

"I'm not really sure," he said slowly. "Big Tree Grove is still there and I guess it's not completely over until it's cut down. Robin's mom always says, 'A way will open.'"

"And do you believe this?"

Did he? He chose his words carefully. "Maybe not on its own. But maybe, if you keep trying to really think about how to make something happen, it could happen. Not always. But if you're lucky."

"And do you think a way will open to save Big Tree Grove?"

"No." And Julian suddenly realized the childishness of all their efforts. He knew in his heart that Big Tree was doomed, that soon it would exist only in his memory.

"Why not?"

"Because the Elders and the scientists did everything they could to save Big Tree and Robin and Ariel and Danny and I did too and none of it worked. And the THP is approved and it's all legal and there's nothing to stop them from logging it."

"But, as you wisely pointed out, it's not logged yet. A way could still open."

"Not unless you're the way," Julian said ruefully.

She seemed delighted with his answer and looked about the table as if the others would share her delight.

"But you see, my dear, I am."

Just then, the door slammed open, and Molly and Jo-Jo ran in with their mother, and behind them, laughing and calling out their names, was Preston, his face shining and his legs strangely bare-looking in shorts and summer sandals.

"Gram!" he said. "I milked a goat! Julian! Daddy—how did you get here?"

29

THE CHILDREN'S EVERLASTING REDWOOD GROVE

Julian sat stunned in the midst of the chatter and buzz that had transformed the room. This formidable woman was Gram? His own grandmother?

She owed him a few computer games, was Julian's first fleeting thought.

Then, suddenly it sank in that she wasn't from IPX, or the police, or the FBI. The truth had been revealed, all his crimes and secrets brought to light, and nobody, it seemed, was going to send him to prison.

Last of all, it dawned on him what she had said. That somehow she was going to help save Big Tree Grove.

"You're Gram?" he said wonderingly.

"It's time we were properly introduced," she resumed, after

smoothing Preston's damp hair away from his forehead. "My name is Abigail Winslow Carter."

A.W. Carter, Julian realized. The one who'd sent the first e-mail.

Sibley cleared his throat. "Mother, I'm going to stop you here. I don't think you—"

"Sibley, just hold on." She turned to Julian. "I thought it was time we met in person. I admire your gumption. Your grandfather had gumption. Whatever he put his mind to, he accomplished. Unfortunately, my sons didn't inherit Jack's character."

There was not a hint of apology in her voice. Julian glanced over at Sibley, who was staring down at his fingers.

She cleared her throat. "My boys never got along," she said in a formal tone. "Sibley resented Billy from the day he was born. And Jack didn't understand your father either. They had a terrible fight, and then Billy just disappeared."

She stared at Julian as though she was trying to read some-thing in his face. "We didn't even know of your existence for years. And then, just when it seemed that reconciliation might be possible, Billy was in that terrible accident. My Jack passed away a few weeks later. I stopped traveling. Oh," she continued in a voice that, for the first time, sounded tired and old, "there's no excuse. I knew you were here, and yet I didn't know you or what you might be like, and I thought your father had brought me enough heartache.

"When I saw your picture in the paper, so like your father—

the shape of the face, something about the eyes—and yet so unlike him, I said to myself, 'Finally, somebody in the family with gumption. It must have skipped a generation.' I read the article from top to bottom—so many mysteries waiting to be solved. I flew out immediately. And piece by piece, I put the puzzle together.

"And then, of course, there was this irresistible piece of fund-raising." She picked up a black leather purse, pulled out a white envelope, and unfolded a piece of lined paper. She passed the paper to Julian and he saw Preston's neat handwriting:

Dear Gram,

I was wondring if you would you like to buy some redwood trees? It's for my cusin, Julian, who you don't know but he is very nice. I did a Final Report at school and for $1 million you can buy 6 whole trees. (Maybe that does not sound like too many, but if you have any friends, maybe they could buy some too.)

Also, thank you for the computer game. I like it a lot.

Love,
Preston

Preston was leaning against Gram and beaming happily.

"I told you I knew somebody who could help," he said in his piping voice. "Wasn't that a good idea I had?"

"Between Preston's letter and the newspaper article," Gram continued, "how could I stay in Boston? Especially when IPX was floundering. I served on the IPX board for years, you know, when Jack was ill. What a shame that Sibley couldn't stand up and protect those magnificent trees."

"Really, Mother. I don't think these personal attacks are necessary—" Sibley began, but she waved her hand dismissively.

"So, now what is to be done? That's the real question. What is to be done with Big Tree?"

Robin had started squirming in her seat and, after a moment, she could no longer contain herself. "Big Tree Grove should be protected," she called out urgently. "It should be protected so that it can never be cut down."

Gram smiled. "Miss Elder. I thought you might have a few ideas to start us off." She began scribbling in her note pad.

"Ever," Ariel added. "Not cut down, ever."

"And you should plant new trees," Julian said.

"Permanent protection," Gram was taking it all down in a neat, slanted cursive. "Replanting."

"And, no offense, but I think you need a new boss," Danny said. "Somebody who actually *likes* redwood trees."

"But Gram," Preston asked, "aren't *you* buying the redwoods?"

"Me? Good gracious, no! What would I do in Boston with a California redwood grove? And then, all those taxes!"

"You could give it to a conservation group, or make it into a park, or something," Robin said.

"But it's our tree house," Molly wailed. "We can't give away the tree house."

Everybody was silent again.

"Perhaps it would be more appropriate to keep Big Tree Grove for the young," Gram said. "The older generations have certainly done enough damage." She sighed. "When I was a girl, the world felt new to me. Untouched. I suppose you don't feel that way anymore."

Julian imagined Big Tree Grove going on and on for miles and miles, the giant redwoods stretching from ridge to ridge. No houses, no roads, no fences. That world wasn't so long ago, he thought. Not even two hundred years ago, the forest had stood fresh and untouched for the next generation.

"What if it were a forest *for* children?" he said.

"We could have school groups come and they could raise money and we could buy more land and more redwoods." Robin's straight eyebrows were knit together and she was twisting her braid around her finger. "Just like they do for the rain forest."

"Zip lines," Danny said. "And bridges to go from one tree to the next. And maybe another tree house."

Ariel frowned. "I don't know. It should be beautiful, like it is now."

"We don't want all the ferns trampled down," Robin agreed.

"The Children's Everlasting Redwood Grove," Ariel said dreamily. Gram continued writing in her note pad.

"No fences," Julian said. "No ticket booths or snack bars or parking lots."

Danny groaned. "No snack bars? That's un-American."

"Definitely no snack bars," Robin said. "And not too big. It'll be educational, for all those poor, ignorant city kids like Julian and Danny."

Danny gave Robin a phony smile. "It's not like everybody's going to be swarming over this place anyway," he said. "I mean, it's about a million miles down a dirt road."

"I don't know." Ariel looked doubtful. "Maybe it should be just for us. I didn't like it with all those people there."

Julian considered. "But what about Jo-Jo? And Preston? And kids who aren't even born, maybe." Kids like him, who never knew that something like Big Tree existed.

"Anything else?" Gram said after a moment of silence. Nobody spoke.

"Then we are in agreement." Gram looked down at her note pad and read aloud: "'Big Tree Grove is to be permanently protected from timber harvesting and replanted with redwood seedlings in appropriate locations. The grove is to be maintained and enjoyed for the education of the young and future generations. Fences, ticket booths, snack bars, and parking lots are strictly prohibited.'"

They nodded uncertainly.

"Julian, I want to make sure that you concur with these conditions."

Julian looked at her, puzzled. "Sure," he said.

"In that case, it's settled." Gram put down her note pad.

There was another long pause. Julian was starting to feel that his new grandmother was a little too fond of mysteries.

"What's settled?" he finally asked.

"The board has already approved the sale."

"For ten million dollars!" As soon as he blurted it out, Julian realized that it wasn't polite to mention what people paid for things.

"Oh, my no! I believe that Sibley's profit estimates turned out to be, shall we say, somewhat inflated. The acreage of old-growth on the property is really quite small. Mr. Elder checked it all out for us."

"You talked to Bob?"

"Of course, it was all quite rush, rush. That's the way it is in the business world. In light of all the controversy, I think IPX got quite a fair bargain."

"But I thought you didn't want a California redwood forest," Julian said. Everything was moving so fast his head was starting to spin.

"That's correct." Gram gave Julian another piercing look. "I'll have the lawyers draw up the papers for you to sign as soon as possible."

"Me?" Julian looked at his grandmother in astonishment.

"Him!" Sibley shouted. "You don't mean to tell me you're transferring the property to—to Julian?" He stared at his mother in outrage.

"With a conservation easement protecting the trees in

perpetuity," she said calmly. "Of course, the easement will reduce the property value. He won't be able to cut down the redwoods later, if he has a change of heart."

"I won't have a change of heart!" Julian said, but his voice was drowned out by Sibley, who roared, "Well, of all the low tricks!" He had risen out of his chair and was pacing up and down the room. Then, abruptly, he unclenched his fists and changed his tone. "Mother, please consider what you're doing. You don't even know this boy. This is a major financial decision."

"If you had shown Julian the least kindness, none of this would have happened in the first place."

"Julian," Sibley said, "is an ungrateful little liar, just like his father."

"All right, Mr. Carter! Now you've crossed the line!" Bob strode to the kitchen door in a fury and opened it wide. "I think it's time for you to go!"

Silence filled the room. It was so quiet, Julian could hear the kitchen clock ticking.

"You will apologize to Julian at once," Gram said in a low voice.

Sibley's mouth was open, his breathing was heavy, his cheeks were flushed and sweaty. "I was out of line," he finally said.

Gram gave him a steely look.

"My apologies," Sibley said, with the pained expression of a person undergoing an uncomfortable medical procedure. Then, abruptly, he straightened his shoulders, picked up his briefcase, and began taking short side steps toward the door. "I can't stay any longer, I'm afraid. I have an important meeting to attend. Mother, let me know the board's decision. I will facilitate to the extent feasible. Preston, I'll see you back in the city." He gave a quick nod to the room and, averting his face from Bob's angry glare, he ducked out of the door.

The children looked nervously from one to another.

"Well!" Gram took a deep breath. "Where were we?"

Robin was looking in bewilderment at Gram. "I don't understand what's going on. Are you saying you're giving away the Greeley property? To Julian?"

"You know, my dear," Gram said, turning to Julian. "Once we found out Billy had a son, Jack talked about providing for you. He would certainly have been proud of what you did. It's a pity he's not here to see it."

"Dad? Is that what she's saying?" Robin asked.

Julian looked up and saw Bob watching him with a wide grin. "Apparently, that's the plan."

Robin started shrieking, "I can't believe it!" She jumped out of her chair and threw her arms around Julian. "You'll be our next-door neighbor!" She started dancing around the room. "Can you believe how lucky we are? Isn't it lucky that I sent that e-mail? And Julian found it? And Operation Redwood worked! I can't believe it! We saved Big Tree!" She ran over to Gram and gave her a huge embrace, which she accepted with somewhat flustered dignity. "Oh, thank you, Mrs. Carter. Thank you a thousand times!" And Robin ran out the door and started ringing the bell again and again.

With the pealing of the bell, everybody started talking at once. Danny gave Julian a high five. The girls all shrieked and hugged each other. Preston leaned against Gram's leg, smiling at all the hullabaloo.

Nancy came up behind where Julian was sitting and put both hands on his shoulders. "You kept saying a way would open," Julian said, looking up at her. "I told my grandmother that—before I knew who she was. I told her a way would open and it turned out she was the way!"

Nancy burst into laughter and gave him a hug. "I just keep remembering the day I met you. When you looked so frightened and hungry and Bob kept going on about how you might be some kind of felon. And look what you've done! Look what you all have done for Big Tree!"

30

TO BIG TREE GROVE

Everyone spent the next day preparing for the celebration. The four operatives trekked happily together to Big Tree Grove, while Preston and Molly ran ahead, swinging Jo-Jo between their arms. When they reached Big Tree, Julian said grandly, "This is it, Preston! A real old-growth forest—just like in your report!"

Preston stood looking up at the giant trees. "You got my wish!" he said. "But you got even more than six redwood trees. You got a whole forest!" He peered through the trees. "Are there any fishers here?"

"Well, I don't know if you'll see a fisher today," Julian said. "But I can take you up in the tree house. I've been wanting to show it to you forever."

Preston walked solemnly around the tree house, examining Julian's freshly carved initials, the storage boxes, the interior of the cabin. Down below, Danny and Robin cleared away the scattered branches on the forest floor and cleaned out the old fire ring. Ariel taped streamers to the giant trunks and Molly blew up the balloons.

As the shadows lengthened, Nancy and Bob trooped in on the Greeley Road trail, carrying folding chairs and card tables, then returned home to haul more supplies. Gram had spent the morning in town, tracking down a "fah-bulous" cake, which arrived in splendor, borne high by two men in white coats, with CHILDREN'S EVERLASTING REDWOOD GROVE written in green cursive over chocolate frosting.

Bob and Nancy returned later in the day, with Popo, Luciana, and Eduardo trailing behind them. They all carried an unbalanced assortment of bowls and pots and, like everybody who entered the grove for the first time, they stopped for a moment, peering up at the treetops. The boys ran over to help them unload.

"Oh, thank you!" Luciana said as she set a heavy pot of beans on the table. She was dressed festively in a flowered dress and red sandals. "Papa and I couldn't stay away from the party! Oh, you must be so excited!" she said, wrapping her arms around Julian. "We're so proud of you. Ooooh, and you too, Danny." She gave him a brief inspection, before squeezing him tightly. "I saw your picture in the newspaper. They hung the article on the bulletin board at work! You guys are like little heroes!"

The two boys stood grinning sheepishly as she hugged them again.

"Now, Danny, you come with me," Luciana said, pulling him by the arm. "Help Papa and me set up all the food."

Popo smiled proudly at Julian. "So, your protest worked. Not exactly how you intended, but even better. That doesn't happen too often!"

"Thanks for sending Bruce!" Julian said. "You saw the article?"

"It's in my scrapbook," Popo answered. "And I e-mailed a copy to your mother. I thought you might want to tell her the end of the story yourself."

Julian imagined how surprised his mom would be when she saw the picture of him and Danny up in the tree house. And she wouldn't even know the half of it.

"If we hadn't been in the newspaper, none of the other stuff would have happened," Julian said. "The protestors and the board getting upset and Gram coming out . . ." He turned to Gram, who had just arrived and was fussing over the cake.

"Gram," he called out, "do you know my grandmother, Eleanor Li?"

"Abigail Carter," Gram said, taking a few steps toward them and casting an appraising eye over Popo. "Unfortunately, we never met. But I'm sure we won't be strangers for long. We appear to have something very significant in common."

Julian stared at the two grandmothers. Gram stood tall and aristocratic in her red suit. A smile played on her lips as though she were contemplating some private joke. Popo peered through her glasses with a journalist's exacting gaze, her dark eyes taking measure of everything she saw. It suddenly struck Julian how strange it was that he should be descended from two such different people, how weird and improbable that their DNA would end up mixed together in his own body.

"So, Julian," Gram said, "Preston and I have a little tradition where he comes to visit me in Cape Cod for the last week in August. If you came, the two of you could amuse each other."

He would fly at last! Julian turned to Popo. "Do you think I could?" he asked.

"Well, your mother will be back on the first of September, so we'll have to check with her," Popo said. "And I was hoping you'd help me go house hunting. I've put in for a transfer to the San Francisco office."

Gram smiled tightly. "You're moving to San Francisco?"

"I'm starting to miss the fog," Popo said. "And I wouldn't mind being closer to Julian and his mother."

"Of course," Gram said. "Though we'll have to discuss Thanksgiving. I'd love to have my two grandsons together. Thanksgiving is a big tradition in the Carter clan."

"Don't forget, Julian is my *only* grandchild," Popo answered.

Julian watched his grandmothers in astonishment. Beneath their courteous veneer, the two of them were practically fighting over him.

"Well, Eleanor," Gram said, with a laugh, "it looks like we'll have to determine how to share Julian. He may end up with quite a few frequent flyer miles."

"Julian! Julian!" Jo-Jo was calling from the pulley seat. "Take me up! Take me up in the tree house!"

Julian shifted Jo-Jo into his lap and hoisted him up to the top where he walked about happily, slamming the lids of all the bins. The three girls sat chatting together on the cabin roof. Danny and Preston were playing rummy. Below them, Big Tree Grove stood transformed. The ancient trees were festooned with green and gold streamers and balloons and every square inch of the tables was covered with food. Luciana was handing out little glasses of grape juice and champagne.

Julian heard a sharp clinking sound and looked down to see Gram tapping a spoon against her champagne glass.

"Good afternoon," she announced in her grand voice. "I would like to officially welcome you all to the unofficial dedication of Big Tree Grove. And to thank you all for responding so generously to my call for a little celebration." She looked about the gathering with a patrician air. "Welcome."

Gram's eyes rested on Popo. She hesitated a moment, then said graciously, "There's one person here today who shares with me the honor of being Julian's grandmother, and I would be most appreciative if she would start us off with a toast."

Popo looked surprised, but she took a step forward and stood for a moment, gathering her thoughts. "To the children!" she said, in a surprisingly loud voice. "May they continue to know what's worth fighting for. And may they continue to explore new places and make new friends. They fought hard to protect this beautiful place. I know their future will be bright!"

"Hear! Hear!" the children shouted from the tree house, and Nancy called out, "When we first met Julian, he kind of washed up on our doorstep." She gave him a fond nod. "But since then, he's won our hearts. We hope he'll come back next summer and every summer! He's like part of the family now!"

"And here's to the rest of them too!" Bob said, lifting his glass to the tree house. "We've watched Robin and Ariel grow up to be the outstanding young ladies they are. And Julian and Danny are pretty terrific too. I knew Ed Greeley all my life, and it would have broken his heart to see these trees cut down. And these four kids—nothing could stop them. Even me!" he said with a grin. "So I would like to give a toast to four fabulous kids!"

"And Molly!" Robin yelled down from the tree house. "She did as much as any of us!"

"And Preston!" Julian called. "Our best fund-raiser!"

"To all the kids, then," said Bob, raising his glass to the tree house. Everybody cheered again and sipped from their glasses.

"Attention! Attention, please!" Danny called out from the tree house deck. "I would like to make a toast to Julian, the new heir to Big Tree Grove! He's been my best friend since kindergarten! He's never let me down! What can I say? He's awesome! He's brilliant! He made me do some things I didn't want to, but I forgive him! Three cheers for Julian! Hip-hip-hooray!" And then from all around, cries of "Hip-hip-hooray! Hip-hip-hooray!" lifted into the air.

After the cheers died down, everybody looked around for the next toast.

Finally, Gram stepped forward again. "If everybody has had a chance to speak, I will take my turn." She cleared her throat abruptly. "It gives me enormous pleasure to dedicate Big Tree Grove to the young people of this great country." She raised her glass to Julian in the tree house.

"Not so long ago, I lost a son. I almost lost my grandson as well." Her proud voice cracked for a moment, and she hastily wiped at her eyes. "But through his actions, he reached across a continent and found me. I hope it is not too late for us to have many fine years together."

The forest glowed in the late afternoon sun. Gram took a deep breath and looked about at the majestic trees, the arching ferns, the tree house perched in midair. "There is no greater legacy I could leave Julian than to preserve and protect Big Tree Grove. It is an extraordinary place. I find my grandson and his friends extraordinary as well—extraordinarily courageous, extraordinarily farsighted, extraordinarily clear-thinking. May they have these qualities always."

The glasses were raised again. Julian drank the sweet grape juice and looked at the faces of the friends and relatives gathered around.

"To grandmothers!" Robin cried out.

"To friends!" Ariel raised her glass high in the air.

"To Big Tree Grove!" Julian called exuberantly from the tree house. "May it stand forever! And now, let the feasting begin!"

The celebration lasted well into the evening. There was all the food to eat. There was a ribbon-cutting ceremony and a formal tree planting, both hastily organized by Robin and Ariel. Then, there was the cake. Julian got the first piece, filled with chocolate and coffee and cream and bits of toffee—every bit as fabulous as Gram had promised.

Nobody wanted to leave. Cups were refilled. The last of the cake disappeared. The pulley seat creaked up and down. As the light faded, the children began gathering wood for a fire. Gram asked to see Julian's pocketknife, and he went to the tree house to retrieve it.

From the top, he could see everybody assembled and he climbed onto the roof for a better view. Standing with a foot on each slanted side, he stretched the happy stretch of a boy filled with chocolate cake, and his fingers grazed a branch above him. With surprise, he realized that by standing on the very tip of the roof, he could just reach his hands around the branch. He hoisted himself up and swung one leg over, and then the other. Now, the slender branches led up and up like a staircase, and Julian climbed until he was high above the ground, high above the tree house, higher even than some of the treetops. The bark was rough and sticky under his hands. In the twilit space between the branches, a distant star blinked into view. Far below, the campfire was shining, and he could hear the sound of singing rising up toward him.

Soon, he would climb down and warm his hands over the bright, smoky fire. But for the moment, Julian stood with a glad heart among the whispering branches, feeling the light wind rocking him to and fro and watching the almost full moon rise in the evening sky.

AUTHOR'S NOTE

While *Operation Redwood* is a work of fiction, the true history of the battle over California's redwoods is a fascinating story of money, courage, greed, protest—and even a few tree-sitters.

In 1848, when gold was first discovered in California, two million acres of redwood trees blanketed the northern coast. Most of this land was bought up (sometimes fraudulently) by large timber companies. The companies proceeded to chop down trees as fast as they could, first using axes and cross-cut saws, then moving on to chain saws and giant machinery. By the 1960s, most of the original redwood forest had been cut down.

One company, Pacific Lumber Company, took a more long-range approach. It had been in the logging business since 1863 and owned more than 200,000 acres of redwood forest along California's northern coast—an area about the size of New York

City. While other companies clear-cut their land, removing every tree over hundreds of acres, Pacific Lumber practiced selective logging—leaving up to 30 percent of the trees in the harvest area standing. By the 1980s, the largest groves of ancient redwoods left on private land ("the Headwaters") were owned by Pacific Lumber.

All this valuable timber caught the eye of an investor from Texas named Charles Hurwitz. His company, Maxxam, Inc., was one of the richest and most powerful in the world. In 1985, he hired consultants to fly over the Pacific Lumber lands. They concluded that the trees were worth a fortune. He began quietly buying shares of stock in Pacific Lumber until Maxxam was ultimately able to take control of the whole company. But there was a cost—$750 million dollars. To make enough money to pay off this debt, Pacific Lumber began chopping down trees twice as fast as it had before. And it began plans for cutting down the Headwaters.

Many people were outraged that one of the most beautiful and rare forests in the world could be destroyed for a single company's profit. Environmental groups filed lawsuits to stop the logging. People chained themselves to the trees. Thousands swarmed a sawmill where the trees were cut into lumber and formed human chains blocking bulldozers and logging trucks. Some activists moved into the trees. The most famous, a young woman named Julia Butterfly Hill, lived in her tree, nicknamed Luna, for over two years, while her friends and fellow activists provided her with necessities such as food, water, clothes, and batteries. Some tree-sitters came down on their own. Others were brought down by "Climber Dan," a skilled tree climber hired by Pacific Lumber to remove the protestors by force.

The fight over Headwaters Forest finally got so big that the United States government and the state of California stepped in. In 1999, they paid Pacific Lumber $480 million in exchange for 10,000 acres of ancient and second-growth redwoods that would be protected in a preserve. Eight additional redwood groves, totaling 8,000 acres, were spared from logging for a fifty-year period. While Pacific Lumber could continue logging on its remaining land, it had to follow a Habitat Conservation Plan—a set of rules designed to protect endangered species like the Northern spotted owl, the coho salmon, and the marbled murrelet, a seabird that nests in old-growth forests.

The story didn't stop with the Headwaters deal. There was continued controversy over whether the Habitat Conservation Plan did enough to protect wildlife and streams and allowed too much logging in the land outside the preserves. In 2007, Pacific Lumber filed for bankruptcy and a year later, its lands were taken over by another company that promised to be a better steward for California's redwood country. Many will be watching to see if this promise is fulfilled.

Today, experts estimate that roughly 100,000 acres of old-growth redwood remain in the world. Fortunately, most is protected in parks and preserves like the Headwaters Forest

Reserve. About twenty percent, however, is located on private lands where it may be subject to logging under state and local regulations. Redwoods continue to need the protection of people, young and old, who care about forests and the diverse life they support.

ABOUT THE AUTHOR

S. Terrell French grew up near Washington, D.C., and spent her summers running barefoot in the forest. She graduated from Harvard College and Berkeley Law, and once spent two months as a Forest Service volunteer in Misty Fiords National Monument in Alaska. She currently lives with her husband and three children in the very foggiest part of San Francisco, where she divides her time between writing and practicing environmental law. She tries to visit the redwoods as often as possible. You can visit her at www.operationredwood.com.

ACKNOWLEDGMENTS

This book would not have been possible without the hard work and optimism of my agent, Kate Schafer Testerman, and the vision of Susan Van Metre, whose editing was always marked by thoughtfulness, flexible thinking, and a sense of humor. Special thanks also to Maureen McLane, my earliest champion and the catalyst for all that followed; to Tina Bennett, for opening a door; and to Charles and Vanna Rae Bello, for sharing their home and work in the redwoods with my family.

I am truly grateful to the friends and neighbors who fed and cared for my family, took walks with me, and generally cheered me on during the writing of this book, as well as to the communities at Clarendon and Shute, Mihaly & Weinberger. I would also like to thank those who took the time to review early (and later) drafts of this book, particularly my young readers, Jules Cowan, Izzy Miller, and Kara Scherer. Françoise and Jim French, Kelly

ACKNOWLEDGMENTS

Kilcoyne and Melissa French, and Chris and Judy White were a constant source of reassurance and encouragement; special acknowledgment is due to my sister for her many good ideas (like tree houses) and my mother, who followed *Operation Redwood*'s progress with unflagging enthusiasm. My husband, Sai, provided frequent logistical aid and whatever else I asked of him. Finally, *Operation Redwood* was inspired by, and is dedicated to, my children, Nathan, Clara, and William, who taught me the value of perseverance and waited patiently for this book to come out.

This book was designed by Maria T. Middleton and art directed by Chad W. Beckerman. The text is set in 12.5-point FF Atma Serif, a modern typeface with transitional characteristics similar to Baskerville. FF Atma Serif was designed by Alan Dague-Greene in 2001.

The interior of this book was printed on recycled paper.

KEEP READING!

Heart of a Samurai
MARGI PREUS

The Sisters Grimm
Book Eight:
The Inside Story
MICHAEL BUCKLEY

Secrets of the Cicada Summer
ANDREA BEATY